DULCIE'S HUNCH—

Dulcie heard a car start and drive away. Her whiskers twitched eagerly; it was time to start her search. There was no mystery a smart cat couldn't solve—even the mystery of the disappearing old folks at Casa Capri Retirement Villa.

A miniature chest of drawers stood next to the hat boxes in the darkened room. Dulcie nosed at the chest and, with a careful claw, pulled a drawer open.

She froze, staring.

Eyeballs. The drawer contained human eyes. . . .

Other Books by
Shirley Rousseau Murphy

Cat on the Edge
Cat Under Fire
Cat in the Dark

Coming Soon

Cat to the Dogs

Cat Raise the Dead

Shirley Rousseau Murphy

AVON BOOKS
An Imprint of HarperCollinsPublishers

AVON BOOKS
An Imprint of HarperCollins*Publishers*
10 East 53rd Street
New York, New York 10022-5299

Copyright © 1997 by Shirley Rousseau Murphy
Cover illustration by Joe Burleson
ISBN: 0-06-105602-2
www.avonbooks.com

First Avon Books paperback printing: July 2000
First HarperPrism printing: July 1997

Avon Trademark Reg. U.S. Pat. Off. and in Other Countries, Marca Registrada, Hecho en U.S.A.
HarperCollins® is a trademark of HarperCollins Publishers Inc.

Printed in the U.S.A.

OPM 10 9 8 7 6

For those who wonder about their cats.
And for the cats who don't need to wonder,
for the cats who know.
And, of course, for Joe Cat.

Cat
Raise
the
Dead

1

Within the dark laundry room she stood to the side of the door's narrow glass, where she would not be seen from the street, stood looking out into the night. The black sidewalk and the leafy growth across the street in the neighboring yards formed a dense tangle, a vague mosaic fingered by sickly light from the distant streetlamp. Pale leaves shone against porch rails and steps, unfamiliar and strange, and beneath a porch roof hung a mass of vines, twisted into unnatural configurations. Beneath these gleamed the disembodied white markings of the gray cat, where it crouched staring in her direction, predatory and intent, waiting among the black bushes for her to emerge again into the night. She stepped aside, not breathing, moving farther from the glass.

But the cat turned its head, following her movement, its yellow eyes, catching the thin light, blazing like light-struck ice, amber eyes staring into hers. Shivering, sickened, she backed deeper into the shadows of the laundry room, clutching her voluminous black raincoat more tightly around herself, nervously smoothing its lumpy, heavy folds.

She couldn't guess how much the cat could see in the blackness through the narrow glass; she didn't know if it could make out the pale oval of her face, the faint halo of gray hair. The rest of her should blend totally into the darkness of the small room, her black-gloved hands, the black coat buttoned to her throat. Even her shoes and stockings were black. She had no real understanding of precisely how well cats could see in the dark, but she imagined this beast's vision was like some secret laser beam, some infrared device designed for nighttime surveillance.

She could only guess that the cat had followed her here. How else could he have found her? Somehow he had followed the scent of her car along the village streets, then tracked her, once she left the car, perhaps by the smell of the old cemetery on her shoes, where she had walked among the graves earlier in the day? Such skill and intensity in a common beast seemed impossible. But with this animal perhaps nothing was impossible.

Earlier, approaching the house, she hadn't seen him, and she had watched warily, too, studying the bushes, peering into the late-afternoon shadows, then had slipped in through the unlocked front door quickly. Not until she had finished her stealthy perusal of the house, taking what she wanted, and was prepared to leave again had she seen the beast, waiting out there, crouched in the night—waiting just as, three times before, it had waited. Seeing it, her mouth had gone dry, and she had wanted to turn and run, to escape.

But now the sounds behind her down the hall kept her from fleeing back through the house to the front; she was trapped here. She was terrified that someone would come this way, step from the brightly lit kitchen, down the hall, and into the laundry room, switch on a sudden light. She could hear the little family, gathered in the bright kitchen, preparing supper, the clang of pans and dishes, the parents and the three children bantering back and forth with good-natured barbs.

Stroking her bulky coat, she fingered the hard little lumps of jewelry and the three small antique clocks, the lizard handbag and matching pumps, the roll of twenties and fifties, the miniature painting, all tucked neatly away in the hidden pockets sewn into the lining. She should be on a high of elation—the day had been unusually profitable. She should not be shivering because a cat—a common, stupid beast—waited for her to emerge into the night. Yet she had never felt so helpless.

The cat moved again shifting among the shadows, and for a moment she saw it clearly, its sleek gray coat dark as storm clouds, its white parts stark against the black foliage. It was a big cat, hard-muscled. The white strip down its nose made it seem to be frowning, scowling with angry disapproval. An easy cat to identify; you would not mistake this one. This cat had no tail, just that short, ugly stub. She didn't know if it was a Manx or if it had gotten de-tailed in some accident. It should have been beheaded.

It was the kind of big, square beast that might easily tackle a German shepherd and come out the winner, the kind of cat, if you saw it slinking toward you through a dim alley, ready to spring, you would turn away and take an alternate route. And the creature wasn't a stray—it was too well fed, sleek, and confident, nothing like the thin, dirty strays her friend Wenona used to feed down around the wharf.

She would not in her wildest dreams ever be a person to get friendly with cats; not as Wenona had. Wenona had seemed drawn to cats. It was Wenona who told her about this kind of beast, told her years ago that there were unnatural felines in the world, sentient animals that knew far more of humanity than they should, knew more of human language and of human hungers and human needs than seemed possible. The tales of those creatures even now terrified her.

Now again the cat's eyes blazed directly at her, its narrow face and hot stare burning into her, shaking her with its strange, unreadable intent. What did it want?

Three times just this last week the cat had tracked her as she approached other houses, had trailed her as she searched for an unlocked door, and had watched her slip inside—had been waiting an hour later when she came out.

The first time she saw it, she assumed it was some neighborhood cat, but days later, when she saw the same distinctively marked tomcat in a totally different neighborhood, following her again, she had thought of Wenona's stories. Oh, it was the same cat, same narrow-eyed scowl, same narrow white strip down its face, same steely fur, thick shoulders, and heavy neck, same stub tail. Encountering that too-human gaze, she had gone back into the house she had just left, back through the unlocked front door, hoping that if a neighbor saw her, they'd think her a guest who had forgotten something.

And there, in a stranger's house, standing at the front window, she had watched the cat pace the sidewalk waiting for her. She had delayed for more than an hour worrying that someone would come home, had used the bathroom twice, cursing her kidneys, and then at last when she looked out and the cat was gone, when she couldn't see it anywhere, she had hastened away down the street, stricken with nerves, had hurried nervously to her car, scanning every bush and shadow, flung herself into the car, locked the doors, and taken off with a squeal of tires.

But she had not gone back to her room, fearing that the cat could somehow follow her there, she had driven mindlessly down into the village. Parking on Ocean Avenue, she had shed her heavy coat, left it folded on the seat, effectively concealing the sterling flatware, the heavy silver nut bowls and sterling side dishes, gone into a little hole-in-the-wall for a cup of coffee, drunk three cups, nursing them, making them last, all the while longing to be home, longing for the comfort of a closed door and tightly pulled shades, for a quick supper and a hot bath and bed. She stayed in the restaurant a long time before she worked up the nerve to return to her car in the gathering dusk.

And when she reached the white Toyota, there on the dusty hood were pawprints. A trail of big pawprints that had not been there before, prints that led across the hood to the windshield, as if the cat had stood looking in, perhaps studying her black coat.

She had driven away sickened.

Wenona said that if such a cat took an interest in you, it would not be easily discouraged. Wenona's tales had made the back of her neck prickle; never since Wenona told her those stories had she been able to abide cats.

The third time she saw the cat she was just approaching her mark, a house she was sure was, for the moment, empty. Suddenly the same beast appeared two doors down, leaping to a porch rail, watching her, same deep scowl, far too intelligent. Glimpsing its yellow eyes, she had panicked.

Oh, she had gotten through her usual routine all right, stripped the house of what she could carry, but by the time she left again she was shaking. She had refused to return to her car, had gone brazenly to a neighbor's house, had rung the bell and asked if she could call a cab, had said her car was stalled.

Now, tonight, she had parked much farther from the neighborhood she had chosen, hoping she could lose the beast.

She didn't usually work at night. The middle of the day was best, on weekends when people were out in back gardening or were out around the pool, leaving the house open. She was in and out quickly, and no one the wiser until hours later.

But tonight, cruising the neighborhood, she'd seen the husband and wife raking the freshly plowed yard in preparation for reseeding the lawn, and she was pretty sure their three elementary-school children would be at the big middle-school ball game—she paid attention to such matters. Parking several blocks away, she'd hoped a change in her schedule might put the cat off.

But again he'd been waiting.

And the irony was, a cat was her alibi. A lost cat. An alibi that had served her very well.

If, in a stranger's house, she was apprehended and confronted, as she had been three times in this village, her story was always the same. She'd been traveling with Kitty, Kitty liked to ride loose in the car, she'd had her dear Kitty since he was just a tiny little ball of fluff, he'd always ridden in the car with her, but this time he'd jumped out and run away. He'd be terrified in a strange neighborhood, she lived a long way down the coast, he wouldn't know where he was, she couldn't bear to think of him lost in a strange town. The story always worked. People were suckers for a pitiful lost cat. But now . . .

Now her carefully prepared lie had turned on her, had begun to taunt her.

On each job she changed her "lost" cat's description just as she varied other details of her operation, but always she played the tearful, lonely woman looking for her lost Kitty; she'd say she'd heard Kitty crying inside the house, that she thought it had slipped in through an open door and was trapped and frightened, so she had gone in to find him. Her story never failed to generate sympathy, and sometimes she was offered a cup of coffee or hot tea, a slice of cake, and a promise of help in looking for Kitty. It amused her greatly to sit in someone's kitchen drinking their tea and eating their cake, her coat loaded down with her hostess's jewelry and money and silver flatware.

It was Wenona who gave her the idea of using a lost cat as cover. Years ago Wenona, if she was questioned while shoplifting along Hollywood Boulevard, said she was looking for her lost cat, that it had jumped out of her car. People always believed her; people were such fools. Wenona had a good job but she adored shoplifting, loved finding a little something for nothing. Now Hollywood Boulevard seemed very far away. Oh, she did miss Wenona. They had been closest friends, and, though Wenona was twenty years her senior, age had never seemed to matter.

From beyond the laundry room, footsteps suddenly sounded, coming down the hall, and she stiffened, ready to bolt out into the night.

But it was only one of the children crossing to the bathroom. She heard him pee, heard the toilet flush. Couldn't people soundproof their bathrooms? So easy to do—the building-supply houses carried a special sheathing board for that purpose. But maybe they didn't care.

From the kitchen the children's voices, shrill and querulous, had begun to set her on edge. All that togetherness. The smell of spaghetti sauce cooking, its thick, rich aroma, made her stomach growl. The older girl must be setting the table; she was arguing that the knives went on the left. Her small brother whined about a television movie he wanted to watch. The father scolded irritably, his voice bored and quick.

Earlier, while she was still upstairs in the master bedroom, she had glanced out the window, watching the parents working away, diligently putting in the new lawn beneath the bright outdoor lights as if following a farmer's almanac instruction to plant only beneath the light of vapor bulbs. People were stupid to try to grow a lawn on a California hillside; there were hardly any lawns in the village. With the increasing shortage of water and California's frequent droughts, any homeowner with common sense planted some hardy, drought-resistant ground cover like ivy or ice plant.

She'd still been upstairs when she heard the tiller stop and, in a few minutes, heard the couple come in, heard them down in the laundry laughing together. They had left their dirty gardening clothes there—the clothes lay in a pile behind her—had come upstairs naked and giggling. She had slipped into the little sewing room down at the end of the hall, had watched them through the crack in the door as they entered the master bedroom, had listened to them showering together, laughing in an excess of merriment.

The three children had come in soon afterward from the ball game—she'd watched from the sewing-room window as they piled out of a van packed with kids. They had come directly upstairs, the older boy grumbling about losing the game. While they were in their rooms and their parents had not yet descended to the kitchen she had come down the stairs, lifted the miniature painting from the wall in the entry, and slid toward the back of the house and into the laundry. She had her hand on the doorknob when, through the half glass of the door, she saw the gray tomcat waiting in the gathering night, his eyes blazing up at her.

She wanted not to be afraid of the cat. She was quite aware that only crazy people had fears such as she was experiencing. Last week, coming out of the Felther house up on Ridgeview, with her inner coat pockets loaded with a lovely set of Rose of Erin sterling and a fine array of serving pieces, when she saw the gray tom watching from atop a black station wagon and she faced him and swore at him, his eyes had flared with rage.

Sentient rage.

The kind of violent anger you see only in human eyes.

She shivered again and touched her coat pocket where the miniature painting rested, wondering why she had lifted it. The primitive picture of a black cat seemed, now, a very bad omen, a symbol of her luck turned awry—as if she were goading fate.

She thought of leaving the painting on top of the washer but decided against doing so. It might give too much away.

She never took large paintings, of course; she took nothing she couldn't conceal beneath her coat, but she could not resist a miniature. Her fence in San Francisco had some good contacts for stolen art, and the village of Molena Point was famous for its small private collections as well as for its galleries. There was, in fact, a good deal of quiet money in Molena Point, a number of retired movie people, their estates hidden back in the hills, though she avoided these. With a household staff in residence, who knew when you'd bump into an unexpected maid lurking in one of the bedrooms, or come face-to-face with the butler in the master's study placing cigars in the humidor as in some forties' movie.

The middle-class houses were better for her purposes, affluent enough to have some nice antiques and silver and jewelry, but not so rich as to include live-in help. And the occasional alarm systems she encountered were usually turned off when people were about the place. Her usual routine was first to slip upstairs into the master bedroom, take care of the jewelry, clean out a purse or billfold left lying on the dresser. She had taught herself well about gems, and could usually tell the real thing.

Looking out through the dark glass, she saw the cat rise suddenly. He flashed her one intent look, his stare so insolent that all of Wenona's lurid stories came back to her. She was, for an instant, almost crippled with fear.

He looked, then moved away into the blackness beneath a neighboring porch, only his white parts still showing, like bits of discarded white paper.

Why was he so persistent? Why did he care about her? Why would a cat—any kind of cat—care what she stole?

So far, the cat seemed the only living presence that had guessed her scam. The Molena Point *Gazette* didn't have a clue; its little reports of local burglaries hadn't printed one word about a woman looking for her lost cat. And, as far as she could tell, the Molena Point cops were equally ignorant. They seemed to have made no connection with her successes up and down the coast—Santa Barbara, San Jose, Ojai, San Luis Obispo, Ventura. Of course the minute the papers blabbed her cat scam she had moved on, checked into a new town, and the furor in the old town quickly died, at least in the press.

She tried to hit each town quickly, work it for just a few weeks, then get out again. Montecito had given her some really nice hauls. She'd chosen its smallest cottages among the extravagant mansions and had made some rare finds. She was amused at herself that she'd saved all her newspaper clippings, like some two-bit actress saving stage reviews—some of them were a real hoot.

But those towns down the coast had been practice runs. Molena Point was the real gem. This village had never been properly worked, and she was enjoying every minute. Or she had been, until the cat showed up.

As she fingered the heavy gold jewelry and stroked the nice fat roll of bills inside her coat, outdoors the gray cat rose again and came out from beneath the porch. And now he didn't so much as glance at her. He turned away, trotted away purposefully up the side street as if she didn't exist, moved off toward the front of the house, prancing insolently up the center of the sidewalk under the streetlight, his stub tail wiggling back and forth, his tomcat balls making him walk slightly straddle-legged. And he was gone, not a glance backward.

She had no notion what had taken him away so suddenly. She did not feel relieved, only apprehensive. When he didn't appear again she let herself out, slipping open the laundry-room door. Listening to the smallest boy's giggles from the kitchen, she engaged the push-button lock, quietly shut the door behind her, and headed up the street for her car.

But approaching her own car in the black night where she'd parked it beneath a maple tree, the Toyota's pale, hulking shape seemed suddenly possessed, as if the cat watched from beneath it. She could not approach. Fear of the unnatural cat gripped her. She turned away from her own car and headed downhill toward the village—a coward's response.

She'd have to get rid of the Toyota. She couldn't

bear that the cat knew this car. Burdened by her heavy coat, she stumped along down toward Ocean Avenue, telling herself she wasn't fleeing from the cat, that she was going down to Binnie's Italian for a nice hot supper and a beer, for a plate of Binnie's good spaghetti, told herself that once she was fortified with spaghetti and a couple of beers she'd enjoy the little climb back up the hill to her waiting car, never mind that the coat weighed a ton. Making her way down toward the village, she fought the urge to look behind her, certain that if she looked, the cat would be there on the dark sidewalk, following her, his white paws and white markings moving like disjointed parts of a puzzle, his yellow eyes intent on her, a beast impossible to believe in—and impossible to escape.

2

Early-morning sun slanted into the Damen backyard, illuminating the ragged lawn, picking out each bare patch of earth where busy canine paws had been digging. Sunlight sharply defined the ragged weeds pushing up among straggling rosebushes along the back fence. Warm sunshine washed across the chaise lounge, where the tomcat lay scowling with anger. Having been rudely awakened from a deep and happy dream, he stared irritably at his human housemate.

Clyde Damen had only recently awakened himself, had brought his first cup of coffee out to sip while sitting on the back steps. He was unwashed, his dark hair resembling an untidy squirrel's nest, his cheeks black with stubble. He wore ancient, frayed jogging shorts above hairy legs, and a ragged, washed-out T-shirt. In the cat's opinion, he looked like he'd slept in a Dumpster. Joe Grey observed him with disgust. "You want to run that by again?" The cat's look was incredulous. "You woke me up to tell me what? You want me to do what?"

Clyde glared at him.

"I can't believe you would even *think* such a thing," Joe said. "Maybe, because I was awakened so unkindly, I didn't hear correctly. What I thought I heard was an amazingly inane suggestion."

"Come on, Joe. You heard correctly." Clyde sucked at his coffee. "Why the indignation? What's wrong with a little charity? I hadn't thought you'd be so incredibly narrow-minded." He sipped his brew, sucking loudly, and scratched his hairy knee. "I think it's a great idea. If you'd try it, you might find the project interesting."

Joe sighed. He'd had a disappointing night anyway. He didn't need to be awakened from his much-needed sleep to this kind of stupidity. "Why me? Why lay your idiot idea on me? Let one of the other cats do it. They won't know they're being used."

He'd returned home last night dismayed at his own ineptitude, and now he wasn't even allowed to sleep out his sulk. He'd been deeply and sweetly down into delightful feline dreams when Clyde came banging out of the house, picked him up, jerking him cruelly from slumber, and laid this incredibly rude suggestion on him. The next instant, of course, Clyde had yelped and dropped him, blood welling up across the back of his hand.

Joe had immediately curled up again and closed his eyes. Clyde had sat down on the step and stared at his hand, where the blood ran wet and dark. But then, guileless, and with incredible bad manners, Clyde made the suggestion again.

"Bloodied hand serves you right," Joe said now. He gave Clyde a narrow, amused cat smile. "I don't come barging into the bedroom waking you out of a sound sleep to tell you how to live your life—not that you couldn't use a little advice."

"I only suggested . . ."

He looked Clyde over coldly. "I can't believe you'd lay that kind of rude, thoughtless request on me. I thought we were friends. Buddies."

Joe knew quite well that the idea hadn't originated with Clyde. And that was what made him really mad.

Cat and human stared at each other as, around them, the morning reeked of sun-warmed grass and rang with birdsong, mostly the off-key blather of a house finch. Joe smoothed his shoulder with a pink tongue. Unlike his human housemate, he was beautifully groomed, his

short coat as sleek and gleaming as gray velvet, his mus-
cled shoulders heavy and solid, his handsome white
paws, white chest and throat, and the white strip down
his nose as pristinely clean as new snow, his eyes as
deeply golden as slanted twin moons.

He knew he was a handsome cat, he knew what a
mirror was for. He knew that look of adulation in his
lady's green eyes, too. But, thinking of Dulcie at that
moment, of her beautiful tabby face and soft, peach-
tinted ears, he was filled with her betrayal. Complete
betrayal. It was Dulcie who had put Clyde up to this
insanity; it was Dulcie and her human housemate,
Wilma Getz, who had hatched this plan.

Irritably he flicked an ear toward the off-key cacophony of the house finch. Didn't those birds know the
difference between sharp and flat? He didn't like to
think about Dulcie's perfidy. Angry, hurt by her
betrayal, he kept his gaze on Clyde.

Clyde shook a tangle of dark hair out of his eyes.
"Just tell me what's wrong with the idea. The venture
would be charitable. It would be fun, and it would do
you good. Help you practice a little kindness, increase
your community awareness."

"What do I need with community awareness?" Joe
sighed, enunciating slowly and clearly, his yellow eyes
wide with innocent amazement. "Let me get this
straight. You want me to join a pat-the-kitty group. You
want me to visit an old people's home. You are asking
me to become part of show-and-tell for the doddering
elderly." He regarded Clyde closely. "Are you out of
your feeble human mind?"

"Dulcie thinks it's a good idea."

"Dulcie thinks it's a good idea because it was her
idea." Joe dug his claws into the chaise cushion.
Sometimes Dulcie lost all sense of proportion. "Do you
really think that I'm going to allow a battalion of
bedridden old people to prod and poke me, to call me
'ootsy wootsy kitty,' and drool all over me?"

"Come on, Joe. You're making a big deal. If you'd just give it—"

Joe's look blazed so wild that Clyde stopped speaking and retreated behind a swill of coffee. The cat treated him to an icy smile. "Would you *submit* yourself to such amazing indignities? Turn yourself into an object of live-animal therapy?"

Clyde settled back against the steps. "You really are a snob. What makes you think those old folks are so disgusting? You'll be old someday. A flea-bitten, broken-down bag of cat bones with a dragging belly, and who's going to be kind to you?"

"You will. Same as you're kind to those two disreputable old dogs."

"Of course I'm kind to them, they're sweet old dogs. But you—when you get old I'll probably dump you at the animal pound."

"Or gas me under the exhaust of that junk-heap Packard you insist on driving."

"That Packard is a collector's model: it's worth a bundle of cash, and it's in prime condition." Clyde regarded Joe quietly. "Those old people get lonely, Joe. I'm not asking you to dedicate the rest of your life. Just a little kindness, a few hours a week. Some of those old people don't have any family, no one to visit them, no one to talk to or to care what happens to them."

Joe washed his left front paw.

"Don't you read the papers? Animal therapy is the latest thing. If those old people can visit with a warm, healthy animal, hold a cuddly dog or cat on their lap, that kind of relationship can really ease their depression, bring a lot of happiness into their dull lives. There've been cases where—"

"*Cuddly?* You think I'm *cuddly?*"

Clyde shrugged. "I don't. But their eyesight isn't too good. You're about as cuddly as a dead cactus. But hey, those old folks aren't choosy. If you could make a few of them happy—"

"What do I care if they're happy? What possible good can their happiness do me?"

"Just a little charity, Joe. A little love." Clyde scratched his dark, stubbled chin.

"*Love*? You want me to *love* them?"

"Can't you even imagine doing something nice for others? If you'd stop thinking about yourself all the time—and stop playing detective, following that damned cat burglar. That's another thing. This whole cat burglar bit. I don't like it that you were eavesdropping on Captain Harper, listening to classified police information."

"Classified? What's classified? The burglaries were in the paper. And I wasn't eavesdropping. You and Harper were playing poker. You're afraid I'll get a line on that woman before the cops do. And who knows, maybe I will. Make Harper's secret undercover surveillance look like a parade down Main Street."

He washed his right paw. "Who knows, maybe I can pass along a little information to Harper. Would he object to that? He hasn't objected in the past; I don't remember any complaints when Dulcie and I solved the Beckwhite murder, or turned up the evidence on Janet Jeannot's killer."

Clyde's dark, sleepy eyes stared into Joe's slitted yellow ones. "I'm not going to discuss that. You go off on these big ego trips. Like you were the only one who ever solved a murder. And if I tell you that stuff's dangerous, that you and Dulcie could get yourselves killed or maimed, you go ballistic, pitch a first-class tantrum."

Clyde stared into his empty coffee cup. "Couldn't you at least volunteer a couple afternoons a week? If your best friend likes the idea, couldn't you try? Try giving something back to the community?"

Joe's eyes widened to full moons. "Give something back to the community? Talk about limp-wristed dogoodism. Why should I give anything to some community? I'm a cat, not a human. What did this village ever—"

"May I point out that Molena Point is an unusually nice place for a cat to live? That you're lucky to have landed here?" Clyde sucked at his empty cup and moved his position on the step, following the shifting path of the sun. "How many California towns can offer you a veritable cat Eden? Where else are there endless woods and hills and gardens to hunt in, and even the street traffic is in your favor. Molena Point drivers are unbelievably slow and careful. Everyone takes great pains, Joe, not to run over wandering cats. Even the tourists are thoughtful. You want to move back into San Francisco's alleys, dodging trucks, avoiding hopheads and drunks? You try living in Sacramento or downtown L.A., see how long before you end up as pressed cat meat."

Joe glared.

"You fell into paradise when you landed in Molena Point. It would seem to me you'd be anxious to pay your dues."

No comment. The gray tomcat washed his shoulder.

"To say nothing of the free gourmet food you village cats indulge in behind Jolly's Deli. Where else are you going to be served free caviar, smoked Puget Sound salmon, imported Brie? You may not have noticed, Joe, but between Jolly's gourmetic freebies and the rabbits and mice you gorge on, you're getting a sizable paunch."

"I wouldn't talk about paunch, the shape you're in." Joe looked him over coldly. His stub tail beat so hard against the cushions that Clyde imagined an invisible tail lashing: the tail that was no longer a part of the tomcat's anatomy.

"Why not give it one visit, just to see what those old people are like?"

"I don't see *you* visiting the feeble elderly. And since when are you so concerned about Molena Point's old folks?"

"If you'll try just one pet visiting day, I'll treat you to

the best filet in Molena Point, delivered to the house sizzling hot."

"Not for all the filets in the village will I be crammed into a bus beside a bunch of yapping stink-a-poos scratching and lifting their legs, hauled away to an institution, locked inside rooms that smell like a hospital, rammed by wheelchairs, shoved into the laps of strangers to be poked and prodded, people I never saw before and don't want to see, people smelling of Vick's VapoRub and wet panties." Joe's eyes burned huge and angry. "Get them a teddy bear. Get them a stuffed cat—one of those cute furry life-size kitties you see on the shelf in the drugstore, but leave yours truly alone." He turned his back, curled up in the warm sunshine, and closed his eyes.

But Joe's reluctance would come to nothing, his stubborn negativism would soon register zero. When soft little Dulcie set her mind to it and turned that sweet green gaze on him, his blustering tomcat resolve would begin to melt. Before another two days had passed, the gray tomcat would find himself enduring with amazing patience the palsied stroking of the old folks' frail, wrinkled hands—and soon would find himself studying the Casa Capri Retirement Villa with intense interest, trying to understand what was not right within that seemingly gentle, cosseting home for aged villagers.

3

 The Molena Point Library, deserted at midnight, was so silent that the book-lined walls echoed with Dulcie's purrs; the little brindle cat lay sprawled on a reference table across a tangle of newspapers. Around her the dim, empty rooms stretched away into mysterious caverns that now belonged to her alone. At night the library's shadowed sanctuaries were hers; she shared her space with no one.

There was no hustle of hurrying feet, no hasty staff, no too-bright lights, no busy patrons, no swarms of village children herded by their teachers in barely controlled and giggling tangles among the brightly colored books. In the daytime library Dulcie was a social beast, wandering amiably among sneakers and nyloned legs, receiving almost more stroking and admiring words than she could handle. She was, officially, the Molena Point Library Cat, appointed so by all but one of the library staff. Library cats were the latest trend in bibliothecal public relations; in the daytime, Dulcie was Molena Point Library's official greeter, collector of new patrons, head of PR. The one librarian who disapproved of her was a distinct minority. Her recent attempts to oust Dulcie had met with villagewide resistance. Through petitions and public hearings, Dulcie's position was now solid and secure. She had seen her own picture in the official newsletter of the Library Cat Society along with pictures of countless other similarly appointed feline dignitaries. She was, in the daytime, a busy social creature.

But at night, she no longer need pretend to dumb ignorance, at night she could do just as she chose, she had only to paw a few selected volumes from the shelves and, *voilà*: she could follow any mystery, travel anywhere, entertain herself with any kind of dream.

Beyond the dark library windows, the village streets were empty. Oak branches twisted black against the moon-washed clouds, their gnarled shadows reaching in across the table and across the pile of open newspapers. Each paper was neatly affixed to a wooden rod by which it could be hung on a rack. Dulcie had, with some difficulty, lifted each from the rack in her teeth and leaped with it to the table, spread it out, taking care not to tear the pages.

Occasionally a light raced across the windows and she listened to a lone car whish down the street. When it had passed, her ears were filled again with the crashing of waves six blocks away against the Molena Point cliffs; and she could hear, from the roof above, a lone oak twig scraping against the overlapping clay tiles of the low, Mediterranean building.

None of the newspapers she had retrieved was a local publication; each had come from one or another California coastal town south of Molena Point. For hours she had studied these, piecing together a history of the cat burglar. Turning the pages with her claws, trying to leave no telltale puncture mark in the soft paper, she found the burglar to be both a puzzle and a grand joke. The woman was completely brazen, walking calmly into unlocked houses in the middle of the day, walking out again loaded down with jewelry, cash, small electronic equipment, and objets d'art. She had robbed some forty residences in a dozen coastal towns. This had to be the same woman who was operating now in Molena Point; though the local paper had made no mention of the cat connection. But Joe Grey was certain of his facts, Joe had a private source of information not open to the general citizen.

Unlike Joe, Dulcie found the woman's methods highly amusing. To use a cat for cover, and to commit her robberies with such chutzpah, tickled her senses, made her laugh.

Though she was stirred by other emotions, too. Just as the antics of a brazen jay were amusing yet made her lust to kill the creature, so the cat burglar's brash nerve, while it entertained her, made her long to track and pounce.

Dulcie's own sharp, predatory lusts were as nothing compared to Joe's interest. He'd been on the trail of the cat burglar for weeks—he was fascinated by the woman, and with typical tomcat ego he was enraged by a burglar who used a cat as her alibi.

Dulcie rolled over in a shaft of moonlight and batted at a moth that had gotten trapped in the room. It kept coming back to the light, darting mindlessly through the beam. She supposed she ought to put the newspapers back in the rack, but that was hard work. If she left them, Wilma would collect them from the table in the morning and put them away; Wilma always picked up after the late-evening patrons who straggled out leaving a mess when the library closed at nine. Wilma might be gray-haired, but she was a whirlwind when it came to work; she could work circles around these younger librarians.

Dulcie's housemate walked several miles a day, worked out at the gym once a week, and could still hit the bull's-eye consistently at the target range, a skill she had acquired in her profession as a parole officer. Wilma's professional interest in helping others had made her a natural to help with the Pet-a-Pet program.

Day after tomorrow would mark their third visit to the retirement center—though Dulcie hadn't told Wilma all that she'd learned there. Best to keep some things to herself, at least for now.

There was, within the sedate and ordered Casa Capri, more going on than the little everyday problems of the cosseted elderly. She hadn't told Wilma the stories she'd heard; she didn't want to upset her. And she wasn't telling Joe, either, but for a different reason.

She wanted Joe to join the Pet-a-Pet program out of kindness, not because he couldn't resist a mystery. If she told him what little old Mae Rose had confided to her, he'd be all over those old folks, be up there like a streak, pawing and snooping around.

No, she wanted him to join Pet-a-Pet out of compassion.

She'd longed to be a part of Pet-a-Pet from the minute she read about it. The half dozen magazine articles she'd found had her hooked—the idea of cat therapists for the elderly and for disturbed children seemed a truly wonderful venture, a way to do some real good in the world.

The trouble with Joe, the only fault he had, was that he didn't give a damn about doing good. Telling him of the cats she'd read about, who had helped people, had no effect but to make him laugh.

She'd told him about the cat who helped Alzheimer's patients recover some of their vanished mental capacity 'through his unconditional love and by spurring fond associations in their minds,' and Joe scoffed. The therapist cat, Bungee, had a special magic, a real curative power for those old people, but when she told that to Joe, he had collapsed with laughter, rolling against a rooftop chimney, shouting with high amusement.

"I don't see what's so funny. The article told how patients who practically never spoke would talk to Bungee, and how several old folks who had to be spoon-fed began to feed themselves, and how the agitated ones were calmer if they could pet and stroke Bungee."

Joe had swatted idly at the roof gutter, dislodging a wad of leaves. "You can't believe that drivel."

"Of course I believe it. It was a legitimate magazine article; it had pictures of Bungee with the old people."

"Hype, Dulcie. Nothing but hype."

"Hype for what? The cat isn't running for president."

"Is he making a movie?"

"Of course he's not making a movie. Can't you understand anything about helping those less fortunate? It must be terrifying to grow old, not to have a strong body anymore, not be able to leap or storm up a tree."

"Since when do humans leap and storm up trees?"

"You know what I mean. Don't be such a grouch. It must be terrible to feel one's joints stiffen and have pains and aches and bad digestion." Her own digestion, as Joe's, was efficient and diverse. Mice, rats, caviar, lizards, Jolly's imported cheeses and pastrami, all were enjoyed with equanimity and no tummy trouble. "I just mean, it's terrible to get old. If we could—"

"So it's terrible to get old. So are you alone going to save the world?" He opened his mouth in a wide cat laugh. "One small tabby cat—what are you, Bastet the mother goddess? Healer of mankind?"

"Just a few old people," she had snapped. "And who are you to say I can't help? What does a mangy tomcat know?"

That ended with claws and teeth and a fur-flying scuffle across the roof. Fighting, they rolled so near the edge that Joe nearly fell to the pavement below. As he hung swinging, and then crawled up again, they'd stared at each other, shocked; then they'd raced away across the roofs, dodging the flue stacks and chimneys.

But no matter how she flirted and teased him, he hadn't changed his mind about visiting Casa Capri. She felt so frustrated she'd been tempted to tell him Mae Rose's story. That would get him up there in a minute.

But then he'd be all fake purrs, fake wiggles, snooping around, caring nothing for the old people, caring for nothing but Mae Rose's little mystery that might, after all, be only a figment of an old woman's twisted imagination.

Mrs. Rose was a tiny woman, a little miniature human like an oversize doll, the kind of life-size old-lady doll you might see in the Neiman-Marcus windows at Christmas. There was no Neiman-Marcus in Molena Point, but Wilma did her Christmas shopping up in the city, returned home to describe the wonders of the store's Christmas windows. Dulcie could just imagine Mae Rose in one of those elegant displays, the little old lady sitting in a rocking chair, her bright white hair all wispy and glowing like angel hair on a fancy Christmas tree, her round face with too much pink rouge on her cheeks, her plump little hands, her twinkling eyes as bright blue as the blue eyes of the finest porcelain doll.

But Mae Rose wasn't all fluff. Not if you could believe the old lady's stories about what went on behind the closed doors at Casa Capri.

Dulcie told herself, when she was feeling sensible, that probably the disappearance of certain patients was the old woman's imagination. Mae Rose said that six patients had vanished, that when a patient had a stroke or became severely ill, sick enough to be transferred from the Care Unit over to Nursing, that was the last anyone ever saw of them. When Mae Rose's friend Jane Hubble was sent to Nursing, Mae Rose claimed she was not allowed to see Jane anymore. Jane had no family to care that she had vanished or to try to find her. Mae said that none of the six who had disappeared had a family.

As Dulcie lay curled on Mae Rose's lap, with Mae Rose tucked into her wheelchair, Mae told her about Lillie Merzinger, too, and about Mary Nell Hook, both of whom had gone to Nursing and were not seen again. Mary Nell Hook, who had cancer, was moved to Nursing where she could be on pain medication. Mae said if Mary Nell Hook had died of the cancer, then why didn't the staff tell them all, and maybe take them in the van to Mary Nell's funeral.

Mae Rose said Lillie Merzinger had owned a cocktail bar when she was younger, and when she came to Casa Capri she brought her record collection from the forties, that she played the old records in her room, and they all liked to listen. But when Lillie had the heart attack and was taken to Nursing, no one ever heard her music anymore. Well of course Lillie was too sick to play her records. But couldn't they have played her music for her, over in Nursing?

Dulcie couldn't point out that there might be reasons for them not to play music in a sick ward, that maybe it would disturb the really ill patients. Sometimes it was all she could do to remain mute. She couldn't argue with Mae Rose that there might be reasons for not letting everyone go visiting over to Nursing, where people would be disturbed; she couldn't say anything. All she could do was purr, hold her tongue and purr.

Mae Rose never mentioned her wild tales to Wilma; probably she thought Wilma wouldn't believe her. The sensible thing to think was that Mae's stories were only an old lady's crazy imaginings, tales woven to keep from getting bored.

But try as she might, Dulcie couldn't leave it at that. She kept wondering how such stories got started in Mae Rose's mind, from what crumb of truth they might have grown. The stories picked and nipped at her as persistent as a hungry flea nibbling.

Lashing her tail, she stared out through the dark library windows, past the knotted oak branches, where the lifting moon beckoned. Midnight was near—hunting time. She needed no clock—her sense of time was far better than the ticking white clock hanging on the wall above the checkout desk; a cat knew when the mice and rabbits stirred. Leaping down, she trotted through the shadows into Wilma's office, hurried past Wilma's desk and out her cat door to the narrow village street.

Moonlight brightened the shop windows and flower boxes and sheltered doorways, sent long shadows stretching out from the potted trees and the tubs of flowers, and from the old oaks that shaded the sidewalks taking up part of the street, narrowing the flow of daytime traffic. Oak branches reached across rooftops and fingered at balconies; and between the knotted limbs the moonlit clouds ran swiftly. The hunting would be fine, the rabbits giddy and silly in the racing light.

She felt giddy herself, felt suddenly moon silly. Felt like rolling and playing.

And, though both cats and rabbits play and dance in the moonlight, that did not prevent her from hungering for rabbit blood. Heading south through the village, she was wild with conflicting emotions—the hunger to hunt, but hunger as well for things she could hardly name. She stopped every few doors to stand upright and stare into a lit shop window.

The little coffee shop kept baked breads and cookies piled in baskets just behind the glass; the scent was heady and sweet. But she stopped for a longer look into the dress shop, admiring a red silk cocktail sheath. For strange and mysterious reasons, the richly draped garment made her little cat heart beat double time.

To the casual viewer Dulcie was only a plain tabby cat. Yet beneath her sleek dark stripes, beneath those neat, peach-tinted ears, fierce yearnings stirred. Longings that had never belonged to an ordinary feline.

Ever since she was a small kitten she had coveted silk stockings, little silky bras, black lace teddies, soft gauzy scarves and the softest cashmere sweaters. By the time she was six months old she had taught herself to claw open any neighbor's window screen and to leap at a doorknob, swinging and kicking until she had turned it and fought the door open. Wilma's neighbors for blocks around were used to Dulcie's thefts. When they missed a silk nightie, or a pair of panty hose which had been hung over the bathroom rack to dry, they had only to walk up the block to Wilma's house, rummage through the wooden box that Wilma kept on her back porch, and retrieve their lost garments. Neighbors, heading for Wilma's porch to look for stolen undies, often ended up in pleasant little social gatherings.

Now, staring up into the shop window at the red silk dress, Dulcie yearned. She thought about the feel of the silk, and about diamond earrings and about midnight suppers at lovely restaurants. Who knew what strange heritage produced such unfeline dreams? Who knew what lineage made the little cat yearn so desperately, sometimes, to be a human person. She knew there were Celtic tales of strange, unnatural cats, stories so old they were passed down and down before history was ever written; she knew folk stories that made the fur along her back stand stiff with amazement and sometimes with fear.

Fear because she longed so sharply for things a cat did not need, longed so intensely for a life she could never know.

Joe Grey's talents were just as remarkable as her own, but Joe was quite content to remain a cat, was totally happy to experience human perceptions and human talents but not have to bother with neckties, income tax, or vicious lawsuits.

Leaving the dress shop, she trotted north up the sidewalk to the Aronson Gallery, and there, pressing her nose against the glass, she enjoyed a moment of pure self-indulgence. Studying the three drawings of her that were exhibited in the window, she let her ego fly, allowed her own lovely likeness, gold-framed and more than life-size, to inflate her feline ego, enlarge her self-esteem like a hot balloon threatening to sail away with her; she imagined herself dangling in the sky, unable to return to earth, hoist on her own silly vanity.

The artist's rendering of her long green eyes was lovely; her peach-tinted paws and her peach-toned ears and little pink nose were a delight. She luxuriated

in the sleek lines of her graceful form, in the curving
mink brown stripes of her glossy tabby fur, and
sighed with pleasure. Who needed red silk cocktail
dresses? Charlie Getz had drawn her with such love,
had made her so beautiful, she should long for nothing more.

Charlie, Wilma's niece, had come to visit early last
fall, moving into Wilma's guest room with her paints
and drawing pads and with a monumental disappoint-
ment in her young life. A disenchanted graduate of a
San Francisco art school, Charlie had discovered only
after completing her courses that she couldn't make an
adequate living at her chosen major, that she was not
cut out for the demands of today's commercial art and
that there seemed little money in a fledgling career as
an animal artist.

After a short sulk, she had started a household repair
and cleaning business, CHARLIE'S FIX-IT, CLEAN-
IT. In Molena Point her services were already in such
demand that she was working ten and twelve hours a
day and couldn't hire enough help. She loved her new
business, loved the hard work, loved the success of her
venture. And she gloated over the growing balance in
her bank account. But belatedly, after giving up an art
career, she found that the Aronson Gallery wanted her
animal sketches. Dulcie knew the gallery well, and it
was highly respected.

Just last fall, she and Joe had broken into the
Aronson Gallery when they were searching for clues to
the murder of Janet Jeannot, one the gallery's best-
known artists. Of course Sicily Aronson knew nothing
of their B&E, or of their involvement in solving the
crime. Who would suspect a cat of meddling?

Smiling, remembering that night she and Joe had
prowled the locked gallery searching for clues, she
dropped down from the windowsill and sat a moment
on the warm sidewalk, washing her paws, then headed
across the village to find Joe.

She made a little detour up Ocean, past the greengrocer's, sniffing the lingering scent of peaches and melons, then the delicious aromas which seeped through the glass door of the butcher's, but soon she crossed the southbound lane of Ocean, crossed the wide, tree-shaded median and the deserted northbound lane. Heading up Dolores toward the white cottage which Joe Grey shared with Clyde Damen, she plotted how best to soften up Joe, get him to join Pet-a-Pet. And she kept thinking about Jane Hubble and the other patients, who, Mae Rose said, had disappeared. Probably she was being silly, believing such stories; probably the old people at Casa Capri were just as safe as babes tucked in their beds, the staff kind and unthreatening—except perhaps for the owner of the care home.

Beautiful Adelina Prior, in her lovely designer suits and her crème-de-la-crème coiffure and makeup, seemed, to Dulcie, as out of place at Casa Capri as a tiger among bunny rabbits. Why would a woman who looked like a model want to spend her life running an old people's home?

Trotting through the inky shadows where large oaks roofed the sidewalk, she thought of being trapped in Casa Capri, behind those tightly locked doors—if there was some criminal activity—and her paws began to sweat.

It was one thing to pry into the crimes she and Joe had solved earlier this year, where they could escape through windows and unlocked doors and over roof-tops. But to be confined within Casa Capri, where the doors were always bolted, made a chill of fear clamp her ears and whiskers tight to her head, made her cling low to the dark sidewalk, in a wary slink.

But yet she wanted to go there. And she knew, if something was amiss, she'd keep digging at it, clawing at it until the mystery was laid bare.

4

 In the hills high above the village a miniature world of tiny creatures crept through the grass, vibrating and humming, a community whose members were unaware of any existence but their own, of any needs but their own to kill or be killed, to eat or be eaten. The two cats, poised above this Lilliputian landscape, waited motionless to strike. Around them the grass stems had been pushed aside to carve out little mouse-sized trails, but some of the paths were wide enough for rabbits, too, major lanes winding away, dotted with pungent droppings. One pile of rabbit scat was so fresh that grass blades still shivered from the animal's swift flight. The cats, leaping to follow, panted with anticipation.

Above them the clouds drew apart, freeing the moon's light, and the moon itself swam between washes of blowing vapor; the dark hills caught the light, humping between earth and sky like the bodies of sprawled, sleeping beasts.

All night they had worked together stalking cooperatively, not as normal cats hunt but as a pair of lions would hunt, hazing and driving their prey. Dulcie's eyes burned toward the trembling shadows, her smile was a killer's smile, her paws were swift. She was not, now, Wilma's cosseted kitty rolling on stolen silk teddies.

But yet as they hunted, a poetry filled her, and she began to imagine she was Bast, stalking among papyrus thickets, clutching live geese in her teeth. Racing through the grass, she was Bast, hunting beside Egyptian kings, Bast the revered cat goddess, Bast the serpent slayer leaping to the kill . . .

The rabbit spun and bolted straight at her and beyond her, exploded away, was past before she could strike. She jerked around streaking after it, hot with embarrassment. Joe had flushed the creature nearly into her paws, and she had missed it. It sped away, kicking sand in her face, dodged, zigzagged, showed her only its white fluff tail, and disappeared into a tangle of wild holly. Her nostrils were filled with its fear and with the smell of her own shame.

But then it swerved out again, and she dodged after it. As it doubled back she sprang, snatched it in midair, clamped her teeth deep into its struggling body.

Its scream cut the night as she tasted its blood, its cry was shrill, as terrified as the scream of a murdered woman. It raked her with its hind claws, slashing at her belly. She bit deeper, opening its throat. It jerked and stopped struggling and was still, limp and warm, the life draining from it.

She carried the rabbit back to Joe, and they bent together over the kill. He did not mention her daydreaming inattention. He scarfed his share of the carcass, rending and tearing, flinging the fur away, crunching bone.

"Someday," she said, "you're going to choke yourself, gorging. Snuff out your own life, victim to a sliver of rabbit bone."

"So call 911. What were you dreaming, back there?" He gave her an annoyed male look, and ripped fur and flesh from the bones.

She didn't answer. He shrugged. The rabbit was succulent and sweet, fattened on garden flowers. Dulcie skinned her half carefully, then stripped morsels of meat from the little bones, eating slowly. Only when the bones were clean, when nothing was left but bones and skull, did they settle in for a wash. Licking themselves, cleaning their faces, then their paws, working carefully in between claws and between their sensitive pads, they at last cleaned each other's ears. Then, stomachs full, they sat in the moonlight, looking down upon the village, at the moonstruck rooftops beneath the dark oaks and eucalyptus.

Because many of the village shops had once been summer cottages, the entire village was now a tangled mix: shops, cottages, galleries, and motels, crowded together any which way. But where the hills rose above the village, the houses were newer and farther apart, with dry yellow verges between. It was here that the cats hunted. Besides the rabbits and ground squirrels, the mice and birds, there were occasional large and bad-tempered rats. Both cats carried scars from rat fights; and Joe remembered too vividly the rats in San Francisco's alleys when he was a kitten, rats that had seemed, then, as big and dangerous as Rottweilers.

It was Clyde who had rescued him from those dark alleys. He'd had a piece of luck landing with Clyde and then the two of them moving down here to Molena Point. Though if he ever admitted to Clyde how much he really did like the village, he'd never hear the last of it.

"What are you thinking?"

"That Clyde can be a damned headache."

She stared at him. "You mean about the Pet-a-Pet program? If Clyde ordered you not to go near Casa Capri, you'd be up there in the shake of a whisker."

"I wasn't thinking of . . . Oh, forget it."

She looked at him unblinking.

"You're going to keep at it, aren't you? Keep nagging until I agree."

"What did I say?"

"Staring a hole through my head."

"You could at least try."

He looked hard at her.

She smiled and licked his ear.

He watched her warily.

"They talk to me, Joe. That little Mrs. Rose, she tells me all kinds of secrets. I feel so sorry for her sometimes." She didn't intend to tell him all of Mae Rose's secret, but she'd like to tweak his curiosity ever so slightly.

He lay down and rolled over, crushing the grass beneath his gray shoulders. Lying upside down staring at the sky, he glanced at her narrowly. There was more to this Casa Capri business than she was saying.

She patted at a blade of grass. "Those old people need *someone* to tell their secrets to."

The cry of a nighthawk swept the moonlit sky, its *chee chee chee* rising and dropping as the bird circled, sucking up mosquitoes and gnats.

She said, "Wilma tells them stories."

"Tells who stories?"

"The old people. Cat stories. About the Egyptian tombs and cat mummies and Egyptian hunting cats and about . . ."

He flipped to his feet, staring at her.

"Not about speaking cats," she said softly. "Just cat stories. She's always done story hour for the children at the library. This is no different. Both our visits, after the cats and dogs were all settled down in the old people's laps, when everyone was yawning and cozy, she told stories.

"She told the little milkmaid cat. You know, *There was a little cat down Tibb's Farm, not much more'n a kitten—a little dairy maid with a face so clean as a daisy but she wanted to know too much. . . . And all was elder there and there was a queer wind used to blow there . . ."*

"Boring. Boring as hell. Probably the old people love that stuff."

But her look iced him right down to his claws.

"And why do they need animals to visit them, if Wilma tells them stories? Isn't that excitement enough? You don't want to overtax those old folks."

She sighed.

"Get her to read that story by Colette, the one where the cat gets pushed off the high-rise balcony, that ought to grab them."

She shivered and moved closer to him in the tall grass. They were quiet for a while, listening to the nighthawk and to the far pounding of the sea. But, thinking of Casa Capri, she felt like the little milkmaid cat. She wanted to know too much. She was certain, deep in her cat belly, that she was going to find, like the little milkmaid, that there was *summat bad down there*.

She could hardly wait.

5

Mae Rose had her good days, when she was able to walk slowly out onto the patio, holding on to the back of the chairs, when she could sit out there enjoying the flowers and the warm sun. But there were days when she was so shaky, when she looked back at herself from the mirror white as flour paste.

Those days she felt vague and afraid, those days she was too weak to walk at all, and had to be helped not only from her bed and to get dressed, but even into her wheelchair. Those bad days, a nurse wheeled her into the social room and through it to the dining room and helped to feed her, and she felt 120 years old.

But the times when she woke feeling strong and happy and ready for the day, she felt as good as she had at fifty. Those times she could even sew a little. Of course, she still made the doll clothes—that was nearly all she had left. All her life she'd made doll clothes, even when she was so busy working in wardrobe before the children were born. After the children came she'd left little theater, and that was when she hit on making a business of designing doll wardrobes. James had laughed at her— James had always patronized her—but she'd had a brochure printed up with pictures of her dressed dolls, and she sent carefully stitched samples of her little doll coats and dresses, too. It didn't take long before she was making enough money from her exclusive toy-store customers to dress herself and their three girls and buy the little extras they wanted. James said she spoiled the children. James thought her impossibly childish just because she loved the little, pretty details of life. If that made her childish, she couldn't help it. James said she would have fit better in the Victorian era, when a woman could be admired for choosing to deal only with the minute and the pretty.

Well she'd raised three children, and not a lot of help from James. He had died when their oldest, Marisa, was only twelve. It wasn't her fault that she hadn't been able to deal with the passions of those children; they were James's children, born and bred. When they got into their teens, and she was trying to raise them alone, it seemed impossible that the little beasts could be her own. The girls' puberty had been a terrible time: she had suffered from too many sick headaches during those years.

But the girls all got married off at last, and whatever went on in between she had wiped from memory. Now, of course, all three girls lived so far away that they could seldom visit, two on the East Coast with their husbands, and Marisa in Canada on a farm and already five children of her own to worry over. Now that she didn't see the girls except every few years, and now that Wenona, her one good friend, was dead these long years, and Jane Hubble wasn't here anymore, the doll wardrobes were all she had.

She missed Jane. She missed Wenona. Years ago, when Wenona died, before she, Mae, ever came to live here at Casa Capri, she had known she would spend the last years of her life alone. Wenona had been her only real friend. In little theater all those years together, Wenona in charge of scenery and publicity, and they'd had such lovely times. Their long walks through the village, and shopping together, going up to the city. Wenona had loved to look at fabrics for the doll wardrobes though she didn't sew. Wenona couldn't really love the dolls, not like she cared about cats.

She had to laugh, the way Wenona always had to go feed the stray cats down at the wharf. As if that were her sole responsibility. And the way she spoiled her own cats, putting in cat doors, buying special food, tramping the neighborhood calling if one of them didn't come home. Always worrying over her cats.

But then Wenona went on down to Hollywood with a wonderful chance to work in the MGM prop department. She'd thought Wenona would be back, that she really wouldn't like Hollywood, but she had stayed. She came up once a year, and they had a few days together, but then the cancer, very quick, and Wenona was gone.

And she was alone again.

Wenona dead. James dead. And her own daughters across the country. When Jane Hubble had come to live here, that was a blessing, but now Jane, too. The nurses said she was over in Nursing, said where else would she be? But she didn't believe them.

She'd given Jane one of her five dolls before Jane had the stroke—they said it was a stroke. Once she asked a nurse if Jane still had the doll, and the nurse had looked so puzzled. But then she said yes, of course Jane had the doll.

If Jane had gone away or died, she'd like to have the little doll back again as a keepsake to remind her of Jane. But she didn't ask. They were so strict here, strict and often cross. They took good enough care of you, kept you clean, changed your linens and washed your clothes, and the food was nice, but she sometimes felt as if Adelina Prior's hard spirit, her cold ways, rubbed off on all the staff. There was no one Mae could talk to.

When she had phoned her trust officer to tell him that she didn't think Jane really was over in Nursing, he treated her as if she was senile. Said he was sorry, that he had talked with the owner, Ms. Prior, and Jane was too sick to have visitors, that he saw nothing wrong. Said that the Nursing wing was too busy and crowded with IV tubes for anyone to visit, that visitors got in the way and upset the sick patients.

Jane would hate it over there. Jane was so wild and full of fun. In that way, Jane was like Wenona. Those years when Mae and Wenona roomed together, Wenona was always the bold one, always making trouble. She would never put up with any kind of rules, from their landlord or from the manager of little theater when she was helping with the sets. And Jane was like that, too, always telling the nurses how stupid the rules were. She made everyone laugh, so crazy and reckless—until they took her away.

Four times Mae had tried to go over to Nursing to visit, and every time a nurse found her and turned her chair around and wheeled her back. So demeaning to be wheeled around against her will, like a baby.

Eula said maybe Jane packed up and walked right out of Nursing, even if she did have an attack. Eula was her only friend now. Eula—so sour and heavy-handed.

She had wanted to tell Bonnie Dorriss, who ran the Pet-a-Pet program, about Jane, but she decided not to. Bonnie Dorriss was too matter-of-fact. That sturdy, sandy-haired, freckled young woman would never believe Jane had disappeared; she'd laugh just like everyone else did.

Well at least when Pet-a-Pet started, she had the little cat to talk to. Holding Dulcie and stroking her, looking into her intelligent green eyes, she could tell Dulcie all the things that hurt, that no one else wanted to hear. Cats understood how you felt. Even if they couldn't comprehend the words, they understood from your voice what you were feeling.

Maybe the little cat liked her voice, too, because she really seemed to listen, would lie looking up right into her face, and with her soft paw she would pat her hand as if to say, "It's all right. I'm here, I understand how you are grieving. I'm here now, and I love you."

6

This was not a happy morning. Joe's stomach twitched, his whole body ached with sorrow. As he watched through the front window, Clyde backed the Packard out of the drive and headed away toward the vet's. Poor old Barney lay on the front seat wrapped in a blanket, too sick even to sit up and look out the window, though the old golden retriever loved the wind in his face, loved to see the village sweeping by. When Clyde had carried him out to the car he'd looked as limp as a half-full bag of sawdust.

Early last night Barney had seemed fine, frolicking around the backyard in spite of his arthritis. But this morning when Joe slipped into the kitchen just at daylight, Barney lay on the linoleum panting, his eyes dull with a deep hurt somewhere inside, and his muzzle against Joe's nose hot and dry. Joe hadn't realized how deeply he loved Barney until he'd found the old golden retriever stretched out groaning with the pain in his middle.

He had bolted back into the bedroom and waked Clyde, and Joe himself had called Dr. Firreti—said he was a houseguest—while Clyde pulled on a crumpled sweatshirt and a pair of jeans. Dr. Firreti said to meet him at the clinic in ten minutes.

Last night Joe'd gotten home about 3:00 A.M., parting from Dulcie on Ocean Avenue so full of rabbit, and so tired from a hard battle with a wicked-tempered raccoon, that he hadn't even checked out the kitchen for a late-night snack. He'd gone directly to the bedroom and collapsed on the pillow next to Clyde, hadn't even bothered to wash the coon blood from his whiskers, had hardly hit the pillow, and he was asleep.

He woke two hours later, puzzled by the faint sound of groaning. The bedroom clock said barely 5:00 A.M., and, trotting out to the kitchen, he'd found Barney hugging the linoleum with pain. Now at five-fifteen Barney was on his way to the vet, to a cold metal table, anesthetics, a cage, and Joe didn't like to imagine what else.

He lay down on the back of his private easy chair and looked out at the empty street. The smell of exhaust fumes still clung, seeping in through the glass. From the kitchen, he could hear Rube pacing and whining, already missing Barney. The black Lab hadn't been parted from the golden since they were pups. Joe listened to him moaning and fussing, then, unable to stand the old Lab's distress, he leaped down.

Pushing open the kitchen door, he invited the big Lab through the living room and up onto his private chair, onto his beautifully frayed, cat hair-covered personal domain. He never shared this chair, not with any cat or dog, never with a human—no one was allowed near it—but now he encouraged old Rube to climb rheumatically up.

The old dog stretched out across the soft, frayed seat, laid his head on the arm of the chair, and sighed deeply. Joe settled down beside him.

This chair had been his own since Clyde first found him, wounded and sick, in that San Francisco gutter. Taking him home to his apartment after a difficult few days at the vet's, Clyde had made a nice bed in a box for him, but he had preferred the blue easy chair, Clyde's only comfortable chair. Clyde hadn't argued. Joe was still a pitifully sick little cat; he had almost died in that gutter. Joe had known, from the time he was weaned, to play human sympathy for all he could get.

From the moment he first curled up in the bright new chair, that article of furniture was his. Now the chair wasn't blue any longer, it had faded to a noncolor and was nicely coated with his own gray fur deposited over the years. He had also shredded the arms and the back in daily clawing sessions, ripping the covering right down to the soft white stuffing. This texturing, overlaid with his own rich gray cat hair, had created a true work of art.

The old dog, reclining, sniffed the fabric deeply, drooled on the overstuffed arm, and sighed with loneliness and self-pity.

"Come on, Rube. Show a little spine. Dr. Firreti's a good vet."

Rube rolled his eyes at Joe and subsided into misery.

Joe crawled over onto the big dog's shoulder and licked his head. But, lying across Rube, Joe felt lost himself. He was deeply worried for Barney. Barney's illness left him feeling empty, strangely vulnerable and depressed.

He stayed with Rube until long after the old black Lab fell asleep. He had managed to comfort Rube, but he needed comforting himself. Needed a little coddling. He studied the familiar room, his shredded chair, the shabby rug, the battered television, the pale, unadorned walls. This morning, his and Clyde's casually shabby bachelor pad no longer appeared comforting but seemed, instead, lonely and neglected.

Joe rose. He needed something.

He needed some kind of nurturing that home no longer offered.

Frightened at his own malaise, he gave Rube a last lick and bolted out through his cat door. Trotting up the street, then running flat out, he flew across the village, across Ocean, past the closed shops, past the little restaurants that smelled of pancakes and bacon and coffee, fled past the closed galleries and the locked post office.

From a block away he saw that Wilma's kitchen light was on, reflected against the oak tree in her front yard. He could smell fresh-baked gingerbread, too, and he raced toward that welcoming house like some little kid running home from schoolyard bullies.

Galloping across Wilma's front yard and up the steps, he shot straight for the bright glow of Dulcie's plastic cat door and through it, into Wilma's friendly kitchen. The aroma of gingerbread curled his claws and whiskers.

Dulcie stood on the breakfast table looking down at him, startled by his charging entry. She watched him with amazement, her green eyes wide and amused, her muzzle damp from milk and flecked with gingerbread crumbs. "You look terrible—your ears are drooping, even your whiskers are limp. What's wrong? What's happened?"

"It's Barney. Clyde took him to the vet."

"But—not a car accident? He's never in the street."

"He's sick, something in his middle, hurting bad."

"But Dr. Firreti will . . ."

"He's old, Dulcie. I don't know how much Dr. Firreti can do." He leaped to the table and pressed against her for comfort. She licked his ear and laid a soft paw on his paw. Around them, Wilma's blue-and-white kitchen shone with warmth and cleanliness.

Above the tile counter, the rising morning light through the clean windows lent a pearly glow across the blue-and-white wallpaper and the blue cookie jar and cracker jars. Behind the clean glass of the diamond-paned cupboard doors, Wilma's blue pottery sparkled. Wilma's homey touches always eased him, eased him this morning right down to his rough cat soul. He sighed and licked Dulcie's ear.

She nosed the gingerbread toward him and bent her head again, nibbling gingerbread and lapping milk from her Chinese hand-painted bowl. Hungrily, he pushed in beside her. Whoever said cats don't like freshly baked treats didn't know much about cats. Not until every crumb had vanished, and every drop of milk, did they speak again. His whiskers and his teeth were sodden with gingerbread crumbs and milk, and he felt infinitely better.

He knew there was nothing he could do for Barney but wait and hope. He wasn't used to praying, but he did wonder if a cat prayer would be accepted by whatever powers—if indeed there were any powers existing beyond the pale.

He looked at Dulcie, sitting so regally in the center of the table delicately washing her face. "I thought you took your meals on the rug. When did Wilma start sharing the table?"

She glanced at her bowl, and grinned. "When I told her you ate on the table. She's not about to let Clyde spoil you more than she spoils me."

"The house looks nice," he said, leaping down. He didn't usually notice domestic details, unless Dulcie called them to his attention, but Wilma had recently redecorated. Her niece Charlie had helped her paint the walls white and replace the lacy curtains with white shutters. Wilma had sold the thick rag rugs, too, and bought deep-toned Khirmans and Sarouks that were luxurious to roll on. A dozen of Charlie's animal drawings, framed in gold leaf, graced the front rooms, several of Dulcie and even one of himself, of which he was more proud than he let on. The couch had been re-covered in a deep blue velvet as silken as Dulcie's rich fur, and Dulcie's blue afghan lay across the arm just where she liked it; the three upholstered chairs had been re-covered in a red-and-green tweed. And over the fireplace hung a large oil landscape of the Molena Point hills and rooftops, all vibrant reds and greens, done by Janet Jeannot some years before she was murdered.

He trotted into the living room, following Dulcie, and leaped to Wilma's desk, where the early light flooded in through the white shutters.

Beneath their paws lay a map of Molena Point, unfolded and spread out flat.

"Wilma left this for us?"

Dulcie smiled. Beside the map lay a stack of newspaper clippings about the cat burglar, machine copies of papers Dulcie had read in the library.

Joe scratched his ear. "If Clyde knew Wilma was leaving out maps and news clippings for us—aiding and abetting—he'd have a royal fit." Clyde did not take easily to Joe's playing detective. For a hard-nosed macho type, Joe's housemate worried too much.

"A few measly clippings and a map," she said. "That's hardly aiding and abetting. And Wilma's never helped us before—not that I wanted her to. She didn't have a clue that we were into the Beckwhite murder."

"Maybe she didn't, but she knew about Janet. She told you afterward she was worried."

"But she stayed out of it—she's sensible, for a human." Dulcie stretched, and curled up on the blotter. "You have to admit, Wilma tolerates our interests better than Clyde does."

"She couldn't spend her whole career working criminal cases without getting some sense of perspective."

Some of the clippings were about the local burglaries, but most of them chronicled the cat woman's thieving progress as she moved up the coast from San Diego, working ever farther north as the summer progressed.

"As if the old gal prefers cooler weather," Joe said. "Southern California in the winter, San Francisco for the summer."

Studying reports of the local burglaries, they inscribed a claw mark on the map at each location but found no pattern. The woman seemed to travel back and forth at random, across the wealthier neighborhoods, perhaps picking out whatever house she passed where people were working outside.

"I like this one," he said, pawing at the newspaper

clippings. "Shell Beach. She goes right on in while the guy's sleeping.

"Guess she thought, if he'd been to a bachelor party, he'd be so drunk nothing would wake him."

The cat burglar, slipping upstairs into the prospective groom's bedroom on the morning of the appointed wedding, had lifted the matched gold wedding rings, laid out for the ceremony, from the dresser.

She took the rings out of the box, left the closed box on the dresser with two coins stuck into the slot, presumably to give the box some weight. The groom, probably hung over and in a hurry, or dazed with the thought of his coming nuptials, didn't have a clue until he opened the box at the church, to give the ring to the best man, and found instead, two nickels.

Dulcie smiled. "The woman's brazen."

"And she's afraid of cats. When she sees me watching, I scare the hell out of her." He rubbed his whiskers against the shutters, staring out through the glass.

The morning was turning golden, the windows across the street reflecting tiny suns mirrored all in a row. He narrowed his eyes against the glare. "We need a lookout; I've about worn out my pads following false leads, when the cat burglar never did show. The roof of Clyde's shop isn't high enough. I can't see half the hills."

His plan, so far, had been to watch from the roof of the automotive shop as the cat burglar drove around choosing her mark, then nip on over to where she'd parked. Trouble was, she ditched her car blocks away, and sometimes she didn't return to it. And that one time, when he thought she was inside a laundry room, she'd slipped away, or maybe had just outstubborned him. He'd waited what seemed hours, until he was faint from hunger, had left at last in a huff, not sure if she'd given him the slip or was still in there, and so hungry he didn't care. Then the next day, sitting on the breakfast table, he'd read the *Gazette* article with a list of what she'd stolen, including a miniature cat painting worth a cool two hundred thousand. He'd really muffed that one—he'd felt stupid as dog doo.

"That brown shingle house," Dulcie said, "that tall one up on Haley with the cupola on top. Except for the courthouse tower, it's the highest point in the village."

"Right on."

"And today's Saturday, half the village will be digging up their yards."

They leaped from the desk and out through Dulcie's cat door, and as they headed up Dolores toward Sixth, she couldn't help purring. She loved this sneaky stuff. Spying was a hundred times more fun even than stalking rabbits.

But as they crossed Danner, the wind quickened, swirling along the sidewalk and ruffling their fur, and above them the clouds came rolling. Joe stared up at the rain-laden sky.

"If that cuts loose, no one will work in their yard. If it rains, that old woman will stay home in her bed."

"Maybe it will blow on out, dump itself in the sea."

Crossing Danner, trotting between morning traffic, they angled through a backyard to Haley, could see the brown house rising just ahead, its cupola thrusting up like a child's playhouse atop the wide roof, jutting up into swiftly gathering clouds. There was no tree by which they could reach the roof. As they circled the shingled walls and stared above for a likely windowsill or vine-covered downspout, the wind gusted sharply, pressing them against the bushes with strong thrusts. "Wind gets any stronger," Joe said, "it'll lift us right off the roof, send us flying like loose shingles."

7

The dark and ungainly old house had been built long before earthquake restrictions decreed that no building over two stories be constructed in Molena Point. With its extra height and poor condition, it was a sitting target for ground temblors. At the first 6.0 on the Richter it would likely topple in a heap of scrap lumber and rusty nails. The roof was ragged. The dark, shingled walls looked as if they were eaten with rot. The FOR SALE sign which had been pounded into the mangy front lawn led one to imagine not a new owner and fresh paint but a future with the wrecking crew.

The house stood just a block off Ocean and a block below the green park which spanned the Highway One tunnel. As the cats circled it, pressing through scraggly weeds, they found at the back a precarious rose trellis held together only by the thick thorny vines. Swarming up, climbing three stories, they gained the steep, slick roof, trotted up across it to the cupola. The old shingles beneath their paws were worn soft. Scrabbling up, gaining the high peak, they pushed into the little open cupola—onto a thick white frosting of bird lime that coated the cupola floor. The place stank of bird droppings, despite a fresh wind that swirled through the four arched openings, bringing the smell of rain.

The swift clouds were fast darkening, the colors of the village deepening, and beyond the village the sea lurched steel gray beneath the heavy, dense sky. The sun had gone; Molena Point's citizens would be indoors checking the *TV Guide* or curled up by the fire with a book. Joe and Dulcie could imagine the cat burglar, perhaps in one of Molena Point's hundreds of little motels, bundled up, ordering room service. The sounds of passing cars rose up to them, muffled by the whine of the wind.

Looking down the steep roof to the sidewalks along Ocean, watching people heading to work or toward some cozy restaurant for breakfast, they could smell pancakes and the sweet aroma of warming syrup. The shop windows reflected the dark, swift sky. Over on San Carlos old Mr. Jolly, swinging open the glass front door of the deli, carried out four pots of bright red flowers.

He arranged the pots two at either side of the door, then paused to look up at the sky, and stood considering.

Finally he knelt again, picked up the pots, and carried them back inside. The cats watched him disappear into the warmth of the deli, then fixed their gazes on the alley behind, licking their noses, thinking of imported salmon or a dollop of warm chowder.

Some of the village shopkeepers claimed that Jolly's gourmetic gifts drew mice. Indeed they might—and what could be nicer than a fat, warm mouse with a bit of seafood quiche or a slice of Camembert or Brie?

The cupola was chill with the sharp wind. Its four open arches looked squarely to the four points of the compass, affording maximum draft, but also fine views of the village streets. Both cats could see their own houses. To their left, beneath the spreading limbs of an oak, shone the shabby roof of Clyde's white Cape Cod. That dwelling was badly in need of professional attention, but what did Clyde care? Clyde tended his cars like newborn babes, alert to the tiniest complaint, but the house—not until the roof leaked or the floor fell in was Clyde going to make any architectural adjustments.

To their right, past the shops and galleries, they could see the back of Wilma's house, its steeply peaked roof and stone chimney just visible above the hill at the back—the front garden belonged to Wilma, but the back hill was Dulcie's, a private preserve, a forest of wild grass rich with game and admirably suited to the quick, spur-of-the-moment hunt. Those mice and birds were strictly off-limits to any other neighborhood cat, if he valued his hide.

Almost directly below them, just across Ocean, shone the red tile roofs of Beckwhite's Foreign Cars and of Clyde's automotive shop. And beyond Beckwhite's, among a sprawl of cottages, was the white frame house which held Dr. Firreti's animal clinic, where Barney now lay. Joe was afraid to know how Barney was doing; something about the old dog this morning had left him coldly distressed—as if Barney had already given up.

And he worried not only about Barney but about Rube. If Barney died, Rube would be a basket case. Old Barney's illness made him think how short was life, how capricious and unpredictable.

Beyond the village to the east, above the rising hills, one patch of sky was still blue between the steely clouds, its clearer light striking down on the hills, picking out every bush, every tree and flower garden. The houses and streets, rising up, were displayed as clearly as a stage set. Between the scattered houses, the grassy fields gleamed golden. And despite the threat of rain, the shadowed, darkened yards, stretching across the hills were not deserted. Three children were playing catch up on Amber Street, and, as a very little boy crouched to dig in the gutter, half a dozen kids flew down the hill on their bikes.

They watched an old man cutting his steep hillside lawn with a hand mower, as if perhaps modern power equipment was not designed for such extremities of terrain. The wind grew colder. Shivering, Dulcie snuggled close to Joe. "Maybe the old burglar'll show up—who could miss that white Toyota?" She snorted. "Mud on its license plate—what a tired old trick."

"It's worked, though. So far. Mud so thick I couldn't even scratch it off."

"Don't you wonder if she noticed?"

He shrugged. "So she noticed. So if she's scared of cats, that ought to chill her."

"Or maybe she'll have some other car. If she can burgle a house, it should be no problem to 'borrow' someone's car for a few hours."

They watched intently each vehicle that moved across the rising hills, watched a station wagon wind back and forth making its rounds, picking up children for some Saturday event, watched a FedEx truck trundle up the hills on its appointed stops, the driver running to each door and leaving his package, racing back to the truck again as if his pay scale was structured on swift timing.

A small red sedan turned up from the Highway One tunnel and parked beneath some maple trees on a residential block, and a lone woman emerged, a dumpy creature; the cats watched her so intently she should have felt their gaze like a laser beam.

She made her way directly up the walk of a two-story green frame house, paused to pick up the morning paper, and appeared to be fumbling with a key. Unlocking the door, she disappeared inside.

Five blocks away, a tan VW climbed the hills and parked before a half-timber cottage flanked by sycamore trees. Another lone woman emerged, a slim, sleek figure in a black business suit. She entered the house quickly, and in a moment lights came on. "If that's the cat burglar," Joe said, "she's done a real state-of-the-art makeover."

In the cupola a bee buzzed, circling their heads and diving at their ears. Dulcie slapped it down, nosed at it, then backed away. Far up the hill, at a yellow cottage, the back door opened and a man and woman appeared, dressed in shorts. Crossing the lawn, they opened a garden shed and pulled out a mower, rakes, a shovel. Above the yellow house, at a new house where the yard was still raw dirt, a woman appeared from around the back with a basket, knelt beside the front walk, and began to dig in the earth, setting out little plants, patting them carefully into the ground. Joe yawned.

"They plant grass, then have to mow it. Plant flowers, then have to weed them."

She cut her eyes at him. "I've seen you rolling on those lush lawns."

"On Clyde's moth-eaten patch of grass?"

"On your neighbors' lawns. I've seen you sitting in the neighbors' flower beds, sniffing the blooms when you thought no one was watching."

"I was hunting; those flower beds are full of moles."

She did not remind him that he hated moles.

They had been on the roof for better than an hour when a blue hatchback came up Highway One from the south and turned up into the hills just before the tunnel. Heading up a winding lane, it cut across the hills and back again, cruising. By now, seven families were working in their gardens despite the dark sky and fitful wind, diligent homeowners too conscientious to spend the morning loafing. *That*, Joe thought, *is one of the main advantages of being a cat. Cats do not have a problem with compulsive personalities.* And now, far out to sea, a web of lines slanted down where rain was pouring.

The blue hatchback paused beside a two-storied Spanish house set well back on a large corner lot. It didn't stop; it crept slowly by as if the driver was looking the place over. The way the house was angled, one would be able to see into a portion of the backyard, where a family of five was planting shrubs and small trees. The hatchback turned at the next corner and parked.

A woman emerged, a dumpy creature dressed in a long, full skirt, a sloppy sweater, and a floppy hat. Joe crept forward, watching her, his stub tail twitching. She glanced around her, studying the houses nearby, then headed up the street toward the white stucco. Approaching from the side street, she would be able to see the backyard, but might not be noticed by the busily gardening family. The cats watched her glance into the backyard then turn away, retrace her steps to the front door.

They didn't see her ring the bell. She tried the knob, glanced around again, and moved right on in. Evidently no one in the backyard noticed her, no one made a move toward the house. Maybe she belonged there. And maybe she didn't. Joe leaped to the cupola roof. Rearing tall, he studied the house, getting his bearings. Standing like a weather vane braced against the wind, he counted the streets.

"Five blocks above Janet's burned studio. Four blocks to the left."

And they fled down the trellis and across yards and sidewalks, up across the grassy park above Highway One and up the winding streets, through the high grass of the open fields, through tangles of broom and holly; across lawns and manicured flower beds, moving so swiftly that when they reached the blue hatchback—which turned out to be a late-model Honda—the motor was still ticking softly, and the tires and wheels were still warm.

Again there was dried mud smeared across the license plate. But this time, pawing together at the caked dirt, they were able to flake away enough mud to reveal California plate 3GHK499.

There was no indication of issuing county, of course. California plates did not include that information. The car could be registered anywhere in the state; only Max Harper would know, when he pulled up the number through DMV. It galled Joe that the cops had access to information the average citizen—average cat—couldn't touch.

But he guessed it had to be that way; a cop's job was tough enough. Give civilians access to the DMV files, and they'd create a ton of mischief.

Leaving the Honda, trotting on up the street to the white stucco house, they found the family still working away, lowering the burlap-wrapped roots of sturdy nursery shrubs into the earth. There the constricted bushes could stretch out their thin white roots like hundreds of hungry tongues reaching for food. A black Mercedes was parked in the drive. The cats jumped to the hood, then to the top of the car, leaving pawprints, and leaped to the garage roof, onto the rounded clay tiles.

To their left, the two-story portion of the house rose above the garage. The windows of both bedrooms were open, the sheer white curtains blowing. Within the front bedroom a figure moved, her baggy skirt and huge sweater catching the light in lumpy folds as she turned to the closet. The cats slipped closer, up across the tiles, and pressed against the wall, glancing around to look warily in through the glass.

The woman had pulled the double closet doors open and was examining the hanging garments. Her ragged gray hair was in need of a good trim and a vigorous brushing. She looked like she'd made her clothing selections from the "latest fashion" rack of the local charity outlet. Her skirt hem dipped so rakishly around her thick-stockinged ankles that one could imagine this style as the precursor of a new trend; and her shoes might soon be the "in" look, too, thick and serviceable and of a variety favored by the unfortunate homeless. Rummaging through the closet, the old lady carefully lifted a little gold lamé dress dangling on its hanger.

As she turned to the mirror above the dresser, they could see clearly her reflection. Smiling with impish delight she held the slim little cocktail number up against her thick body, turning and vamping, pressing the svelte garment against her lumpy form.

Watching her, Joe choked back a laugh. But Dulcie crept closer, the tip of her tail twitching gently, her green eyes round with sympathy, with a deep female understanding. The old woman's longing filled her to her very soul; she understood like a sister the frumpy lady's hunger for that sleek little gold lamé frock. Watching the dumpy old creature, Dulcie was one with her, cat and cat burglar were, in that instant, of one spirit.

"What's the matter with you?"

Dulcie jumped, stared at him as if she'd forgotten he was there. "Nothing. Nothing's the matter."

He looked at her uneasily.

"So she makes me feel sad. So all right?"

He widened his eyes, but said no more. They watched the old woman fold the gold dress into a neat little square, lift her baggy sweater, and tuck the folded garment underneath into a bag she wore against her slip. They watched, fascinated, as she searched the dresser drawers, lifting out necklaces and bracelets, stuffing them into the same bag, watched her tuck away two soft-looking sweaters, a gold tie clip, a gold belt, a tiny gold evening clutch. When she moved suddenly toward the window, coming straight at them, the cats ducked away, clinging against the wall. She flew at the open window uttering a string of hisses so violent, so like the cries of a maddened tomcat that their fur stood up. In feline language this was a grade-one kamikaze attack. This woman knew cats. This old woman knew how to communicate the most horrifying threat of feline violence, knew something deep and basic that struck straight at the heart of cat terrors, knew the deep secrets of their own murderous language. They stared at her for only an instant, then fled down the roof tiles and onto the Mercedes. Racing its length, they hit the ground running, heading straight uphill, past the white house, into a wilderness with bushes so thick that nothing could reach them.

Crouching in the dark beneath jabbing tangled branches, they watched the old woman leave the house smiling, watched her slip away up the street looking as smug as if she had swallowed the canary.

Dulcie shivered. "She scared the hell out of me." She licked her whiskers nervously. "Where did she learn to do that?"

"Wherever, she's out of business now. As soon as we call Harper with the make on that blue Honda, it's bye-bye, cat burglar."

But Dulcie's eyes grew huge, almost frightened. "Maybe we . . . She's just an old lady." She paused, began to fidget.

"What are you talking about?"

"Will the court . . . Do you think the court would go easy with her? She's so old."

"She's not that old. Just frowsy. And what difference does it make? Old or young, she's a thief."

He fixed a piercing yellow gaze on Dulcie. "This morning you were plenty hot to nail the old girl. *You're* the one who always wants to bring in the law. 'Call Harper, Joe. Give the facts to Captain Harper. Let the cops in on it.'

"So why the sudden change? You're really getting soft."

"But she's so . . . They wouldn't put her in jail for the rest of her life? How could they? To be locked up when you're old, maybe sick . . ."

He narrowed his eyes at her.

"Maybe we shouldn't tell Captain Harper. Maybe not just yet."

"Dulcie . . ."

"They wouldn't keep her in jail until she's feeble? Maybe in a wheelchair, like the old folks at Casa Capri?"

"I have no idea what the court would do. I don't see what difference." He looked at her a long time, then turned his back and crept out of the bushes. Of course they were going to tell Harper.

He heard Dulcie crawl out behind him. They crouched together, not speaking, looking down the hill where the blue Honda had driven away. Just below them, the little family was still planting their trees and bushes. Neither the two adults nor the children seemed to have any notion that their house had been burglarized. That made him smile in spite of himself. The old girl was pretty slick.

But slick or not, she was still a thief.

Dulcie didn't speak for a long time, but at last she gave him a sideways look. "I guess, with the number of burglaries that old lady has pulled off, and all the valuable things she's stolen, I guess maybe jail will be the last home she ever has."

"Can it, Dulcie. Let it rest. One look at the old lady mooning over that glittery little dress, and you sell out."

He looked her over. "Sisters under the skin, is that it? You and that old lady, two of a kind, two avaricious, thieving females."

Her look was icy. "It was a lovely gold dress." Her green eyes stared him down, her glare as righteous as if *he* were the criminal.

8

Dulcie wasn't much into cars, but she had a keen eye for luxury. The sleek red convertible that slipped by, moving like a whisper down the southbound lane of Ocean, left her gawking, her green eyes wide. The tip of her pink tongue came out, ears and whiskers thrust forward, and she took a little step along the sidewalk, twitching her tail, staring after the car's beautifully molded rear and sleek black convertible top.

"It's a Bentley Azure," Joe whispered against her ear. He twitched a whisker and pretended to lick his paw; there were people around them on the sidewalk, pedestrians, shoppers. "To quote the publicity, 'the newest, fastest model in the Rolls Royce line.'"

They watched it turn at the corner and head back up the northbound lane of Ocean. Joe's yellow eyes widened. "That's Clyde driving. *Clyde*. Driving that silky beauty. Look at him tooling along—as if he owned the world." Passing them, Clyde turned into the covered drive of the automotive shop, beneath the wide tile roof of the Mediterranean building that housed Beckwhite's Foreign Car agency.

Near the cats, several pedestrians had paused, gawking, as the lovely red car slid by. Joe ducked his head, pretending to nibble another flea. "That color's called pearl red. That's Adelina Prior's new car. Three hundred and forty thousand bucks, paid for by the old folks up at Casa Capri."

Dulcie's eyes blazed in disbelief.

He gave her a narrow leer. "You hadn't thought of that, had you? You don't know anything about how rich Adelina Prior is. That car just arrived from the factory. White leather upholstery, CD changer, inlaid walnut dash, a bar in the back, the works. Clyde was supposed to install her phone; that's probably why he has it." He led her toward the shop, adroitly dodging pedestrians, then, crossing Ocean, dodging slow-moving cars.

But as they trotted into the covered drive, a Molena Point police car turned in, parking just behind Clyde. The static of the police radio made their ears twitch.

Max Harper stepped out of his patrol unit, leaned into the Bentley's open window. Neither man saw the cats. The engine of the red Bentley Azure idled as softly and luxuriously as the purr of a jungle cat.

"Nice wheels," Max said. The police captain's scent drifted to them pleasantly on the little breeze that sucked in through the open drive. He smelled of horses and cigarettes, with a hint of gun oil. His thin hands, resting on the car door, were as gnarled and dark as Clyde's old hiking boots.

"Adelina Prior's." Clyde leaned back into the soft upholstery and grinned, stroked the steering wheel. Harper looked the car over, took out a pack of cigarettes, then changed his mind and put them back in his pocket. As if he didn't want to smoke up that pristine beauty. His thin, lined face was drawn into a scowl. "Got another line on that green truck that hit Susan Dorriss. Not much. And not much chance it'll show up here, but thought I'd pass the word.

"Man came in the station yesterday. Seems our last newspaper article jogged his memory; he recalled an old green truck cruising the hills about the time Susan was hit, says he saw it three times that week, up around his place." Harper nodded vaguely toward the hillside residences. "Green step-side. He thought it was a Chevy but wasn't sure, didn't know what year, didn't get a plate number.

"Didn't know it was important until he read yesterday's paper. He was out of town when Susan's car was hit, and he didn't see the original newspaper story."

Again he took out a cigarette, slipping it from the pack in his pocket in an automatic reflex. He started to tamp it on the door of the Bentley, then put it back again. "Why the hell does an accident like that happen to someone like Susan?"

Clyde turned off the Bentley's engine. "I'll watch for the truck, though not likely we'll see it at Beckwhite's. Green. A step-side. Not much to go on."

Harper nodded. "Likely it's down in L.A. by now with a new paint job, new plates, or it's been junked."

"And no idea of the year?"

"None. And Susan only got a glimpse before it hit her. She thought it was American-made, a full-sized pickup, not new. Faded green paint, and with fenders, she thought. Those models can fool you, can look older than they are."

Harper eased his weight, as if perhaps his regulation shoes were uncomfortable. "I hate a hit-and-run, that was too damn bad. Susan's a really nice woman; she used to walk that big poodle all over the village—before that guy put her in a wheelchair. You'd see her go by the station, Susan and the dog swinging along happy as a couple of kids.

"Tell you one thing," Harper said. "That daughter of Susan's isn't going to give it up. One way or another, Bonnie Dorriss means to nail the guy that busted up her mother." He managed a lean, leathery smile. "Bonnie's really on my back, calls in every couple of days. Have we got anything new? Just what are we doing?"

He glanced up, saw Joe and Dulcie sitting in the wide doorway to the automotive shop. "You're bringing your cat to work?" He raised an eyebrow. "I'd think you'd keep him out of here, after he nearly got himself blown into fish bait."

Joe and Dulcie glanced at each other, and Joe watched Harper carefully. Max Harper never could figure out why his old beer-drinking buddy, his ex-rodeoing buddy, was so dotty about a cat. And he knew he made Harper nervous; twice this past year he and Dulcie had upset the police captain pretty badly.

Though whatever suspicions might needle Harper, they could be no more than suspicions.

Highly amused, laughing inside, he gave Harper a blank and stupid gaze. He loved goading Max Harper. On poker nights he always tried to have some new little routine, some subtle new irritant to taunt the captain— not because he disliked him, only because he enjoyed Harper's stern discomfiture.

And what difference, if Harper was suspicious? No matter what he might suspect, if Max Harper breathed a word about intelligent cats, about crime-solving cats, to his fellow officers, he'd be off the force quicker than he could spit.

Dulcie nudged Joe, and he came alert, saw Clyde's meaningful look, realized he must have been staring too hard at Harper, maybe smirking. Clyde's look said, watch yourself, buddy. And to distract Joe, Clyde leaned over and opened the passenger door of the Bentley.

"Come on, cats. Come on, kitty kitty," Clyde said sarcastically.

Glancing at each other, they lowered their eyes demurely and trotted around the front of the Bentley. Stood staring up through the open door as Clyde carefully arranged his clean white lab coat across the front seat. When he had suitably covered the creamy leather, he shouted, "Come on, dammit." And they jumped up onto the coat, the three of them playing the master-and-cat game perfectly for Harper's benefit.

"You two make one claw dent, you leave one cat hair

anywhere near this upholstery, and you're dog meat. Two little portions of Ken-L Ration."

Harper observed this little tableau with only the faintest change of expression on his long, cheerless face. Whatever he was thinking didn't show.

Clyde patted Joe roughly, and grinned at Max. "I volunteered the cat to Bonnie Dorriss for that Pet-a-Pet group she's organized, to visit up at Casa Capri."

Harper raised an eyebrow, but nodded. "She started the project for her mother, only way she could think of, to take the poodle up there. Thinks the dog'll cheer Susan, help her recover. Susan loves that big poodle."

"Bonnie told me the plan; she's sure the dog can help Susan get through the pain of the therapy, keep her spirits up while she heals." Clyde ruffled Joe's fur in an irritating manner. "Bonnie wanted some cats in the group, so why not? Let the little beggar work for a living."

Beneath Clyde's stroking hand, Joe held very still, trying to control his rage. Clyde could be a real pain. *Let the little beggar work for a living.* Just wait until they were alone.

Pulling away from Clyde's stroking hand, turning his back, he pictured several interesting moves he might pursue to put Clyde Damen in his place.

Harper said, "I can't believe she'd take cats up there. A dog, sure. You can train a dog, make him mind. But a cat? Those cats will be all over; you can't control a cat.

"But hey, maybe a few cats careening around will give those old folks a little excitement, anything to break the boredom." Harper frowned. "When old people get bored, they can turn strange. We've had some real nut calls from up there."

"Oh?" Clyde said with interest. "What kind of nut calls?"

Harper shifted his lean body. "Imagining things. One old doll calls every few months to tell us that some of the patients are missing, that her friends have disappeared."

Clyde settled back, listening.

"When someone gets sick, Casa Capri moves them from the regular Care Unit over to Nursing. More staff over there, nurses who can keep them on IVs or whatever's needed. They don't encourage people from Care to visit the patients in Nursing, don't want folks whipping in and out. I can understand that.

"So this old woman keeps calling to say they won't let her see her friends, that her friends have disappeared. She got on my case so bad that finally I sent Brennan up to have a look around, ease her mind."

Harper grinned. "The missing people were all there, their names on the doors, the patients in their beds. Brennan knew a couple of them from years ago. Said they were pretty shriveled up with age."

He shook his head. "I guess that place takes as good care of them as you'd find. But poor Mrs. Rose, she can't understand. Every time she calls, she's bawling."

"Damned hard to get old," Clyde said.

Harper nodded. "Hope I go quick when the time comes." He ducked a little, for a better look at the interior of the Bentley, at the soft white leather, at the tasteful and gleaming accessories and the sleekly inlaid dash. "How much did this baby set Adelina back?"

"Three and a half big ones," Clyde said. "Poker this week?"

"Sure, if we don't have a triple murder." Harper glanced at the cats lying sedately on Clyde's lab coat, shook his head, and swung away to his police unit. Stepping in, he raised a hand and backed out. Within thirty minutes of Max Harper's departure, Joe and Dulcie were taking their first, and probably only, ride in Adelina Prior's pearl red, $340,000 Bentley Azure convertible. Heading up into the hills, sitting in the front seat like celebrities, Dulcie sniffed delicately at the inlaid wood dashboard, but she didn't let her pink nose touch that maple-and-walnut work of art. Carried along in that soft, humming, powerful palace of luxury, she felt as smug as if she were dining at the finest hotel, on a silver bowl of canaries prepared in cream.

Heading high up the hills toward the Prior estate, Clyde slowed as he passed Casa Capri. Following him at some distance was his own antique Packard, driven by his head mechanic. That quiet man had made no comment about Clyde giving two cats a joyride. Clyde was, his employees knew too well, touchy about the tomcat.

As they passed Casa Capri, Joe asked, "Did Harper mention anything more about the cat burglar?"

"Matter of fact, he did. He thinks she's moving on up the coast. She's started working Half Moon Bay."

"Really," Joe said, and shrugged. "Well she ripped off another Molena Point house just this morning."

Clyde turned to stare at him, swerving the Bentley. But at his touch the car responded like a thoroughbred, righting herself with superb balance. "How do you know she ripped off another house? What did you do, follow her?"

Joe looked innocent.

"Can't you two stay out of anything?"

Joe said, "She lifted a gold lamé dress and some jewelry from that new two-story Mediterranean house up above Cypress."

"Harper'll be thrilled that his favorite snitch is on the case again. I suppose you got a make on her car."

"Not a thing," Dulcie said quickly. "Didn't see the car. But the gold lamé dress was lovely."

Joe gave her a narrow look. He didn't like this; Dulcie had turned completely sentimental about the old woman. He didn't like this soft, sentimental side of his lady. What had happened to his ruthless hunting partner?

Clyde turned into a wide, oak-shaded drive. No house was visible; the curving lane led up over the crest of the hill. They drove for some time through the deep, cool shade beneath the overhanging branches of a double line of ancient oaks, then the drive made a last turn, and the house appeared suddenly, just on the crest of the hill. The two-story Mediterranean mansion was sheltered by oaks so huge they must have been here long before the house was built. The cats could see, far back behind the house, what appeared to be a much older structure.

The Prior house was two-storied, its thick white walls shadowed beneath deep eaves and beneath a roof of heavy, red clay tiles laid in curved rows. The front door was deeply carved, the main floor windows had beautifully wrought burglar bars, and each upstairs bedroom had French doors standing open to a private balcony.

"Five acres," Clyde said. "All that land back behind belongs to Adelina, and this is just the tiny remainder of the old land grant. Worth several million per acre now, plus the house and the original farmhouse and stables.

"This house was built in the thirties, but the estate goes back to the early eighteen hundreds. It belonged to the Trocano family, was a Spanish land grant. All the hills, every bit of land you can see, was Trocano land, thousands of acres. The buildings behind the house date from then."

Dulcie tried to imagine the distance in years, back to the early part of the last century. Tried to imagine Molena Point without houses, just miles of rolling hills and a few scattered ranches, imagine longhorns roaming, wolves and grizzly bears, where now she and Joe hunted the tiniest game. The terrible distance in time and the incredible changes made her head reel.

The grounds of the Prior estate were well tended, the lawn thick and very green. To the left of the old original house lay a wood, and they could see dark old tombstones between the trees.

"Family burial plot," Clyde said, "from when families were laid to rest on their own land." He parked the Bentley just opposite the front door. The cats could smell jasmine flowers, and the rich aroma of meat and chilies from somewhere deep within the house. Clyde picked up the two of them unceremoniously, carried them to the Packard, and deposited them in the back-seat.

But on that brief journey as she was carried, Dulcie took in every possible detail she could see through the broad front windows of the house, a glimpse of library with walls of leather-bound books; pale, heavy draperies; the gleam of antique furniture; oriental rugs on polished floors. Dulcie's green eyes shone with interest, her pink tongue tipped out, her dark, striped tail twitched.

The mechanic, slipping over into the passenger seat, turned to look back, watching the little cat, puzzled. As if he'd never seen a cat so interested in fine houses. And quickly she began to wash, trying to look uninterested and dull.

She had no idea that her interest in the Prior home, her desire to see inside those elegant rooms, would soon be more than satisfied—and in a way she would not have imagined.

9

Susan Dorriss regarded her lunch tray, which had been fixed across the arms of her wheelchair, with disgust. At least she'd wangled a meal alone in her room, though to gain that privacy she'd had to pretend a pounding headache. Solitary meals were against policy at Casa Capri unless you were fevered or throwing up. The home's owner-manager considered anyone who liked to be alone as mentally crippled or suspect. "We put a high value on everyone making friends; we're one big family here." The longer she was in Casa Capri—and Thursday would mark her second month—the less she could abide this enforced closeness. The whole structure of Casa Capri seemed to her rigid and heavy, reflecting exactly Adelina Prior's overbearing manner.

And today the food was just as unpleasant, the plate before her loaded with a pile of overdone roast beef and gluey mashed potatoes and canned gravy that smelled like sweet bouillon cubes. She knew she was being a bitch, but why not? There was no one to hear her even if she grumbled aloud.

Usually the meals were wonderful, when Noah was in charge of the kitchen. Lunch would be a fresh salad, plenty of fruits, and a variety of crisp greens, and for the entrée something light and appealing, a small portion of light lobster Newburg or a nice slice of chicken with asparagus or sugar peas. You paid enough to live in this place that the food ought to be thoughtfully prepared. She'd forgotten this was Noah's day off.

She ate some of the hot bread and forced down a bite of limp salad swimming in Thousand Island dressing, then pushed her plate away. She set the dessert aside, shoving the heavy bread pudding onto the night table next to her glasses and a stack of books. She was watching *Tootsie*, an old favorite. She loved the fun Dustin Hoffman had with this role, loved the way he handled his disguises. Bonnie had brought the video yesterday when she came; her daughter knew which movies she liked and she brought several each week. *Tootsie* would finish up about one-thirty, and Bonnie would arrive at two with Lamb.

The big, chocolate-colored poodle was Susan's ticket to freedom for a little while; it was Lamb who would take her out of here, away from the nurses and the regimentation and rules.

Bonnie had organized the Pet-a-Pet program mainly for that purpose. With the accompanying favorable publicity for Casa Capri, there was no way Adelina could refuse. Publicity meant money, and money was what Adelina Prior was all about.

On Bonnie's first Pet-a-Pet visit, Lamb had been so happy to find Susan, had been so playful, overjoyed, acting as if she'd been hiding from him. And she'd had no trouble at all teaching him, that first day, to pull her along the deserted lanes of the adjoining, wooded park, using the harness Bonnie had fashioned. The acreage beyond the Spanish-style complex was large, and the path through the oak woods was shaded and pleasant, scented with the perfume of rotting leaves, peopled with a dozen varieties of birds flashing among the oaks and rhododendron. And with the cool wind, and with Lamb's damp nose nudging her hand, after those afternoons she returned to the villa refreshed, renewed, quite ready to be calm and patient for a few days.

And then after the Pet-a-Pet session Bonnie had

taken her out to dinner, folding her wheelchair into the backseat, tucking Susan herself into the leather front seat and gently fastening the seat belt around her, careful of the bones that had been broken. Dinners out were a real treat since she had come to Casa Capri. The evenings they spent sipping wine and enjoying lobster or scallops at The Bakery, or cosseted within the luxury of the more expensive Windborne, those evenings, and these afternoons with Lamb, were what made her long days at the nursing home bearable.

She removed her loaded lunch tray and set it on the bed. Wheeling her chair to the low dressing table, she began to brush her short white hair. She had been so excited about moving down here to Molena Point from San Francisco when she retired from Neiman-Marcus. She had always loved the village, loved its oak-wooded hills and the hillside views of the village's rooftops gleaming red against the blue Pacific. She loved the upstairs apartment she had rented from Bonnie; it had a wonderful view. But she had hardly been moved in, half her boxes still unpacked, when the car accident changed everything.

She had run out to the store for some more shelf paper for the kitchen before she unpacked her dishes, and as she turned off Highway One just north of the tunnel, the truck came around a curve, crossing the center line. The driver hit his brakes, skidded, spun out of control, and hit her car broadside.

When she came to at the bottom of a ten-foot embankment, her car on its side, she had been conscious enough to dig the phone out from under her injured legs and dial 911. Had been very thankful for the phone. She'd given it to herself as a birthday gift, and that day it probably saved her life.

The police never had found the old green pickup. Bonnie said they were still looking, that they still had it on their list. But after all this time, what good? Certainly her insurance company would like to find the truck. Two weeks in the hospital, four more weeks in a convalescent wing, and then here to the nursing home, and a visit every day from a physical therapist, all this was terribly expensive. She spent an hour a day doing resistance exercises that hurt so badly they brought tears spurting.

But the exercises were strengthening her torn muscles, and that would help support her healing bones. She had metal plates everywhere. Bonnie kept saying she wanted to hug her hard, but she couldn't—a hug would hurt like hell. Bonnie said she was like a poor broken bird one was afraid to pick up, and that had made her tears come in self-pity until she shouted at Bonnie to stop. If Bonnie had a failing, it was too much feeling for others, too much pity.

Bonnie was so much like her father. She had George's way of looking at life just as she had inherited his square, sturdy build, his sandy hair and freckles. She had nothing of Susan's own long, lean body that never seemed to take on weight. Bonnie had always had trouble with weight though she didn't seem to mind. She was always reaching out, as George had, so eager to be with people and to help them.

When Susan came to Casa Capri, Bonnie had been appalled at the sense of depression among the patients. And Bonnie was constitutionally unable to leave any unpleasant situation alone. That, too, had propelled her into organizing the Pet-a-Pet program, though her plan was born primarily so she could bring Lamb to visit. The big, easygoing standard poodle had become as much Susan's dog as Bonnie's. From the day she moved into the hillside apartment, Susan had walked him twice a day, up among the village hills and down among the shops, her pleasure complete at having a dog to walk after so many years in a San Francisco apartment that wouldn't accommodate a big dog. She didn't like little dogs. Might as well have a cat, and her opinion of cats wasn't high.

She loved Lamb's steady, happy disposition. He was

such a delightful and handsome dog. Bonnie's down-stairs apartment had a nice yard, and Bonnie kept Lamb's chocolate coat clipped short, in a field cut, no ruffles or pompoms, no nonsense. One of the worst things about the aftermath of the accident was not having Lamb warm and pressing against her leg, looking up at her, sharing her lonely moments.

When the pain was at its worst, she kept thinking, *Why me? Why did this happen to me. What kind of God would let this happen?* But what stupid, pointless questions.

God was not to blame; God had nothing to do with accidents. Things just happened, and no use fretting. If she made the best of it, if she did the painful therapy and got herself back in shape, she'd be out of here.

That was what God looked at, how you responded to the random bad times that might hit. God could see if you were a fighter. He was pleased if you were, and disappointed if you didn't fight back against life's bad luck. She'd always known, ever since she was a little girl, that God didn't like quitters.

And she was tremendously lucky not to be here for good like the other residents. She was only sixty-four and had plenty of plans for her remaining years. She was going to heal herself and be out of this place by the end of summer.

But for now she needed the extra care that the retirement home offered and which Bonnie couldn't manage, working all day. For the first weeks she could hardly move. She'd rather be here with a regular staff who were used to giving care than at home trying to deal with some hired woman. She had spent her first three days in the Nursing wing at the other end of the block-long building, before she was moved over here.

At least in this wing the outer doors weren't kept locked during the day, as they were in Nursing. That had given her the willies. Bonnie had really climbed the fire marshal about that, but he said they had Alzheimer's patients over there and had to keep the doors locked. He swore that every person on duty carried door keys at all times in case of fire or earthquake.

But locked doors or not, there was really no reason why the Nursing unit should be so strict about visitors. What did Adelina Prior think, that someone was going to pull out a sick patient's IV or feed him poison? No wonder little Mae Rose got upset and let her imagination run wild.

Casa Capri was one of those complexes known as three-stage living. Residents could progress from retirement living in a private cottage, to assisted living here in the Care Unit, with twenty-four-hour service available, then on to Nursing, where you retired to your bed for good.

That was fine for some people, though in her view such careful planning for every remaining moment of your life was like living in a cage.

Many of the cottage residents still drove their own cars and jogged and traveled, but wanted the extra security and services such a place offered. They didn't have to cook, didn't have to worry about housecleaning or maintenance. Old Frederick Weems lived over in Cottages, while his wife Eula lived here in the Care Unit. And who could blame him, with Eula's nagging? If they had the money, more power to him.

But maybe she was unfair in her assessment of Casa Capri. The car accident had allowed her no time to work up a mind-set that would help her adapt to these rigid group rules. She was never much for rules; during her years working in retail sales she constantly had to rein in her passions and her temper.

Now she no longer cared if people thought her abrasive—she'd be rude when she chose. That included, to Bonnie's distress, being rude to Adelina Prior.

If she didn't dislike Adelina so deeply, she'd get friendly and try to figure out what made the woman tick. Why would a woman as beautiful, as expensively groomed and elegantly dressed, want to spend her life running a nursing home?

But though the puzzle nagged at her, she didn't have the patience to fake friendliness with Adelina. It was all she could do to deal with the pain; that alone, when it was at its worst, could turn her as short-tempered as a caged tiger. She dreamed of being free of pain and home again in her new apartment, she dreamed of wandering the village, with Lamb walking at heel.

She loved the fact that in Molena Point people shopped with their dogs. Anywhere in the village you might see a patient, obedient dog tied outside a shop in the shadow of an oak tree while his master or mistress did errands. It was such a casual, lovely little town. She burned to know Molena Point better, to discover more of the hidden galleries and boutiques which were tucked away in the alleys, to browse the bookstores and enjoy the many small restaurants. These were her retirement years. What was she doing in a wheelchair? She had been so glad to move away from the heart of San Francisco, from its growing street crime, to a village devoid of that kind of violence. Molena Point was a walking village, a safe and friendly place where one felt nothing bad could happen.

It was their first night out for dinner after the accident, the first night she was able to lift herself from the wheelchair into Bonnie's car, that Bonnie told her about the Pet-a-Pet idea. Sitting in the Windborne at a window table, looking down at the sea breaking on the rocks below, Bonnie said, "You need a friend in that place. You need Lamb."

"I wish. Bring him on over, we can share a room."

But Bonnie laid out her plan with childlike enthusiasm; she had worked out all the details, even to convincing Adelina Prior of the positive public relations and advertising value of such a venture. The owner-manager of Casa Capri was not an animal lover, not that cold-eyed woman. Bonnie promised Adelina she would get articles about Casa Capri's exciting Pet-a-Pet venture in several specialty magazines; she had some connections among the clients of the law firm she worked for that would help. No special favors, just casual networking. There was, at the time, a Pet-a-Pet group based in San Francisco, and a branch in Santa Barbara, making regular visits with their well-mannered animals to local nursing homes, and the local newspapers had done great human-interest articles with lots of pictures.

Bonnie said, "Halman and Fletcher is getting me an assistant, and I'll be working Saturdays for a while with John Halman on this land-swindle case. That frees me up two afternoons a week, to bring the Pet-a-Pet group out to Casa Capri. I've already contacted the San Francisco chapter, and they're sending instructions about testing the animals for sweet dispositions and gentleness. They suggested five Molena Point pet owners they thought might like to join us, and one is the reference librarian you met, Wilma Getz."

The waiter brought their salad and filled their wineglasses; beyond the windows the sea had darkened.

"Lamb misses you, Mama. I swear he's pining, he's so sulky. And you miss him; so what could be more perfect?" She broke her French bread, looking out at the heaving sea, its swells running swift beneath the restaurant's lights. "I have the plan all in place. Three hours each visit, two afternoons a week. One owner-handler for each pet.

"A reporter has already interviewed us. Of course, Adelina was there." Bonnie grinned. "Guess who took all the credit. The *Gazette* is sending a photographer later, when we get settled in. I don't want the animals bothered until they're used to the routine."

Though Adelina Prior had been prominent during the newspaper interview, she had not been in evidence during the first two Pet-a-Pet sessions. Several nurses had worked with the group, attending each patient as an animal was brought to an old man or woman. The nurses brought water bowls for the pets, too, and after the session they vacuumed up whatever loose dog and cat hair might offend Adelina.

Of course when Adelina learned that Susan had taken Lamb outside into the oak-shaded park alone, the woman pitched a fit; but Bonnie calmed her with promises of a possible *Sunset Magazine* spread. Bonnie's boss had gone to school with one of the attorneys who handled the *Sunset* account. The only sour note was the attitude of young Teddy Prior, Adelina's cousin. Like Adelina, the young wheelchair patient had no use for animals. The difference was, Teddy made his sentiments clearly known. She thought it strange that Teddy Prior, though he drove his own specially equipped car, occupied a room at Casa Capri rather than his own apartment, or rather than living with his cousin. Though he had many amenities here—all the advantages of a hotel, maid service, and meals, while enjoying many privileges forbidden to the other residents.

She was ashamed of herself for faulting Teddy. He was only twenty-eight, and the accident that crippled his spine had caused damage beyond repair. Five bouts of surgery had been of no use. She should feel empathy for him—or at least pity, not annoyance. In fact, Teddy was to be admired. He had disciplined himself well against the pain; she saw no signs of stress in his smooth face and clear blue eyes. He had a sweet smile, too, as charming as a young boy's, and he had a nice way with the old people. He was always interested in their personal lives, in their complaints and their family stories. Teddy had that rare gift of making each person feel he was their special friend.

But yet she couldn't bring herself to like him.

He was particularly attentive to Mae Rose, too, though who wouldn't be? Little Mae was a dear—if she just wouldn't worry and fuss so. But Mae Rose did seem to have calmed, with the Pet-a-Pet visits—just as some of the other residents had become more lively and talkative, more outgoing.

Putting down her hairbrush, she turned off the video and tied a soft red scarf around her throat, tucking it beneath her white blouse. Maneuvering her wheelchair so she could pull open her door, she fastened the door in place with the little hook provided, and headed down the hall. It was time for Bonnie and Lamb, time to get out of this prison for a little while, time for a few hours of freedom.

10

The car was too hot—Joe felt steam-cooked clear to his whiskers. And the little girl's lap, on which he had been encouraged to sit, was incredibly bony and uncomfortable. Setting out in Wilma's car for Casa Capri, he hadn't expected to ride in some kid's lap; this was not part of the deal. And why would Wilma invite a twelve-year-old kid on this excursion? Was the child some new kind of pet to be added in with the dogs and cats? And did the kid have to keep petting him? Her hands were hot and damp and made him itch. Irritated out of his skull, suppressing a snarl, he crouched lower and squeezed his eyes closed.

The kid hadn't messed with Dulcie for long. One green-eyed venomous glance from the little tabby, and the girl had jerked her hand away fast.

Dulcie stood, with her paws on the dash, staring out the window totally enthralled, as she always was in a car, watching the hills, watching eagerly for the first glimpse of Casa Capri, as if the retirement villa was some really big deal, as though she'd been invited to high tea at the St. Francis or the Hyatt Regency.

Dillon Thurwell, that was the kid's name. Who would name a female child Dillon? Her black hair hung stringy and straight beneath her baseball cap. Her dark eyes were huge. She began to scratch behind his ear, but kept staring ahead expectantly as if she, too, could hardly wait to get to Casa Capri, all set for a fun afternoon.

She was dressed in jeans and one of those T-shirts that made a statement, a shirt she had obviously selected as appropriate for the occasion. Across her chest four cats approached the viewer, and on the back of the shirt, which he'd seen as she came around the car to get in, was a rear view of the same four cats walking away, as if they were stepping invisibly through the wearer's chest, their tails high, and, of course, all their fascinating equipment in plain sight.

Abandoning his ear, she began to scratch his cheek just behind his whiskers. Couldn't the little brat leave him alone? He was doing his best to be civil. It was enough that he had condescended to sit on her lap—and that only after dour looks from Dulcie and Wilma. Under her insistent scratching, he shook his head and got up, pressing his hard paws into her legs, and resettled himself dourly on her bony knees. He hated when people touched his whiskers.

But then she found that nice itchy place by his mouth, and she scratched harder, and that did feel good. Slowly, unable to help himself, he leaned his head into her hand, purring.

Wilma glanced down at the child, gave her a long look. "What made you dye your hair, Dillon? What's that all about?"

Dillon shrugged.

"I always envied your red hair; I hardly knew you today. What did your folks say?"

"Mama said I might as well get it out of my system— I cried until she had to say something." Dillon grinned. "It'll grow back, it'll be red again. I just wanted to try it."

Wilma stopped at a red light, pushed back a strand of her long gray hair, and refastened the silver clip that held it. Then, moving on with the traffic, she turned up Ocean toward the hills, following the little line of vehicles, a cortege of five cars and a white Chevy van, headed for Casa Capri.

"Come on, Dillon, what's the rest of the story?"

"What story? I don't know what you mean." The kid was cheeky, for being only twelve.

Wilma sighed. "Why change your looks the day before you join Pet-a-Pet? What's the deal here?" Wilma Getz wasn't easily taken in; she hadn't spent her professional life listening to the lies of parolees without gaining some degree of healthy skepticism.

"I just wanted to try it," Dillon repeated. "I wanted to do it now during spring break, so I can go back to school looking different. So I can get used to my new look before the kids see it." The kid was, Joe felt, talking too much. "How could my hair have anything to do with Pet-a-Pet? My friend Karen has black hair, and she's so beautiful." Her little oval face was bland as cream, her brown eyes shone wide and honest.

Wilma shrugged and gave it up, said nothing more.

Joe figured that dyeing her hair was just a stupid kid thing, but he did wonder why Dillon had joined Pet-a-Pet. What twelve-year-old would elect to spend spring break making nice to a room full of geriatric couch potatoes? She ought to be biking or swimming or playing ball.

He knew that Dillon Thurwell was a favorite of Wilma's. Dulcie said she'd been going to the library ever since she could toddle, and when she asked to join Pet-a-Pet, Wilma was delighted. Never mind that the kid didn't have a dog or cat; she could be in charge of Clyde Damen's gray tomcat. Don't ask him, just appoint the kid surrogate cat handler for yours truly, just plan his life for him.

The little entourage of cars trundled along up a steep, narrow side street like a third-rate funeral procession, and turned into a long, private drive. Ahead, on the crest of the hill, Casa Capri sprawled in Mediterranean splendor, a one-story villa as imposing as a Spanish monastery, pale walls and red-tile roofs all shadowed beneath the requisite oak trees, its deep-set windows guarded by handsome wrought-iron grilles, their intricate curlicues designed to prevent illicit entry. Or maybe illicit escape?

On beyond the buildings, up along the hills, ran a narrow street, but there were no houses near, just the round green hills dotted with old sprawling trees. To Joe's left rose an oak wood, a little private park. He could see a path winding through it among beds of ferns, and he imagined the frail residents taking little walks there, in the cool shade, accompanied by attending nurses.

They parked at the beginning of a circular drive, and Dillon disembarked, clutching him tightly against her kitty T-shirt, holding the nape of his neck in her fist in a maneuver designed to prevent him from running away, a technique she had undoubtedly learned from some book on cat care. The full instructions would direct the handler to grip the nape of the neck firmly in one hand, grip the base of the tail in the other hand, and carry kitty away from one's body to avoid being scratched. If Dillon went that far, she'd find herself dangling two bloody stumps.

Dulcie rode limply over Wilma's shoulder, all sweetness and smiles, looking ahead to Casa Capri, her green eyes glowing with anticipation. All ready for a fun afternoon frolicking with the cat-loving elderly. Their party was made up of fourteen humans and the same number of household pets, a remarkable assortment of dogs, mostly tiny, and cats-in-arms. One small woman toted a plastic cat carrier with air holes, through which two enraged blue eyes glowered.

In the center of the circular drive was a raised fish pond with a little cupped birdbath at one side, and burbling fountain in the center, a little oasis for our aquatic and avian friends. A flock of sparrows and finches rose lazily away, birds perhaps fed by the residents until they had lost all fear of other creatures. Joe looked after them hungrily. This would be a prime hunting preserve if he could ditch the Pet-a-Pet crowd.

Flanking the walk and drive, regiments of stiff bird-of-paradise plants grew, their dark leaves thrusting up like swords, their red and orange bird heads turned stiffly to observe new arrivals. The walk was mosaicked with tiny stones set in a curving pattern, rising in three steps to a wide landing. The double doors were dark and ornately carved. The resemblance of Casa Capri to the Prior estate in architectural style, even to the doors themselves and the window grilles, led one to conclude that Adelina had ordered the plans and the architectural accessories at a two-for-one sale.

To his left, through long French windows, Joe could see white-clothed tables set with glasses and flatware, as if the help liked to get an early start on the evening meal. To his right, within the nearest window, he glimpsed a window seat scattered with a tangle of bright pillows. Dillon let go of his neck but continued to hug him, pressing him to her like a cuddly toy until he growled at her.

She cut her eyes at him, but loosened her grip only enough to let him breathe.

The group's leader, Bonnie Dorriss, stood above them on the steps, smiling down as if she were a schoolteacher waiting for a gaggle of five-year-olds to gather. Her short sandy hair was the same color as the freckles which spattered her nose and cheeks. Her stocky figure was encased in tight, ragged jeans and a faded green sweatshirt. But she wore a good stout pair of Rockports.

Joe looked around him at their motley group of four-legged recruits, the little lapdogs fluffy and shivering and as useless as whiskers on a toad. But there were two big dogs as well; and the sappy-faced golden retriever looked so much like Barney, with that big silly smile, that Joe felt a lump in his belly the size of a basketball.

Clyde had brought Barney home that morning, had got him settled on his blanket on the bottom bunk of the two-tier dog and cat bed in the laundry room. Barney had seemed glad to be home, but the outlook wasn't good. The problem was his liver. He was on medication; Clyde had come home again at noon to give him his pills and try to get him to drink; all morning, Barney hadn't moved from the bunk.

Joe had hated to leave him all alone in there except for the other animals, because what could they do? Rube and the cats would be no help if he took a turn for the worse. Clyde said he'd run home a couple of times during the afternoon. He and Dr. Firreti were waiting to see if the pills would snap Barney out of it. It was midafternoon now, and he wondered if Clyde was at home. Worrying, he said a little cat prayer for Barney.

And he turned on Dillon's shoulder so he wouldn't have to look at the golden retriever; the dog made him feel too sad.

The other big dog was the brown poodle that belonged to Bonnie Dorriss. The poodle appeared totally aloof, paid no attention to any of the animals. Either he was extremely dignified or bored out of his skull. He must have felt Joe staring, because he glanced up, gave him a completely innocent look—as if to say he never, never chased cats.

Oh sure. Turn your tail, and you'd have poodle teeth in your backside before you could bare a claw.

Their little group consisted of eight dogs and six cats, including a black-and-white cat who could use some advice on the principles of a slimming diet. The long-haired white cat had one yellow eye and one blue, but she was totally color-coordinated: blue collar and a natty yellow name tag. Cute enough to make you retch.

The big yellow tom glowered threateningly at him, as a tomcat is expected to do. But beneath the show of testosterone he looked both sleepy and bored.

Joe could see into the plastic cat carrier now, where a scruffy-looking tortoiseshell huddled, her blue eyes not angry now, but only painfully shy. This was the Pet-a-Pet group? These scruffy cats and puny little lapdogs were expected to play skilled therapist to a bunch of needful humans? And, of course, among the mixed participants, Joe and Dulcie were the only nonhuman members who could have carried on a conversation with the old people.

That would generate some excitement.

Led by Bonnie Dorriss, their group moved on through the wide doors into the entry, the golden retriever gawking and stumbling over its own feet. The big poodle stepped lightly beside Bonnie into the spacious reception area and sat down at her heel. Impressive, Joe had to admit.

The entry was even more elegant than the carved double doors had implied, the blue tile floor gleaming, the small potted trees in hand-painted containers fingering their delicate leaves against the white walls. The heavy ceiling beams looked hand-carved, and to his right hung an old, antique oil painting of the Molena Point hills as they must have looked before any house marred the wild sweeps of grass and young oaks.

Directly ahead through an archway shone a well-appointed sitting area. This faced, through wide French doors, a sunny, enclosed patio surrounded by the wings of the building and planted with flowers and miniature citrus trees. Charming, totally charming. He wondered if the staff would serve tea, maybe little sandwiches of smoked salmon or imported sardines and liver paté.

But then he caught a whiff of medicines and pine-scented cleaning solution; of boiled beef and onions; a mix of smells that implied actual living went on beyond the pristine entry, implied a condensed, crowded occupancy involving many more people forced together than a cat found acceptable.

Dillon, carrying him, wandered away from the others toward the parlor, but she did not enter that elegant, perfectly groomed space. She stood at the edge of the cream-and-blue Chinese rug, looking. The area was too formal to be inviting—the couch and upholstered chairs done in pale silk damask, the little mahogany tables teetering on spindly legs, the damask draperies perfectly pleated. He could imagine digging his claws into that thick fabric and swarming up, laying waste to thousands of dollars worth of thoughtful design. This must be where the residents of Casa Capri entertained their relatives and visitors, away from hospital beds and potty chairs. The room smelled faintly of lavender. Joe found himself observing the furnishings not from his own rough, tomcat frame of reference but from Dulcie's view. Dulcie loved this fancy stuff. He even knew from listening to Dulcie that the four stiff-looking chairs were of Hepplewhite design—chairs as rigid and ungiving as four disapproving spinsters.

The room, in short, might impress, but it did not welcome. There were no cushiony places to cuddle the body, no gentle pillows to ease tired old bones. Casa Capri's parlor looked, to Joe, as if a sign should be placed at the edge of the Chinese rug warning all comers not to touch.

But beyond the stiff parlor, the bright patio was inviting, sunny and lush, the walled garden filled with pastel-colored lilies and low beds of pansies, with intimate arrangements of wrought-iron patio chairs fitted with deep, soft-appearing cushions that just invited a nap.

Surely, out there in that warm and protected setting the frail elderly could take the sun and gossip and doze in peace, comfortably sheltered from the chill sea wind and from the outer world. Sheltered within those walls . . .

Or imprisoned. Joe felt his fur rise along his back.

But maybe his sense of entrapment was only a recurrence of his own kittenhood terrors, when he had been trapped by screaming kids in San Francisco's alleys. Thinking of those nasty small boys with bricks, and nowhere to escape, he found himself clinging hard to Dillon's bony shoulder.

He was still clinging to the child when the big front doors opened behind them and a mousy little woman

stood looking in, a pale, thin creature dressed in something faded and too long, and little flat sandals on her
thin feet. Behind her, through the open door, on the
wide sweep of curved drive, parked just before the door,
stood the pearl red Bentley Azure.

And now the driver's door opened and Adelina
Prior herself stepped out. This could be no other: a
sleek and creamy woman, slim, impeccably dressed in
a little flared black suit and shiny black spike heels,
her jet hair smoothed into an elegant knot—chignon,
Dulcie would call it—which was fastened with a clasp
that glittered like diamonds. She carried a black
lizardskin briefcase with gold clasps, a small matching
handbag.

This was the grand dame of Casa Capri, and she was
everything that Clyde had described, her arch look at
the gathered Pet-a-Pet group, as she entered, was cold
with superiority and distaste.

Allowing her pale companion to hold the door for her,
she swept past them, lifting one perfectly groomed eyebrow, her perfume engulfing dogs and cats in a subtle
and expensive miasma of heady scent that overrode all
the others. Joe supposed that her faded companion, who
trailed away after her, was Adelina's sister, Renet. Nor
had Renet appeared impressed by their little Pet-a-Pet
gathering; she had remained as far from them as she
could manage, quickly fading to invisibility beside
Adelina's blade-perfect presence.

As the two women moved on down the hall to his
right, toward what seemed to be offices, Adelina paused,
turned briefly to survey them—as if hoping they had
somehow vanished.

From Wilma's shoulder, Dulcie stared back at her,
green eyes blazing as if she were reading Adelina's
thoughts, and taking in the woman's sleek hair and slim
expensive attire, her shapely legs and sheer black stockings, her spike heels sharp enough to puncture a cat's
throat.

It was Dulcie who glanced away.

This was the woman who could afford a three-hundred-thousand-dollar Bentley Azure but who presumably spent her days among bedpans counting soiled sheets and inspecting medication charts. A woman who had to be driven totally by love for humanity; why else would she do this? The woman who, Clyde had told him, supervised every detail of the retirement villa like an army general. As she disappeared into an office, Joe shivered, and he, too, looked away.

11

To Joe's right, where Adelina Prior had disappeared, the admitting desk dominated a portion of the villa that was less fancy and smelled strongly of various medicines, of human bodily functions, and of a harsh disinfectant that made his nose burn. A nurse stood before the admitting counter writing on a clipboard, stopping frequently to push back a lock of bleached hair. A wheeled cart loaded with medicine bottles and various pieces of equipment that he didn't recognize and with which he didn't care to become familiar was parked beside the high desk.

The walls were plain and unadorned, the carpet of a dark commercial tweed that looked as durable as concrete. He supposed that on around the corner the hall would lead away between rows of residents' rooms, rather like a hospital on TV. He imagined open doors revealing stark hospital beds and various uncomfortable-looking contrivances constructed of plastic and chrome, and perhaps an occasional closed door behind which a patient was indisposed or sleeping in the middle of the day. From that direction came a tangle of excited television voices, a mix of daytime soaps.

Their group did not approach the admitting desk but headed in the opposite direction, down the hall to the left, where a pair of double doors stood open revealing a shabby sitting room very different from the elegant reception parlor.

In the open double doors, Bonnie Dorriss paused, waiting for them to assemble, the big poodle sitting sedately at her heel in what was beginning to be, in Joe's opinion, an excessive display of overtraining. Did the animal have no mind of his own? But then what could you expect from a dog?

He heard a phone ring behind them, probably at the admitting desk, and in a moment it went silent. He wriggled around on Dillon's shoulder to get a better view of the social room. The decor was early Salvation Army. Mismatched couches and chairs in faded, divergent patterns, a pastiche of varied colors and styles stood about in vague little groups. The multicolored carpeting was of a variety guaranteed to hide any possible stain. Probably only a cat's or a dog's keen nose would detect the spills of cough syrup, oatmeal, and worse embedded in that short, tight weave. Surveying the room, Joe got the impression that when prospective clients were welcomed to Casa Capri to discuss the placement of an elderly relative, these sliding doors were kept closed.

An arrangement of several couches faced an oversize television set, and next to it a weekly TV schedule done up in large print had been taped to the wall. The other seating groups circled scarred coffee tables piled with wrinkled magazines and folded newspapers. There were no fancy potted trees or elegant little touches such as graced the entry and parlor. And the pictures on these walls were dull reproductions of dull photographs of dull landscapes from some incredibly tedious part of the world—the kind of cheap reproductions the local drugstore published for its giveaway Christmas calendar. A pair of lost eyeglasses lay under a coffee table, and a lone slipper peeked out from beneath a couch, implying that the room had not been recently vacuumed.

The few old people who were already in attendance, scattered about in the soft chairs, seemed to have dozed off. They were settled so completely into the faded furniture that occupant and chair might have been together for decades, growing worn and shabby as one entity.

The focal points of the room, besides the TV, were a set of wide glass doors leading out to the inner patio and, at the opposite side of the room, through an arch, the dining room, its tables laid with white cloths, its wide windows looking out through decorative wrought iron to the drive, the fountain, and the gardens beyond. A pair of swinging doors led to the kitchen, from which wafted the pervasive scent of boiled beef and onions. But it was not the kitchen that drew Joe. He looked away longingly toward the sunny patio, where, it seemed, freedom beckoned.

Off to the left of the patio doors, a second long hall led away. The two long wings, separated by the patio, were joined far at the back by a third line of rooms, completing the enclosure of that garden. Glass doors led from each bedroom into the sunny retreat.

As they entered the social room one of their group, a tiny fluff of dog, whined with eagerness. Immediately the dozing old folks stirred. Rheumy eyes flew open, little cries of pleasure escaped as the residents saw their visitors. A waxen-faced old man grinned widely and hoisted himself up from a deep recline, his faded eyes lighting like a lamp blazing.

Dillon's response was surprising. Squeezing Joe absently, hardly aware of him, her body went rigid as she studied the approaching residents.

As patients rose from the deep chairs, others straggled in from the far hall, some led by nurses, some wheeling their chairs energetically along or hobbling in their walkers, converging toward the Pet-a-Pet group moving in slow motion but as eagerly as if drawn forward by a magnetic force.

The animals' responses were more varied. While the little dogs wiggled and whined, hungering for the lavish attention without which, Joe was convinced, the miniature breeds would wither and die, and while the golden retriever, grinning and tugging at his lead, plunged ahead toward his geriatric friends, the cats were sensibly restrained, waiting circumspectly for further developments.

Bonnie Dorriss's poodle remained sitting at heel in an attitude of total dullsville. This was why cats were not given obedience lessons—no cat would put up with this smarmy routine.

But suddenly the poodle stiffened. His short tail began to wag as a wheelchair approached bearing a thin, white-haired woman. His mouth opened in a huge laugh. Sitting at heel, he wiggled all over.

Bonnie spoke a single word. The poodle leaped away, straight at the wheelchair, and stood on his hind legs, prancing like a circus dog around it, reaching his nose to lick the woman's face. His front paws didn't touch the chair until the white-haired woman pulled him to her for a hug.

Within minutes, the pair had whisked away out the front door, the dog pulling the wheeled chair along as the woman held his harness, the two of them heading for some private and privileged freedom.

And now their little group began to disperse as each animal was settled with an old person. And the assorted cats surprised Joe, settling in calmly with one patient or another, relaxed and open and loving. Joe watched them with uneasy interest. It appeared that each cat knew why it was there, and each seemed to value the experience. For a moment, the simpler beasts shamed him.

Dulcie had coached him endlessly about his own deportment. *Don't flinch at loud noises, Joe. Don't lay back your ears even if they pinch you, and for heaven's sake don't hiss at anyone. Keep your claws in. Stay limp. Close your eyes and purr. Just play it cool. Don't snarl. Think about how much you're helping some lonely old person. If you don't pass the test, if you fail, think how ashamed you'll be.*

That was her take on the matter. If he didn't pass the test, he'd be out of here, a cause for wild celebration. If he didn't pass muster, he'd be free, a simple but happy reject.

Bonnie Dorriss had helped with the testing, and that had been all right, but the two women who came down from San Francisco were another matter, two strangers poking and pushing him and talking in loud voices, deliberately goading him. He'd responded, he felt, with admirable restraint, smiling up at them as dull and simple as a stuffed teddy bear.

He'd passed with flying colors.

So I'm capable of equanimity. So big deal. So now here I am lying across this kid's shoulder wishing I was anywhere else because in a minute she's going to plop me down in some old lady's pee-scented lap. The approaching group of duffers that now converged around them thrilled him about as much as would a gathering of vivisectionists.

An old man in a brown bathrobe toddled right for him, pushing his chrome walker along with all the determination of a speed runner. Watching him, Joe crouched lower on Dillon's shoulder. But then the old boy moved right on past, heading for the black-and-white cat, his sunken, toothless grin filled with delight. "Kittie! Oh, Queen kitty. I thought you'd never get here."

Joe watched Bonnie Dorriss take the old man gently by the arm and settle him into a soft chair, setting his walker aside. When the cat's owner handed down the black-and-white cat, the old man laughed out loud. The cat, a remarkably equable female, smiled up at him with pleased blue eyes, and curled comfortably across his legs, reverberating so heavily with purrs that her fat stomach trembled.

This was all so cozy it made him retch. He changed position on Dillon's shoulder, turning his back on the gathering. This was not his gig.

He wasn't into this do-good stuff, had no interest in the therapeutic value of cat petting. Absolutely no desire to cheer the lonely elderly. He'd come only because of Dulcie, because of the bargain they'd made.

You mind your manners at Casa Capri, not embarrass me, really try to help the old folks, and you can give Max Harper the make on the cat burglar's blue Honda. Okay?

He had agreed—with reservations. Now he watched Dulcie, listened to her happy purring as Wilma lifted her down to the lap of a tiny, wheelchair-bound lady. This had to be Mae Rose, and she really did seem no bigger than an oversize doll. Her short frizzy white hair was like a doll's hair, her bright pink rouge rendering her even more doll-like. She sat stroking Dulcie, smiling as hugely as if someone had plugged in the Christmas lights.

He watched Dulcie reach a gentle paw to pat the little woman's pink cheek. Then, curling down in Mae Rose's lap on the pink afghan, Dulcie rolled over, her paws in the air waving limply above her. The little woman's thin, blue-veined hands shook slightly as she stroked Dulcie. What a fragile little human, so thin that Joe thought a hard leap into her lap would break her leg.

He stiffened as Dillon lifted him down from her shoulder. She held him absently, like a bag of groceries, as she stood looking around the room, preoccupied with some private agenda. Irritated, he mewed to get her attention.

She stared down at him, as surprised as if she'd forgotten he was there. Shifting his position, she fixed her sights with purpose on a big lady coming toward them.

She was going to dump him on that woman, he could feel it; all the kid wanted was to get rid of him.

The solid woman approached, leaning on the arm of Bonnie Dorriss, a big square creature clumping along, making straight for the empty overstuffed chair beside Mae Rose's wheelchair. The old woman's face was molded into a scowl. She walked like a rheumy ex–football player, rocking along. Why didn't Dillon move away from her, get him away from her? The kid couldn't dream of dropping him in the lap of that creature. That lady was not in any way a promising candidate for feline friendship therapy.

As the old lady descended on them he couldn't help the growl that escaped him, it rumbled out of his chest as uncontrolled as an after-the-hunt belch. A growl that made the old woman's eyes open wide and made Bonnie's blue eyes fix on him with surprise.

"Oh," Dillon said, "I squeezed him too hard. . . ." She petted him furiously as the old woman settled weightily into the easy chair. "It's all right, Joe Cat, I didn't mean to hurt you." Dillon's face was so close to his that their noses touched. She snuggled her cheek against him, and gently scratched under his chin, whispering almost inaudibly.

"Just play along, Joe Cat. Please just play along?" And she petted him harder. "Just make nice," Dillon breathed. "I wish you could understand."

He was trying.

As Dillon approached the woman's chair, the old lady scowled deeper and pulled her maroon woolen shawl tighter around her shoulders. "I don't want a cat. I don't like cats, take it away." The old girl looked like a hitter. Like someone who would happily pinch a little cat and pull its tail, particularly a stub tail.

But Dillon lifted him down to the old woman's lap and stroked him to make him be still, keeping a tight grip on his shoulder.

The woman glowered and moved her hands away from him as if he carried some unspeakable disease. She smelled of mildew. Her face was thick and lumpy. Her voice was as harsh as tires on gravel. "I want a dog, not a cat. I want one of those fluffy little dogs, but you gave them to everyone else."

Her angry stare fixed hard on Bonnie, as if all the ugliness in her life might be Bonnie's fault. "That fluffy little French dog, Eloise got it. She always gets the best. Gets the biggest piece of cake and the best cut of roast beef, too. Gets to choose the TV programs because no one will dare argue with her. No one asked me if I wanted a little dog." She flapped her hands at Joe as if she were shooing pigeons. "I want that French dog. Take the cat away." Joe crouched lower, determined not to move.

Bonnie told her, "The last time, Eula, when you held that little fluffy Bichon Frise, you pulled his tail and he snapped at you." She smoothed Eula's iron gray hair.

"Is that why you gave me a cat without a tail? So I won't pull its tail?" Eula laughed coarsely. "Is this supposed to be one of them fancy breeds, them Manx cats? Looks like an alley cat to me."

She stared past Bonnie, at Dillon. "Why would you bring a mean old alley cat?" She studied Dillon's faded jeans and T-shirt. "And why can't you wear a skirt to visit? That's all you girls wear, jeans and silly shirts. I see them all in the village when Teddy takes us shopping. Why would you bring this bony cat here? No one would want to pet this mean creature." She peered up harder at Dillon. "Do I know you, girl? You look familiar, like I know you."

Two spots of red flamed on Dillon's thin cheeks, but she knelt beside Eula, stroking Joe.

"The creature is going to scratch me. It's just laying to scratch me."

Joe raised innocent eyes to her, giving her his sweetest face, fighting the powerful urge to nail her with a pawful of sharp ones. He was at a crossroads here. He could show this old woman some teeth and claws and get booted out on his ear—in which case he'd be free to go home. Or he could make nice, stay curled up in her lap, and endure, thus effectively keeping his bargain with Dulcie.

The bargain weighed heavily.

With Dulcie's eyes on him, warily he settled down again. He hadn't called Harper yet to give the police captain the make on the blue Honda. So he could still back out, cut out of here.

"If I had a dog instead of this alley cat," Eula said, "I wouldn't let anyone else pet it, certainly not Frederick. Frederick can get his own dog. Where is Frederick? It's criminal for that Prior woman to move me right out of my own apartment and make me stay over here in a hospital room like a prisoner and give Frederick all the fun in that apartment alone just because I had a little blood pressure."

Bonnie said, "Frederick will be over pretty soon. Pet the cat gently, Eula. Maybe he'll purr for you; he has a lovely purr."

Joe sat up clamping his teeth against any hint of a purr. But Dulcie's look said, *You promised. If you didn't mean to be nice, why did you promise?* And, reluctantly, he curled down again, into a rigid, unwilling ball.

Dulcie was so sure that this gig was important, that a dose of feline therapy really would help these old folks—help them be happy, help them deal with thoughts of death.

Personally, he didn't agree. *You get old, you get feeble. Pretty soon you check out. That's the program. That's how nature works, so why fight it. Let nature take its course, don't screw things up with some kind of newfangled therapy.*

Thinking about getting old, he tried hard not to dwell on Barney's plight. After all, Barney was just a simple, lovable dog, he had no need for—and no way to acquire—some fancy philosophy, some comforting idea of an afterlife the way Dulcie believed.

Dulcie was convinced there was an afterlife for all creatures. So, fine. So who said the next life would be all sardines and cream? That realm could be anything, any number of terrors could await the unwary voyager.

He had, earlier this summer, after a few weeks of thinking seriously about such matters—and growing incredibly nervous and irritable—decided that this starry-eyed dream of eternity was not for him. That he was not constitutionally equipped to maintain on a long-term, conscious level, Dulcie's idyllic and nebulous dreams.

He'd rather believe in nothing. Rather subscribe to plain uncomplicated termination, than keep wondering about a chancy unknown.

Soon Bonnie Dorriss left them, moving quickly across the room to attend to a pair of ladies who both wanted the yellow cat and were arguing loudly. The cat, smiling up from the lap of one of the participants, looked unaffected by their furor, lying limp and relaxed, enjoying every moment.

Dillon paid no attention to the battle; she stood scanning the room, intently scrutinizing each newcomer who appeared belatedly from down the hall. The kid was wired, so intense she made his whiskers itch.

"Stuck here all day alone," Eula said, "and Frederick over there in the apartment doing who knows what. Likely over there with some woman. Or reading some storybook. Always getting out of bed before it was decent to read a storybook. Sun not even up, but he's out there making coffee and reading, I could always smell the coffee. Hiding in the kitchen wasting his time." Her stomach shook violently against Joe.

Dillon glanced down at Eula, hardly listening. And Mae Rose and Dulcie seemed oblivious, engaged in some silent communication of their own. Mae Rose kept smiling and petting, and Dulcie had that beatific look on her face. Mae Rose's overburdened wheelchair was fascinating. The vehicle was hung all over with bags: cloth bags, flowered bags, red bags, blue ones hung from the arms of the chair and from the back, all of them full to bulging. He could see magazines sticking out, a copy of the Molena Point *Gazette*, the sleeve of a blue sweater, a box of tissues. A clear plastic bag contained little bits of bright cloth, and he could see the end of a Hershey bar, a single white glove, and the smooth porcelain face of a doll.

Dillon sat down on the arm of Eula's chair. She wiggled some, getting settled. She did not seem so much relaxed as determined.

"I bet," she said to Eula, "you have a lot of friends in here."

Eula looked at her, surprised.

"Did you live in Molena Point a long time before you moved to Casa Capri?"

Eula didn't answer. She stared hard at Dillon. "I know I've seen you somewhere."

"I guess," Dillon said, "if you go into the village much."

"No, not in the village. I remember a face, girl. Forget a name but remember a face.

"But then," Eula said, "there's always some child visiting out in the parlor.

"Though my nieces don't come. Never bring their children. Only came here twice, both times to find out what's in my will." She glowered at Dillon. "Well I never told them. None of their business."

"I bet you and Mrs. Mae Rose are good friends, too," Dillon persisted. Joe had to smile. The kid wasn't subtle. Someone ought to have a talk with her; she wasn't going to get anywhere in life without a little guile.

She leaned closer to Eula. "I bet you and Mrs. Rose watch TV together." Joe had no idea what she was after, no notion where she was headed with this interrogation, but she meant to hang in there.

"No TV," Eula grumbled. "All *Mae* does is play with her dolls." She scowled deeply at Dillon. "You have as many questions as my old mother. Dead now. Dead a hundred years." She cackled wickedly.

"I didn't mean to be nosy," Dillon said, "but I bet you know everyone, though. Everyone here at Casa Capri. I bet you know if they lived in the village, and all about them."

Eula shut her mouth, leaned her head back, and closed her eyes. Dillon sank into a quiet little funk, realizing she had pushed too hard. But then soon she rose, leaning to stroke Joe. "Would you hold him a little while longer? Don't let him get away? While I go to the rest room?"

The old woman snorted, but she took such a good grip on the nape of Joe's neck that he had a sudden flash of her reaching with both hands and squeezing; her fingers were as strong as a man's. "I won't be long," Dillon said, and she was gone down the hall toward the entry. Joe stared after her wondering what she was up to. Maybe the kid was going to skip—beat it out the front door.

"That's not . . ." Eula called after her, but Dillon was gone.

Joe could see the rest room in the opposite direction, a door clearly marked, just outside the dining room. He listened for the front door to open, but he heard nothing. Where was the kid headed, acting so secretive?

12

"That cat killed an entire litter of newborn pigs," Eula Weems said. "Biggest cat on the farm. So mean even the sow couldn't run it off.

"And after it killed those pigs it kind of went crazy. From that day, it just wanted to bite your bare toes. You couldn't go barefoot all summer, had to wear shoes. Terrible uncomfortable and hot." Eula stared accusingly down at Joe, where he crouched rigid in her lap, glowering at him as if the dead pigs were his fault.

Mae Rose said, "If they won't let us see Jane or Darlene or Mary Nell, then I say they aren't here. Not in Nursing, not anywhere in Casa Capri."

"Maybe in the county home," Eula said helpfully. "Maybe they couldn't pay. County home is free. When that cat got run over by the milk wagon everyone celebrated. It sure did feel good to go barefoot again. Took a month, though, for my feet to harden up on them tar roads. Burn your feet right off you."

Mae Rose pawed through the contents of one of the hanging pockets attached to her wheelchair until she found a handkerchief. She blew her nose delicately. Joe watched the arch where Dillon had disappeared, listening for the front door to open and close, convinced the kid was going to leave. He'd like to beat it, too. Mae Rose blew her nose again and wiped her eyes, then wadded up the handkerchief. "Maybe they're dead."

Eula Weems snorted. "How can they be dead? You know Darlene Brown was in the hospital with cataracts, and you saw her yourself when her cousin came. Right there in that corner room with the dark glasses. You're not making sense, Mae. And you know James Luther's trust officer was over there all one afternoon with him talking and signing papers."

"That's what they told us." Mae Rose glanced across the room toward the open double doors, where a nurse had appeared.

The white-uniformed woman propelled Dillon along before her, clutching the child's arm. Dillon balked and twisted, trying to pull away, her thin face splotched with anger.

"I was only looking for the rest room," the child argued, "I don't see . . ."

"The rest room is there, beside the dining room, not a block down the hall in the private wing. That area of the building is reserved for the very sickest patients, and they must not be disturbed."

"But—"

"You'll remain here in the social room as you were told, or you cannot come back to Casa Capri. You will not disturb the residents." The thin woman dropped Dillon's arm, stood staring down at her as if to make her point, then turned away. Dillon's face was red, her scowl fierce.

Across the room a man in a wheelchair watched the little exchange with interest, and as Dillon sat down on the couch across from Eula, he headed in their direction.

Though he was wheelchair-bound, he seemed too young to be living here among the elderly. Joe thought he couldn't be out of his late twenties—though Joe admitted he was no authority on human age. The man's smooth, white face was lean, his blue eyes friendly, but his body was puffy from inactivity. The roll of fat around his middle, beneath his white cotton shirt, looked like a soft white inner tube. Wheeling his chair toward them, he swerved around couches and chairs with a flashy disregard for the occupants. Coming to rest beside Mae Rose, he gave his chair a final twist like a young man spinning his sports car, and parked beside her chair. He looked Dillon over with curiosity, winked conspiratorially at Eula, then leaned toward Mae, looking hard at the tabby cat in her lap. Dulcie looked back at him warily.

"What's that, Ms. Rose, a fur neckpiece? Did someone drop a moth-eaten fur piece in your lap?"

Eula Weems giggled.

Mae Rose's painted cheeks flamed brighter, and she petted Dulcie with quick, nervous strokes. Dulcie didn't move; she lay stretched out across the pink afghan coolly regarding the young man, and definitely not looking moth-eaten—her dark stripes gleamed like silk. She was very still, and nothing about her seemed to change except that her green eyes had widened; only Joe saw her stiffen imperceptibly, as if to strike.

Eula smiled coquettishly, stroking Joe. "Look, Teddy. I have an old fur piece, too."

Teddy laughed. "Or is that one of those moldering gray union suits you tell about on the farm, that your mama sewed you into?"

Eula favored him with a girlish guffaw.

Teddy said, "Mae, you're hugging that cat like it was a baby. Or like one of your little dolls."

"Leave me alone, Teddy. I shouldn't wonder if it was you that drove Jane Hubble away."

The young man's eyes filled with amazement. His smile was sunny and very kind; he looked as if Mae Rose could not help her aberrations.

But Dillon, watching them, was suddenly all attention. Gripped by some inner storm, Dillon raised her eyes in a quick, flickering glance at Mae Rose and the pale young man; then she looked down again.

Eula said, "Everyone knows Jane Hubble's right over there in Nursing." She looked to Teddy expectantly.

"Of course she is," Teddy said kindly. "They can't let us visit them, Mae. It's too hard on sick people to have us underfoot going in and out, getting in the way. Of course she's there. Where else would she be? Ask Adelina." He put his arm around Mae. "I know you miss her. Maybe when she's better, something can be arranged."

Dillon had turned away, seemed to have lost interest in the conversation. She was all fidgets, moving restlessly, and when she settled on the arm of Eula's chair and leaned down to pet Joe, her fingers were rigid, tense; she was filled with hidden excitement—or apprehension.

"She could send word," Mae said. "The nurses could at least bring a message."

"She's too sick," Eula said. "So sick she has tubes in her arms. They wanted to send me over there with the blood pressure, but I wouldn't have it. I won't have all those tubes stuck in me."

Mae Rose's wrinkled face collapsed into a hurt mask. "I'd only stay a minute."

"The doors are locked," Eula said. "That's all I know. That's all there is to know."

Mae Rose said nothing more, sat quietly stroking Dulcie.

"If she's sick . . ." Dillon began, "if this Jane Hubble is sick . . ."

Teddy turned to look at her.

Mae Rose burst into tears, covering her face with her hands. Dulcie sat up and touched a paw to the old lady's cheek as the little woman huddled, sobbing.

"How long since you've seen her?" Dillon said to Mae, ignoring Mae's tears. "How long since you've seen your friend Jane?"

"Mae doesn't remember," Eula said. "She gets mixed up—in this place all the days run together. She knows Jane's all right; she just likes to make a scene."

But when Mae Rose finished crying and blew her nose, she fixed Eula with an accusing stare. "Your own husband went over to see her. He tried to see her. He was angry, too, when they wouldn't let him in."

"I told Frederick, don't you go over there." Eula's fat fingers pressed irritably along Joe's back. "I told him, you're not to go over there alone to see that woman."

Dillon looked at Eula uncertainly. "You didn't want your husband to see Jane? But . . . ?" She looked blank, then looked shocked suddenly. Then fought to keep from laughing. "You didn't want your husband . . ." She swallowed, then began again. "Does your husband—does he live here, too?"

"Lives over in Cottages," Eula said. "You can have your own car, very stuck-up. Then if you get sick you come over here. Frederick says he can't stand it over here, says it's depressing. If you get real bad sick, like Jane with a stroke, then you go into Nursing. I don't know what Frederick does over there in that cottage all day. He says he goes into the village on the bus, to the library. I don't know what he does. I don't know what goes on over there with those women."

Dillon rose and turned away, smothering a laugh.

But after a moment she turned back, gave Mae Rose a little smile. "You must miss your friend. I had a friend once who went away."

"Her room was next to mine," Mae said. "The corner room, the one they use now for visiting. When Jane . . . When they moved her to Nursing," Mae said doubtfully, "they closed that room, and now they use it for visiting."

"Which corner room?" Dillon asked.

"The one behind the parlor right next to my room." Mae pointed vaguely out through the glass doors toward the far side of the patio.

Dillon walked over and peered out. Turning back, she said thoughtfully, "I don't understand. You mean visitors stay overnight?"

"They—" Mae began.

"No," Eula said irritably. "No one comes overnight. But if you're in bed all the time—bedridden—and you have a dinky little room, you have your visitors there in the big room, it makes a better impression. Those corner rooms are the biggest, private bath and all. If you have a little poky room, or if you're in Nursing, they move you into the corner room to entertain company. Your relatives come, it looks grand. They figure you're getting a good deal for what they pay.

"But when they're gone again, it's back to your own dinky room, and they shut the big room. It's all for looks. Everything for looks." Eula yawned and settled deeper into her chair, shaking Joe. He rose, turned around several times against her fat stomach. Teddy left them, spinning his chair around and wheeling away. From the kitchen Joe could hear a clatter of pots and then a nurse came out, rolling a squeaky metal cart with a cloth draped over.

"Meals for the Nursing wing," Eula said. "Not many of 'em can eat solid food. They get fed early, then get their medicine and are put to sleep."

Joe shivered.

Dillon watched the white-uniformed nurse push the cart away toward the admitting desk. And, ducking her head, pretending to scratch her arm, she kept glancing out the patio doors.

But not until Eula loosed her grip on Joe and began to snore, did Dillon pick Joe up in her arms and head for the patio. His last glimpse of Eula Weems, she had her mouth open, huffing softly.

Pushing open the glass slider, Dillon slipped out into the walled garden, into patches of sun and ragged shade. Joe sniffed gratefully the good fresh air.

Along the four sides of the building, the rows of glass doors reflected leafy patterns. Most stood open to the soft breeze. In some rooms a lamp was lit, or he could see the shifting colors of a TV. The corner room was dark, the glass sliders closed and covered by heavy draperies. Dillon, tightening her hold on him, pressing him against her shoulder, headed quickly for Jane Hubble's old room.

13

Up in the hills above Molena Point the Martinez family was gathered at the pool, Juan and Doris Martinez sitting at their umbrella table wrapped in thick terry-cloth robes, their hair streaming from their swim, the two children still doing laps, skimming through wisps of chlorine-scented steam. The harsh light of afternoon had softened, and the shadows stretched long. Though the wind was chilly, the spring day was bright and the pool was comfortably heated—the water was kept all year at an even seventy-eight degrees. The couple sipped their coffee, which Doris had poured from a thermos, and watched ten-year-old Ramon and seven-year-old Juanita swim back and forth the length of the long pool as effortlessly as healthy young animals. The adults had already completed their comfortable limit for laps. Doris's limit most days was about twenty, Juan's twice that. The kids would swim until hunger drove them out.

With careful attention to the changing times even here in Molena Point, to the increase in household burglaries even in the village, they had left only the patio door unlocked, and it was in plain view behind them. They were discussing an impending trucker's strike, which would delay deliveries of window and wall components for Juan's prefab sunroom company. This, in turn, would delay scheduled construction and throw the small firm behind in its work for the next year or more, depending on how long the strike lasted.

While the adult Martinezes were thus engaged discussing alternate sources of income to tide them through the coming months, a woman entered the yard behind them, making no sound, and slid open the glass door, timing its soft sliding hush to the noisy rumble of a passing UPS truck.

Slipping inside, she found herself in the large, comfortably appointed family room, all leather and soft-toned pecan woods. Crossing the thick, soft carpet, she headed for the front hall and moved quickly up the stairs; she liked to do the upstairs first. Usually, when people were in the pool or the yard, there would be a billfold left on the dresser, perhaps a handbag. Or she would find the handbag in the kitchen when she went down. Climbing the stairs, she thought about making a trip soon up to the city. She didn't like keeping such a large stash of stolen items. She liked to move the goods on, dump the take—all but those few pieces that were so charming she couldn't bear to part with them.

She thought of these as keepsakes. She was not without her sentimental side. She enjoyed the houses she entered, liked looking at the furnishings and getting to know the families, if only superficially, by the way they lived. Each new house, while offering fine treasures, offered also a little story about the residents. And though she knew it was foolish to hang on to keepsakes, she did love the little reminders she had saved, the lovely Limoges teapot from the McKenzie house, the five porcelain bird figurines carefully packed, and the little Swiss clock with a white cloisonné face that she couldn't bear to part with. She had yet to determine the value of the clock, but she thought it would be considerable. She needed more specific information on these miniature clocks; she was finding quite a few. The cloisonné clocks, imported from Europe, were big in California just now. She'd take care of the research up in the city at the main branch of San Francisco Public, not here in Molena Point, where someone might recognize her; she felt particularly wary of that ex–parole officer in the library's reference department.

She'd like to drive up to the city early, spend several hours with Solander; Solander's Antiques was the most reliable fence, and she didn't have to hobnob with little greasy shoplifters. No, Solander was strictly first-class. Then a stop at several banks to get rid of the cash, and a nice lunch, maybe at the St. Francis. Then the remainder of the day in the art reference room of San Francisco Public. The trips made a really nice change from her everyday routine. Maybe she'd stay over, catch a play, do a little shopping.

Though before she left, she did want to get her map of Molena Point in better order. She'd nearly made a bad mistake yesterday, had really scared herself when she realized she was in the Dorriss house. And she had forgotten, if she'd ever known, that the upstairs was a separate apartment.

But no matter, she hadn't gotten that far. Though not until she saw Bonnie Dorriss's car pull into the drive, saw her getting out with that big brown dog, that poodle, did she realize where she was. Luckily the young woman had taken the dog around to the backyard, and she had slipped out the front. She hadn't time to lift anything, and the experience had left her unsettled.

Upstairs, in the Martinez master bedroom, she found a billfold containing something over two hundred in small bills. She didn't find a purse, but she did find a jewelry box and picked up a nice pearl choker and a lovely antique emerald necklace. This last could be a real find—it must be well over a hundred years old and was probably Austrian by the looks of it. If those tiny emeralds were real, she had a fortune in her hands. But even if the emeralds were only chips, or even paste, the finely made antique piece would still be worth a nice sum.

She found a few gold and silver coins in a cuff-link box, none of them in protective envelopes, but found nothing else of value. She was checking the other bedrooms when, in what appeared to be the guest room, she came on a glass case containing five big dolls.

These were not children's toys, but replicas of adult women, works of art so lifelike that at first sight they shocked her. As if, peering into the case, she was looking into a tiny alternate world, spying on live miniature people. The doors of the case were locked.

Each female figure was a very individual little being, her skin so real one wanted to feel its warmth, her tiny fingers perfect. And each lady was totally different from the others, each face different, registering very different human emotions. She could not resist the Victorian woman's aloof smile. Each tiny woman was so alive that even their individual ways of standing and looking at her were unique. In their lovely period lace and satins, these lively ladies were surely handmade. She wondered if they were one of a kind; certainly they were collector's dolls.

Thinking back, she could remember glancing at magazine articles about doll shows, and at ads for dolls, but obviously she hadn't paid sufficient attention. She had missed a whole movement here.

Well she would pay attention from now on, close attention. Her fingers shook as she fished out her lockpicks.

The operation took forever, and she was growing nervous that some member of the family would come slipping in from the pool and up the stairs before she had the glass case open. Her hands were trembling so badly that when she did get the lock open she almost dropped the first doll. The little lady's full silk skirts rustled, and her direct, imperious gaze was disconcerting.

Each doll was over twelve inches tall. They were going to make a huge bulge under her coat. But at last she got them tucked away in the deep pockets that lined the garment, and, still in the guest room, she checked herself before the full-length mirror.

Not too bad, if she stood with her shoulders hunched forward to make the coat fall away from her. She could hardly wait to research these beauties and get them up to the city.

She would take these to Harden Mark; he was the best with the real art objects. And, of course, before she saw him she needed to educate herself. There wasn't a fence in the world who wouldn't rip you off if he could.

She had finished upstairs, was downstairs in the kitchen going through Mrs. Martinez's purse, when she heard the sliding door open. She stuffed the bills in her coat and closed the purse. On her way out the back door she snatched up a handful of chocolate chip cookies.

Silently closing the door, she let her body sag as if with fatigue and discouragement, shrugging deeper down into the lumpy coat, and slowly made her way along the side of the house ambling heavy and stiff, peering into the bushes, calling softly, "Kitty? Here, kitty. Here, Snowy. Puss? Puss? Come on, Snowy. Come to Mama, Snowy." Her old voice trembled with concern, her expression was drawn with worry. She did not let down her guard until she had left the Martinez residence unchallenged—really, this was a great waste of talent—and had ambled the three blocks to her car.

Driving home along Cypress, up along the crest of the hills heading for Valley Road, passing high above the sprawling wings of Casa Capri Retirement Villa, she slowed her car, pulled onto the shoulder of the narrow road for a moment. Sat looking down with interest at the red-tile rooftops softened by the limbs of the huge old oaks and at the tangle of cottages climbing up the hill; even those small individual houses gave one a sense of confinement.

From this vantage she could look almost directly down into the patio. Though the garden was charming, shadowed now, and the lemons and the yellow lilies shining almost like gold, the high walls made her shiver. Casa Capri was beautiful, but it was still an institution, sucking dry your freedom. As the poem said, she could wear red rubber boots to dance in, she could drink wine on street corners if she chose and laugh with the bums, and who was to stop her?

Parked above Casa Capri, she eased off her heavy coat, folded it carefully with the five dolls protected inside, and laid it on the seat. Studying the sprawling complex, she laughed because she did not belong there, then headed away thinking of supper and a hot bath.

14

The patio doors were securely closed and partly obscured by the drawn draperies. Dillon could feel her heart pounding as she pressed her face against the glass, cupping her hands—and ramming the cat's face against the doorframe. Growling, he backed away as if to jump, but she grabbed the nape of his neck. "I'm sorry, Joe Cat, you have to stay here." She stroked him and hugged him, and he settled down again. He was really a good cat. She rubbed his ears, then cupped her hands once more to peer in.

The room showed no sign of life, no lamp burned, no TV picture flickering, no figure moving about or seated in a chair reading. She could see a dresser and a chair, and a bed neatly made up with a white spread, its corners tucked at exact angles. There were no clothes lying around, nothing personal, no glasses or book or newspaper, not a stray shoe, not even a wadded tissue. The surfaces of the dresser and nightstand were bare. The room was definitely empty.

Mama said they charged a bundle to stay here at Casa Capri. So why would they keep a room empty, even for the reason Eula gave? She was so intent on the room that when Joe turned to nibble a flea, jerking around to bite his shoulder, she grabbed at him again, startled.

Pressing him against her cheek, she looked behind her, glancing toward the social room. Making sure no one was watching, she tried the door, testing the latch while pretending to smell the blooms on the lemon tree.

It was locked. Well she'd known it would be. She tugged and jerked to be sure, then turned away.

Moving on down the brick walk close to the row of glass doors, she paused to look in through each, searching for a familiar face, for Jane's tall straight figure, and knowing she wouldn't find her.

At home, the minute she and her folks had gotten back from living in Dallas after their year away, the minute they pulled in the drive, with the car still loaded with suitcases, she had run up the street to Jane's house. They'd lived in Dallas while Dad did a special project at the university, and she'd really missed Jane, specially after Jane stopped writing to her, because at first they'd written every week. Four times while they were living in Texas she'd tried to call Jane, but there was never any answer. Mama tried twice, and then Jane's phone was disconnected, and she didn't know what had happened. By then it was time to come home, so Mama told her to wait, that she'd see Jane soon. But she hadn't seen her; when she got home, Jane was gone.

That afternoon, when they pulled into the drive and she ran down the block, there was the FOR SALE sign pounded into the lawn in Jane's yard. And all the curtains drawn. The neighbor said Jane was in Casa Capri with a stroke and that a trust officer was selling the house.

She had run home, gotten her bike, and come up here to Casa Capri, but they said Jane was too sick to see anyone. They said children weren't allowed in the Nursing wing because of germs. They weren't very nice about it.

As she moved down the patio beside the glass doors, Joe Cat began to wriggle. Though his whiskers tickled her ear, he was being really careful not to dig in his claws. The old people sitting in their rooms watching TV made her sad; they looked so lonely and dried up.

Jane wouldn't be watching TV—she'd be reading or doing exercises or out walking, shopping in the village, maybe buying some little trinket; she loved the antique stores. Jane might be wrinkled, but she'd never be old like these people. Moving along, peering in through the glass, she approached the end of the patio, where sunlight slanted in through the panes across the carpets and beds, across the unmoving old folks as though they were statues—virtual reality that didn't move, figures in stage sets, like the animal dioramas in the museum. Each old person looked back at her, but no one changed expression, no one smiled. One old man sat propped in a reclining chair, sound asleep, with his mouth open, under a bright reading lamp. She was never going to get old.

She knew that the Nursing rooms were directly behind this row of rooms. The second time she came up on her bike, she'd tried to get in there, had gone around to the little street in the back between the main building and the retirement cottages. She'd tried to go in that door directly to Nursing, but it was locked. She'd looked in the windows of the rooms, and they were like those in a hospital, with metal beds and IV stands and bedpans. And then today, when she went down the hall and tried to get into Nursing, that nurse made her go back. She didn't see why everything was so secret, and everyone so grumpy. Unless there was something to hide. And that was what she meant to find out.

Before she started back up the third side she sat down on a bench beneath an orange tree and pulled Joe Cat off her shoulder down into her lap, petted him until he lay down. She supposed it was hard for a cat to be so still. She'd like to let him loose, but she'd been told not to. She could imagine him scorching away up a tree and over the roof and gone, and it would be her fault.

That first time when she came to see Jane and she told Mama they wouldn't let her in, Mama called Jane's trust officer. He said Jane was too sick to have company, and that was the policy here, that they allowed no visitors into Nursing, that only the family could come.

He said Mama could take his word that Jane was doing as well as could be expected, whatever that meant, and that he was in constant touch with the doctor who cared for Casa Capri's patients. And Mama believed him. With Mama going back to work, she didn't have time to go up to Casa Capri and raise a little hell, which Mama really could do when she wanted.

Mama's office, the real-estate office where she worked before she took leave of absence to go to Dallas, wanted her back right away. Three people were out sick, and the office was having a Major Panic. And after that, Mama hardly had time to pee. She did the laundry at midnight, or left it for Dillon and Dad, and they ate takeout most nights, or Dad made spaghetti. All you could hear around the house was "deeds" and "balloon loans" and "termite inspections" until even Dad was tired of it. Mama did talk to the doctor, though, and he said exactly the same thing, that Jane was too sick for visitors, and she was getting excellent care at Casa Capri.

Any sensible child, Mama said, would believe the combined word of several responsible grown-ups.

But she didn't. She didn't believe any of them.

Sliding Joe back onto her shoulder, she rose, catching her hair in a branch of the orange tree. Working it loose, she almost let Joe leap away, but then he settled down again, nosing at her hair, and began to purr. She hated her hair black. But if she'd come up here with red hair again, the nurses would have recognized her. Everyone remembered red hair.

Freeing her ugly black hair, petting Joe Cat, she moved toward the third wing of the building that would lead back to the social room. Moving along the row of mostly open glass doors, she tried the screens.

The third screen was unlocked, and the room empty. Dillon slipped inside.

"Just a little look around, Joe Cat. Who's to care?"

He purred louder, and seemed to be looking, too.

This was a man's room, a pair of boxer shorts tossed on the chair, a man's shoes under the dresser, and that made her sort of uncomfortable. Across the unmade bed lay a rough navy blue robe, and on the dresser beside a little radio, was a pile of paperback books with covers of tigers, grizzly bears, and half-naked women. When she opened the closet, his slacks and shirts hung loosely and smelled sour. Closing the closet again, she slipped on through the too-warm room and out into the hall, turning down toward Nursing.

The door at the end of the hall was locked. She pushed, and pushed harder, then turned away.

Moving back up the hall she inspected every room she could get into, slipping quickly from one side of the hall to the other. She and Jane used to read *Alice in Wonderland*, where Alice tried all the doors, like this, never sure what she would find inside.

But there was no magic mushroom here to make her a different size and maybe give her special powers.

The lady's clothes in one room were all purple, purple satin robe, purple slippers, a lavender nightie tangled on the floor. On the nightstand a stack of romance novels teetered beside a vase of purple artificial flowers, their faded petals icky with dust. She picked up a worn paperback and read a few lines where it flopped open. And dropped it, her face burning.

Did old people read this stuff?

She wanted to look again, but she didn't dare. Reading that stuff, even in front of a cat, made her feel too embarrassed. And strange; she could feel Joe Cat peering over her shoulder staring.

What was he staring at?

She put the book back on the pile and left the room quickly, before someone caught her here.

She thought the occupant of the next room must be moving in or out. At least all her possessions were in boxes. Shoe boxes were neatly lined up on the dresser, and bigger boxes lined up on the floor, all stuffed with sweaters and books, with little packets of letters tied together with ribbon, with lace hankies and little china animals wrapped in tissue. This room faced the outside of the building, toward a narrow terrace.

At the outer edge of the terrace ran a tall wrought-iron fence, separating it from the lawn and garden beyond. Farther away rose the oak grove, and in the wood among the shadowed trees a figure moved swiftly, rolling along in a wheelchair, her short gray hair lifting in the breeze, her chair pulled by the big brown poodle. The dog trotted along happily, pulling her, the two of them looking so free, as if they never had to come back inside Casa Capri. She pretended that the woman was Jane. But of course that woman was Bonnie Dorriss's mother. Dillon turned away, feeling lonely.

Each patio was separated from the next by a low stucco wall, with an open space at the end so you could walk from one patio to the next. But when she tried the wrought-iron gates that led outside, they were all locked. *All our nurses are required to carry keys*, that's what Ms. Prior said. The wrought-iron fence ended just where Nursing began, turning at right angles to join the building. The Nursing wing went on beyond. Its wall had only high, tiny windows. There was one outer door, like the emergency exit door in a movie theater. From this, a line of muddy wheelchair tracks led away, cutting across the grass and across the concrete walk to the blacktop parking lot. The nine cars in the lot looked new and expensive.

She stroked the tomcat lightly. "I never told them my name. When I was here before, I told them my name was Kathy.

"Jane Hubble was my friend ever since I was seven. We read the Narnia books together, and she took me horseback riding my first time and talked Mama into letting me have riding lessons.

"Jane let me ride Bootsie, too." She sighed. "That trust officer sold Bootsie. I hope he got a nice home. I wish my folks could have bought him, but no one told us, no one called us when Jane got sick."

Joe yawned in her face and wiggled into a new position. She was sure he'd like to run and chase a bird. When he started squirming again, she gripped the nape of his neck. "I can't let you loose, I promised. Please, just stay quiet a little while longer, then we'll go back to Eula." She gave him a sidelong look. "Eula will love holding you."

She left the row of terraces, moving back inside to the hall, and wandered up the hall in the direction of the social room, stopping to check each open room. Hoping maybe she'd see something of Jane's in one of the rooms, a sweater, a book. But she knew she wouldn't.

"Somehow, Joe Cat, I have to get into Nursing. Find Jane for myself—if Jane is there."

Joe was, he thought, maintaining a high level of patience considering that he hated being carried, particularly by a child, and that prowling these small cluttered rooms where lonely old folks waited out their last years, was infinitely depressing. He might tell himself that he took a realistic view of getting old, that getting old was just part of living, but this Casa Capri gig was more tedious than he cared to admit.

As for Dillon playing detective, whatever the kid was up to with her intense search for Jane Hubble, the project had begun to wear. He felt as nervous as fleas on a hot griddle. By the time they returned to the social room he was ready to pitch a fit, so strung out that he actually welcomed being dropped down into Eula Weems's lap. Maybe if he just lay still, he could get himself together.

It was not until late that night, as he and Dulcie

hunted across the moonlit hills, that he learned more about Dillon's missing friend. And that he began to wonder if Jane Hubble, and maybe those five other old folks, really had disappeared.

15

Cloud shadows ran along the street where Dulcie trotted, skittish in the wind. Ahead, moonlight shifted across Clyde's cottage. She approached through uncertain heavings of darkness and moonlight; above her the oak's twisted branches plucked at the porch roof, scraping and tapping. But beneath the roof the shadows were deep and still, framing the lit rectangle of Joe's cat door.

Slipping across the damp grass, she leaped to the steps, watching the smear of pale plastic, willing Joe to hurry out. Midnight was already past; the small wild hours, in which the dull and civilized slept, in which the quick creatures of the night crept out to feed and to bare their tender throats for the hunter's teeth, lay before them. The hour of the chase waited, the hour of adrenaline rush and fresh blood flowing.

But as, above her, the moon swam and vanished, and the clouds ran unfettered like racing hounds, the cat door remained empty.

Waiting, she sat down to lick the dew from her claws.

Soon, then, the deepest shadows fled, the moon appeared suddenly again, and at the same instant the plastic door darkened, struck across by a sharp-eared shadow.

The door flipped up. Joe's nose and whiskers pushed out, and he thrust out into the night, jerking his rump through, shaking himself irritably as the plastic flopped against his backside.

She was so glad to see him. "About time! Come on—
I'm wired, let's go, the mice will be out in droves."

But Joe had stopped within the shadows of the porch,
his ears down, his shoulders and even his stub tail
drooping. He looked like an old, old cat, an ancient
worn-out relic, a sad cat skin filled with weariness.

She approached him warily. "What?" she said softly.
"What's happened?"

He did not move or speak.

She pressed against him, her nostrils filled with the
scent of mourning. "Barney? It's Barney."

His eyes were filled with pain.

She sat down close to him, touched him with her
nose, and remained quiet.

"His liver gave out. The pain was terrible. There was
nothing . . . Dr. Firreti gave him pain pills, but there
was nothing else he could do. It was terminal. He gave
him . . ."

"He put him down?"

Joe nodded. They sat looking at each other. Clyde
and Dr. Firreti had done what was needed.

"He's somewhere," she said at last.

"I don't know."

"Remember the white cat. The white cat could not
have come to me in dream if he wasn't somewhere. He
was already dead when I dreamed of him, and he told
me things I couldn't know."

The white cat had led her to the final clue, led her to
Janet Jeannot's killer. And this happened long after he
died—his flesh was rotted when they found him, his
bones bare—yet she had dreamed of him only days
before.

There was, Joe knew, no other explanation but that
the white cat had spoken to Dulcie from beyond the
grave. Yet as they had stood over the white cat's desic-
cated body, over his frail, bare bones with the little
hanks of white fur clinging, a hollowness had gripped
him. He had not experienced Dulcie's joy at proof of

another life. He had been filled with fear, with a sudden horror of the unknown. Terror of whatever lay beyond had ripped through him as sharp as the strike of a rattlesnake.

She nudged against him, and licked his ear. "Barney is somewhere. He's somewhere lovely, Joe. Why would a sweet dog like Barney go anywhere but somewhere happy?" She pressed against him until he lay down, and she curled up close. "He doesn't hurt anymore. He's running the fields now, the way he was meant to do." And lying tangled together in the shadows of the little front porch, comforting each other, they remained quiet for a very long time.

But at last Joe rose and shook himself. "He was such a clown," he said softly. "Every time I came home from hunting he had to smell all the smells on me, the stink of rabbit, the smell of bird, every trace of blood. He'd get so excited, you could just see him sorting out the scent of mouse, raccoon, whatever, wanting to run, wanting to retrieve those beasts the way he was bred to do."

Dulcie swallowed.

"He'd know when I stopped by Jolly's, too. He went crazy over the smells from the deli; he always had to lick all the tastes off my face."

She said, "He did that, once, to me. It was like sticking my head in a hot shower." She rose. "Barney knows we miss him. Maybe he knows we're talking about him." She nudged him until, at last, they left the porch, Joe walking heavily as if he were very tired.

Ignoring the little side streets and alleys where they sometimes liked to prowl, she led him straight for the open hills. They passed the little tourist hotel, where an elegant Himalayan presided over the clientele, a cat whose picture was featured on the hanging sign and in the inn's magazine ads; they could smell her scent on the bushes. The inn's clients liked to have the Himalayan in their rooms at night to warm their feet and sleep before the fire, and perhaps to share their continental breakfast. She, and all Molena Point's cats, were as revered in the little village as were the felines of Italy, taking the sun atop a bronze lion or stalking pigeons across Venice's ancient paving.

"She's a snob," Joe said.

"Not at all. She just fell into a good thing. If she knows how to milk it, more power to her." She nudged him into a trot, and soon they had crossed above Highway One and into a forest of tall dry grass that rustled overhead, casting weavings of shadow across their faces and paws.

It was much later, after several swift chases, after feasting on half a dozen mice and a ground squirrel, that Dulcie, too, began to feel uncertain and morose. Pausing in her elaborate bath, she flicked her pink tongue back into her mouth, licked her whiskers once, and stared at him.

He stopped washing, one white paw lifted. "What? What's with you?"

"I was thinking. About Mae Rose."

"Don't start, Dulcie. Not tonight."

"Mae Rose thinks maybe Jane Hubble ran away. That the home didn't look for her, that they didn't want to tell the police that someone ran away."

"Mae Rose is bonkers. How could an old woman run away from that place, an old woman who'd had a stroke? How far would she get before she collapsed somewhere, or someone brought her back?"

"Mae Rose says Jane got better after her first attack, that she was getting really restless. Then she had the second attack, and they moved her over to Nursing."

He just looked at her.

"She might have run away. I read once about an old woman who—"

"Probably she couldn't even get out of bed, let alone out of the Nursing wing." He gave her an impatient glare. "If the doors to Nursing are all locked, as Dillon says, and with nurses all over thick as a police guard, you think Jane Hubble got out of bed by herself, got dressed by herself, picked up her suitcase, and walked out."

She lowered her ears and turned away.

Joe sighed. "She's there. In Nursing. Safe and sound. Too sick to have visitors. Mae Rose has latched onto one fact, that they won't let anyone visit Jane, and she's turned it into a disaster."

The moon behind them had dropped below the clouds, turning the tomcat into a silhouette as dark and rigid as an Egyptian statue. "Mae Rose is full of fairy tales. Old people get childish, they imagine things."

"But she isn't childish, she's still very sharp. She's told me all about her life, and she isn't imagining that. She showed me her albums, she remembers every play she sewed for, every costume, she showed me the pictures, told me the characters' names and even the actors' names, she remembered them all. She—"

"She showed her albums to a cat? She showed pictures to a cat, told her life history to a cat?"

"No one else is interested; they're tired of hearing her."

"Dulcie, normal people don't talk to cats, not like the cat can really understand."

"But we do understand."

"But no one *knows* that." He hated when she was deliberately obtuse. "Mae Rose doesn't know we can understand her. Anyone—except Clyde and Wilma—who thinks a cat can understand human speech is bonkers. If Mae Rose thinks you can understand her, that old lady is certifiably round the bend."

She crouched down, deflated. "I'm all she has to talk to; everyone else treats her like she's stupid."

"Dulcie, the old woman is in her second childhood. For one thing, what sane, grown woman would carry a doll around with her? Does she talk to the doll, too?"

"She makes doll clothes; that was her living. If she still has dolls of her own, if she still sews for them, I don't see anything strange. She supported herself doing that, the clothes are all silks and handmade lace. She said Jane Hubble loved her dolls."

"Dulcie . . ."

The moonlight caught her eyes in a deep gleam, her pupils large and black, the thin rim of green as clear as emeralds. "No one understands how she feels; she's so terribly alone, and Jane was her only real friend. We could at least try to help her—try to find Jane."

"Can't you understand that she's making this stuff up? That no one is missing?" He moved away through the grass, irritated beyond toleration, so angry that he didn't want to talk about it.

He didn't want to admit his own unease.

Mae Rose was not the only one who thought Jane Hubble was missing. Whatever the truth turned out to be, he didn't think little Dillon Thurwell was bonkers.

Nor had Dillon and Mae Rose invented this story together. The two hadn't met each other until today, yet both were possessed with this fixation that Jane Hubble had met with foul play.

"I want to help her, Joe. Somehow I'm going to help her."

"Dulcie, we're cats, not social workers. We weren't born to help little old ladies, we were born to hunt and fight and make kittens."

"Fine. You go make some kittens." She lashed her tail, her green eyes blazing. "You do what you were born to do, act like a stupid tomcat. And I'll do what I think is right."

"Dulcie—"

"You were eager enough to solve Samuel Beckwhite's murder."

"But there hasn't been a murder."

Her ears went flat, her whiskers tight to her face, her tail lashing. "And you're anxious enough, now, to spy on that harmless woman burglar just because she loves pretty things."

"Come on, Dulcie. The woman is stealing." Dulcie's logic—female logic—drove him crazy.

"I suppose," she said, "it makes no difference that Jane Hubble isn't the only one who's missing. That there are five other patients who were moved to Nursing and haven't been seen again."

"That old woman ought to write for Spielberg. And you heard what Eula said, that some of those people have been seen—the one with the cataract operation, and the man who spent all afternoon with his attorney."

She gave him a dark look. She didn't have an answer; but that didn't change her mind. Exasperated, he stared down the hill toward the lights of the village.

She said, "If I can help you stalk the cat burglar, which I think is stupid, then you could help me search for Jane Hubble."

"If it's so stupid, why did you read all those news clippings? Why . . . ?"

"Will you help me look? It's safer with two," she said softly.

Joe knew he was defeated. She always knew how to push some vulnerable button.

"For starters, I want to search the Nursing wing." She assessed his mood through narrowed eyes. "If we can get into Nursing," she said softly, "we can see for ourselves if Jane and those other old people are there. And that should settle it." She lay down in the grass watching him, all gentleness now, quiet and submissive.

He was beaten. She wasn't going to let go of this; when she got her claws in like this, and then turned gentle, she'd hang on until her quarry—him—was reduced to shreds. "All right," he said, ignoring the uneasy feeling in his belly. "Okay, we'll give it a try."

She smiled and rolled over, and leaped up. Sooner than he liked they had licked the last dribbles of mouse blood off their whiskers and were headed across the hills for Casa Capri.

Trotting across the grassy slopes between scattered houses, as he looked past Dulcie, down the hill, watching the tiny lights of a car leave the police station, heading away toward the beach, he thought about Dillon Thurwell.

Dillon had joined Pet-a-Pet so she could look for Jane Hubble; she had dyed her hair so the nurses wouldn't recognize her. And maybe because of Dillon more than any other reason, he'd let himself get hooked into a predawn break-and-enter that could get plenty hairy. He thought of getting locked into that hospital wing among half a dozen antagonistic nurses, nurses who could wield a variety of lethal medical equipment, and he could almost feel the needles jabbing.

16

 The doll lay in a small dark enclosure just large enough to accommodate her eight-inch height. Her blond hair was matted. Her blue eyes, dulled by grime, stared blindly into the blackness. Her little hands were raised as if she reached but there was no one to pick her up and cuddle her or to examine the knife slit across her belly beneath her little dress.

Her porcelain skin, which had once been clear and translucent, was grayed with dust. Her flower-sprigged blue-and-white frock, made of the finest sheer lawn, and her white lacy slip, all hand-sewn with tiny, even seams, now hung yellowed and limp. And beneath her pretty dress, where her cloth body had been ripped, the three-inch gash had been sewn up again with ugly green thread in large, ragged stitches jabbing any which way into her white muslin body, and the thread knotted with a heavy, lumpy closure.

The walls around the doll were of thick oak, and the container bound outside with brass corners. Someone had hidden the doll well. If anyone had ever loved this doll, she lay forgotten, abandoned. If someone should find her there, they might have no notion of her significance—she was simply a grimy old doll ready for the trash or the Goodwill. Very likely, if she had a tale to tell, no one would know or care. No one would question who had ripped her apart and sewn her up again, or question why. And if there were significant fingerprints remaining on her porcelain face or arms, who would think to look for such a thing? She was not, at this juncture, a clue to any known crime.

17

As the cats crouched on the moonlit hillside, above them the high grass stems thrust black and sharp as knives against the moon. Through the grass they looked down onto the rooftops of Casa Capri, the sloping tiles struck into patterns of curving shadow. Far down beyond the retirement villa and beyond the village roofs, the moon's path cut like a yellow highway across the dark Pacific.

Nothing moved. No wind. The night was still and bright.

Just above the main building of Casa Capri, the rows of small retirement cottages climbed up toward them, their moonlit roofs gleaming pale, their little streets lit at intervals by the decorative lamps spaced along the winding lanes. But the cottages themselves were dark. No light shone, no curtain stirred where retirees slept. The time was 4:00 A.M.

The main building of Casa Capri was dark at the front. Along the sides, a thin glow from the softened hall lights seeped out from the residents' rooms. At the back of the building, in the Nursing wing, bright lights burned. One imagined sleepless patients suffering late-night changes of IV bottles, or perhaps restless with pains and discomforts and with the fears which can accompany old age.

Glancing at each other, the cats slipped on down through the grass, down between the dark cottages, and

across the little narrow streets. Pausing in a geometri-
cally neat bed of pansies, they studied the Nursing wing.

The windows in Nursing were high and securely
closed, as if perhaps those shut-in patients disliked the
cool night air. There was no access there, through those
windows. They had crossed the last street into the
shadow of the building when suddenly a clashing explosion of sound hit them, loud as the crash of wrecking
cars. Metal clanging against metal. They crouched belly
down, staring wide-eyed, frozen to the earth, ready to
run.

But then they identified the harsh metallic music of a
radio booming out from the Nursing wing, a blare of
Spanish brass, of trumpets blasting and snorting, and
they crept on again, ears tight to their heads, slinking.

The next instant someone turned the volume down,
and the noise subsided to a nearly tolerable decibel level.

Eight cars stood in the parking lot, their metal bodies
pale with dew from having been parked most of the
night. Not a car among them was more than two years
old, and they were all top-of-the-line Buicks, Chevys,
even two Mercedeses. Skirting the parking lot, the cats
headed for the Care Unit, and there, slipping in through
the wrought-iron fence that guarded the little terraces,
they searched for an open glass door, for access to a bedroom and the hall beyond.

Most of the glass doors were closed. The two that
had been left open a few inches were secured in place by
a bar, and the screens were latched. As if the occupants
worried seriously about human intruders scaling the six-
foot fence and strangling them in their beds.

The cats could hear the soft breathing of the shad-
owy sleepers, but some of the occupied beds looked
hardly disturbed, the covers nearly flat and only a small,
thin mound where the sleeper lay. Other occupants had
tangled their covers and twisted them or thrown them
on the floor. One old man, wrapped in a cocoon of
blankets, snored like a bulldog with bad tonsils.

Trying each door and screen, they were nearly to the end of the row before they found a glass standing open and the screen unlatched, or perhaps the latch was broken. The room smelled of cherry cough syrup. Slipping inside, they crept past the bed and its mountainous occupant. A metal walker with rubber feet stood beside the open door to the hall. They crouched beside it, looking down the empty corridor, then fled along it toward the social room.

In the darkness, the room seemed huge, the hulking shapes of couches and overstuffed chairs looming like fat, misshapen beasts. Beyond their hunching black forms, the white-clothed dining tables were moonlit, the moon itself shining in through the glass. To the left of the dim room, the patio gleamed pale through its glass doors. They leaped to the back of a dark sofa, listening.

From down the hall, toward the admitting desk, two women were talking; and the cats could smell coffee. Leaping from the couch to a chair, and to a couch again, they moved in that direction, then quickly through the open doors and down the hall.

At the parlor they slipped into the deep shadows beneath a chair. Staring out, they studied the brightly lit admitting desk and the open doors of the two lit offices.

The admitting desk was deserted, but in one of the offices the two women were laughing, and a coffee cup rattled. The cats fled past and down the hall, toward the closed door of Nursing, where they could hear the brassy music playing softly. Sliding into the nearest darkened bedroom, they sat close together, looking out through the crack of the door, studying the secured entrance to Nursing.

The door was one of those pneumatic arrangements which, the cats knew from past experience, was beyond their strength to open. If they waited long enough, someone had to come through; all they needed was patience. Behind them, in the dark bedroom, the sleeper moaned and turned over; the room smelled sour, of sleeping human, and was too warm. Soon Dulcie began to fidget, and then a flea began to chew at Joe's rump. He bit at it furiously, easing the itch, trying in vain to catch the little beast. Lately he'd begun to think of his minor but stubborn flea infestation as a serious breach of personal hygiene, a scourge on the civilized being he had become, a source of deep embarrassment.

Clyde had suggested that if he hated flea spray so much, he might try a daily shower. Well, of course, Clyde would offer some incredibly stupid solution. Joe was surprised Clyde hadn't bought him a razor, encouraged him to take up shaving; certainly that would get rid of the fleas.

They waited, watching the lit crack beneath the door to Nursing for what seemed an endless time before suddenly that space darkened, and footsteps hushed on the carpet within.

The pneumatic door sucked inward, and a nurse hurried out past them, her white shoes flashing along, inches from their noses. Before the door sucked closed they bolted through.

They nearly rammed into the heels of a second nurse. Crouching behind her, their hearts pounding, they stared around for a place to hide, but the best bet, the only real option, was the cart beside her. She stood with her back to them, arranging something on its metal shelves. They could smell hot cocoa and buttered toast, and, as she turned toward a counter, they fled underneath, between the chrome wheels.

Soon they were creeping along beneath the moving cart as she pushed it down the hall, their ears flicking up against the cold metal. The rubber tires made a soft pulling sound on the carpet, like tape being ripped from a fuzzy surface. Around them they could see only the wheels, the wooden molding along the wall, and the bottoms of the evenly spaced doors. If there were charts on the doors presenting the patients' names, they could see nothing of these. They might be passing Jane Hubble's room at this moment and never know. This procedure wasn't going to cut it. If they could ride on top the cart, that would be an improvement. Dulcie glanced at him with impatience, her tail twitching nervously against the metal wheel.

Some of the rooms were dark, but most were lit, and in some the voice of an elderly occupant groaned or called out. The smells of medicine and of sick people made them both want to retch. They could see the bandage-wrapped feet of one patient who was out of bed sitting in a chair. Halfway down the hall the cart stopped, the black rubber tires were stilled, and the nurse's white shoes padded away into a softly lit room. Behind her, they crept out to look.

Through the open door, a bedside lamp threw a narrow glow across the metal bed and across the thin, wrinkled occupant; he had an obedient, gentle face, as if he had long ago resigned himself to the entrapments of old age. As the nurse turned to straighten his nightstand, the cats slipped in behind her and under the bed.

Crouching beneath the dusty springs, they were only inches from her size five white oxfords, so close they could smell the mown grass through which she must have recently walked. This blended pleasantly with the smell of cocoa and buttered toast, and they could hear her arranging a tray before the patient, could hear the plate slide on the metal surface. She spoke to the old man in Spanish, but he answered her in English. Both seemed comfortable with the arrangement. They could hear her fluffing his pillows, then she braced her feet as if helping him into a sitting position. When she had him settled she left the room, wheeling her cart away.

The patient ate with little sucking and clicking sounds, as if his teeth didn't fit very well. They could see no chart on the inside of the partially open door, to tell his name. They had started to creep out when another nurse came down the hall.

Retreating again beneath the bed, Dulcie hunched uncomfortably, her paws tight together. She didn't like this part of Casa Capri—the Nursing wing was a full-blown hospital, reminding her too sharply of the vet's clinic. The disinfectant and medicinal smells and the cold, hard surfaces brought back every dreadful moment of her five days in Dr. Firreti's animal hospital, when she was sick with a respiratory infection.

She had, over in the social room, been able to maintain the illusion of happy days for these old folks, in a comfortable little world set aside just for their nurturing. But suddenly illness and the failure of the body were too apparent. In this wing of Casa Capri, all she could think of was sickness and dying.

Still, though, the old people were cared for, their meals were prepared, and they were warm and clean. If they had no one at home to look after them, and if they could not care for themselves, then where else would they be happier?

The cats remained beneath the bed until the hall was silent again, until they could no longer hear the rubber tires of the cart working its way from room to room. Above them, each time the old man set down his cocoa cup, it rattled as if his hand was shaky. He spilled a few crumbs of his toast, which rained down over the edge of the bed. He coughed once, then gulped cocoa. When he picked up the remote from the nightstand and turned on the TV, when presumably his attention had become fixed on an ancient John Wayne film, they slipped away, streaking out of the room.

Surely he hadn't seen them; behind them he raised no cry of surprise. Gunshots cut the night, and a horse whinnied.

They fled down the hall without the cover of the cart, repeatedly looking behind them, and quickly scanning the charts affixed to the patients' doors. Looking for Jane, Lillie, Darlene, Mary Nell, Foy Serling, and James Luther. They were just at the corner where the hall turned to the right when someone spoke behind them. Joe careened against Dulcie, shoving her down a short, side corridor.

The voices came closer, two nurses speaking casually as they approached on some routine business. The end of this little hall was blocked by a door which must lead back to the Care Unit. They sucked up against the wall as two nurses passed, their white-stockinged legs and white oxfords marching in rhythm. One heel of the taller woman's size nine shoes had a minute speck of dog doo. The cats wrinkled their noses at the smell. Speaking Spanish, the women turned down the longer hall, passing a fire door. As they moved away the cats followed. Joe paused at the heavy, closed door.

"Teddy went out here. Spice shaving lotion."

"So?"

"So when Dillon was dragging me all over, I saw wheelchair marks going out the fire door and into the parking lot."

"Mae Rose said he drives a car, one of those specially equipped cars. If he's Adelina's cousin, probably he comes and goes as he pleases."

"Then why does he live here? Adelina Prior is loaded. Why wouldn't she get him a nice apartment and hired help? Or why doesn't he live on that big estate with her?"

"Maybe he's sort of unofficial social director. Mae Rose says most of the old people like him, that he's always doing little favors, asking for the special foods they want, remembering their birthdays. He doesn't seem as sarcastic with the others as he is with Mae Rose."

Someone changed the Spanish radio station to hard rock, and the thudding drummed at the cats' nerves like a distant demolition crew. Over the din they heard another nurse coming, the sticky sound made by her rubber-soled shoes on the carpet, and quickly they slid into a darkened bedroom.

Immaculate white shoes and red-tasseled sox passed them at a trot, trailing the scent of Ivory soap. Then two more nurses, their snowy Oxfords flitting like two pairs of white rabbits hopping along the hall.

When the way was empty again the cats moved fast, looking up at the names on the charts. The hall formed a rectangle around a block of center rooms, so that only the outside rooms had windows. By the time they had rounded the last corner and could see the nursing station again, they had found not one of the six residents that Mae Rose claimed were missing.

The nursing station ahead was so busy they might never get past it and out the door. Nurses moved swiftly between two counters, which were covered with medicine bottles and boxes and cartons and a stack of paper towels, with a large stainless-steel coffeepot and a tray of ceramic mugs. As they slipped into yet another darkened room, they were beginning to fidget with impatience. Staring out at hurrying feet and listening to disjointed snatches of conversation, both in English and in Spanish, they felt completely surrounded. Trapped. They grew so irritable they nearly hissed at each other.

Someone changed the radio station back to Spanish music. One of the nurses began to sing with it in a sultry voice. When at last the hall was clear for an instant, they fled for the nursing station, running full out, pausing only to scan the remaining charts, then slide beneath the counter.

Crouching under the crowded shelves that lined the back of the counter, they were hardly out of sight when Size Nine returned, moving in near them, smelling of dog doo. She had only to glance down beneath the shelves to see them huddled. Standing inches from their noses, she began to stack papers, tamping the stacks against the desk. The air under the shelf was hot and close. They heard the pneumatic door to the hall open, and someone wheeled the food cart away, presumably back toward the kitchen.

A nurse came to the counter, there was a short conversation about medications, then Size Nine went away with her, down the hall. The instant she left, they reared up to examine the contents of the shelves, looking for some record of the patients' names.

They found boxes of syringes, tongue depressors, small packets containing artificial sweetener and fake coffee cream. There was a row of nurses' handbags lined up, fat and wrinkled, smelling of peppermints and makeup and tobacco; but no files, no list of patients.

"Come on," Joe said. "Check out the other counter. You watch the hall while I look." Leaping to the counter among the medicine bottles and IV tubes and the makings for a hot cup of coffee, he sorted through the tangle, patting irritably at the boxes.

"Here we go," he said softly, pawing a small file box out from behind the coffee canister.

She leaped up, watching the hall, watching him impatiently as he clawed through the alphabetized tabs. The cards contained patients' names and their medication information, the dosage, times per day, and for how many days.

They found no Jane Hubble, no Darlene Brown or Mary Nell Hook. They had no time to look for the others. Dulcie hissed, and they leaped down, dived back beneath the shelves as three nurses appeared.

"I'm beginning to feel like a windup toy," Joe said. "Programmed to jump at the sight of a human. I need a good run, need to clear my head."

"Shh. They're coming."

The nurses moved back and forth. Medicine bottles clinked. Someone sneezed. Coffee was brewed, and the radio station was changed again. They waited nearly half an hour before Size Nine returned to pick up her stack of papers, thumped them on the desk again, and headed for the pneumatic door.

They followed behind her heels and fled into the hall. For an instant, behind her, they were as visible as dog turds on a white sidewalk. If she had turned to look back, it would have been all over; they'd have had the whole staff chasing them.

They dodged into a bedroom, and in the dark, Joe paced. He couldn't settle. When something furry touched his nose, he jumped and raked at it, hissing.

But it was only a furry slipper. He shook it and shoved it aside. Out beyond the glass the moon was setting, its slanting light fading into the blackness of predawn. When the nurse vanished down the hall, they fled for the admitting desk.

In less time than it took for the moon to sink beyond the windows, they had searched not only that tall counter but two nearby file cabinets, clawing open the drawers, pawing through the folders. The procedure gave Joe fits—he'd been creeping and stealthy too long. All this snooping made him feel as if he was going to jump out of his skin. He needed to storm up trees, yowl at the moon. His mood would be considerably improved by a good bloody tomcat brawl.

But Dulcie pressured him on. She was most interested, of course, in the one office that was locked. They could smell Adelina's scent beneath the door, the same expensive perfume that had accompanied her into the entry the first time they saw her. The same scent which had already settled faintly into the leather upholstery of her new red Bentley the day Clyde took them for that memorable ride. Dulcie tried the door, leaping and fighting the knob, but at last she turned away.

In the two open offices they clawed open the desk drawers and file drawers, pawing through, flipping the file tabs with their claws.

They found the patients' full-sized record files, each set of documents in its own manila folder, but they found no record of any of the six missing residents. If those people had ever really existed, they weren't here now. Or at least their records weren't here.

"Maybe Jane took off for Tahiti, booked a cruise.

Maybe right this minute she's paddling her feet in some balmy tropical bay, eating coconuts."

"Very funny." Dulcie leaped down from where she had been balancing on the last file drawer.

"There have to be records, even if those people aren't here. Dead files." She shivered.

"Whatever secret this place is hiding. I'm betting it's in Adelina's office." She leaped up onto a desk. "That would be the . . ."

She paused, looking down between her paws at the glass-covered desk top. Beneath the glass, the desk was overlayed with photographs.

"Movies—they're movie stills. All the old reruns. Look at this, here's Clint Eastwood before he had any wrinkles. And Lindsay Wagner—she can't be more than twenty."

Joe leaped up. Strolling across the desk, he nosed at the pictures. "Who's the washed-out blonde? She's in every shot."

The thin woman appeared in the background behind Clint Eastwood, and at a restaurant table with a very young Jack Nicholson. Joe twitched a whisker. "She looks familiar, but I . . ."

Dulcie studied the lank-haired woman, frowning. "That's Adelina's sister."

"Come on. Why would Adelina's sister have her picture taken with Clint Eastwood?"

"It is her, only younger." The pale blond appeared as a maid standing stiffly beside a fireplace, appeared in several group scenes, and in the backgrounds behind the stars. "She's a bit player. Or she was—she's really young, here."

Beyond the office windows the wind had quickened, and the sky was beginning to pale, the branches of the oaks twisting black against the running clouds. Joe turned, watching the office door. "What time does the shift change?"

She shrugged, lifting a tabby shoulder.

"I don't relish getting caught in here. Like flies stuck to the chopped liver."

"We can have a little nap in the parlor while we wait. We can see the front door from there."

"While we wait for what?"

"For Adelina to get here. Don't you want to search her office? As soon as she unlocks her door, we—"

"Sure, we'll nip right on in, she'll be so pleased. Dulcie, I want into that woman's office like I want into the rabies lockup at the city pound."

She gave him a cool look, leaped down, and trotted away toward the parlor. Bellying beneath the damask sofa, she curled up yawning.

He gave it up and joined her. Far be it from him to back out. If they ended up murdered by Adelina's stiletto heels, there was always, presumably, another life. Unless, of course, they'd already used all nine.

They were cuddled together dozing beneath the sofa when Joe glimpsed movement beyond the black glass. Waking fully, he watched something shiny flickering through the heavy shadows beneath a lemon tree. Quickly he slid along beneath the couch for a closer look, pulling himself across the Chinese rug. Why did people make couches so low? How many cats in the world had to scrape their backs every day, every time they crawled under the family sofa? Where were people's minds? Didn't they think about these things?

Again the movement, glinting and dancing through the dark: the metallic flash of spokes.

Chrome spokes—the spokes of a wheelchair. He watched the chair turn and wheel away into the heavy shadows of the dark, predawn garden. Dulcie was beside him now, peering out. They could see, deep within the blackness, a figure standing, facing the wheelchair, as if the two were talking softly, their voices inaudible through the glass.

The cats looked at each other and slid back deeper under the couch. "I didn't hear the wheels," Joe said nervously. "And I didn't hear footsteps. I don't like when I can't hear something that's moving."

Dulcie stared out at the patio. "Maybe Teddy doesn't sleep well at night; maybe he and some other patient like to roam the halls." Uneasily, she curled up close to Joe, trying to purr, to calm herself. And at last they slept.

Joe woke to the first chirping of birds from the garden. The leaves of the lilies and azalea bushes shivered with activity, forcing Joe's eyes open wide, his metabolism to swing into high, and he crept out from under the couch.

The branches were full of birds. Flitting wings, hopping little bodies. Rigid, his muscles geared immediately into the kill mode, he crouched, staring out at that fluttering feast, at that brazen display of fresh meat, inches from his waiting claws. These birds, reared in that sheltered garden without a cat in sight, would be as stupid and tame as pet chickens.

18

It was early morning when she passed Police Captain Harper; he was just coming out of the drugstore as she went in. He smiled and nodded, and she turned away, hiding a laugh. He'd looked right at her, didn't guess a thing. Not a clue.

But why should he? If she went clanking by him in her black raincoat loaded and lumpy, he'd be onto her like an ambulance chaser onto a five-car collision. But dressed as she was, she could safely pass any village cop or, for that matter, could likely walk right by any hillside resident who had seen her looking for poor lost "Kitty." People weren't that observant. Who would connect?

In the drugstore she made her purchases, thanking fate that there were three druggists in town, so frequent purchases of certain items would not be easily noticed. She returned directly to her car, dropped her packages on the seat, and drove west down Ocean. Turning along Shore Drive, she cruised slowly, admiring the large and expensive beach homes. Out over the sea, the sky was blue and clear, not a cloud. Going to be a bright, boring day. Too much sunshine, the kind of day that seemed to turn the village into a featureless cardboard diorama. She was getting tired of Molena Point. When a town began to pall on her like this, it was time to move on, time to scratch these itchy feet.

Surveying the two- and three-story residences that

faced the sea just across Shore Drive, she slowed and parked for a moment, letting the engine idle. She was powerfully tempted to give one of these beauties a try.

But every time she headed down here, she turned back again. The houses were expensive and well furnished, but the area made her nervous. Too much activity, too many tourists on the beach and wandering the sidewalks. Tourists provided good cover, but idle people saw a lot, too. And tourists drew police patrols; there were always cops cruising, checking the teenagers, spotting for possible drug sales or some unlawful sexual display; and keeping an eye on the dangerous and illegal swimming areas.

Watching the oceanfront houses, she considered several other areas of the village that she had so far neglected. She had, in fact, restricted her work entirely to the newer houses up in the hills, had stayed away from the village proper, from the cottages which flanked and were mixed in with the shops and restaurants, mainly because of the street traffic.

Putting the car in gear, she cruised Shore Drive. Where the houses ended, giving way to rising sand dunes, she turned back again, driving slowly, studying the three houses that interested her the most, houses where she had never seen more than one car in the drive, and never seen much activity—not a lot of people going in and out.

It wasn't hard to check out such a house—a look at the city directory, then a few phone calls to see how many different people answered; but she seldom bothered. So far, her routine had worked fine without making all that fuss.

Turning off Shore Drive up Ocean into the village, she headed for the library. Wouldn't hurt to run in for just a minute, take care of that last bit of research. She wanted more information on the cloisonné clocks. Once in a while, using this library wouldn't hurt, as long as she kept an eye on who came in and didn't get involved with the librarians. Yesterday, in the San Francisco library, she'd been too busy learning about handmade dolls, trying to assess the value of the five dolls from the Martinez house. This whole business of handmade dolls was fascinating.

But the pricing range was incredibly large, their value depending on the skill and creativity of the artist and on his reputation, just as in the art world, where a painter spent years building a following. The price depended, as well, on whether the doll was one of a kind, or whether it had been produced in a limited edition, as was an etching or serigraph.

She had made quite certain of what she had before she approached Harden Mark. All five dolls were by a well-known name and were of small, limited editions, the retail price of each doll ranging close to five thousand.

She'd had the dolls only overnight before she packed them up to take to the city, but just having them propped on the dresser overnight she'd hated to part with the perfect little ladies. At the last minute, she'd kept one back, the blond sixteenth-century lady in the blue silk. She could always sell her later.

In the city she had come away from Harden Mark's office with ten thousand in cash, half the dolls' retail value, which was fair. She'd gone directly to her three banks, distributing the cash among them to avoid undue interest on the part of some nosy teller.

Now she drove on past the library and parked a block beyond. The library's pale stucco walls and sheltering oaks looked incredibly boring. She was getting tired of this faux-Spanish architecture. Maybe she was taking an unfair and warped view of the small coastal towns, but she found more color in San Francisco. The skies were more fitful, the wind-driven clouds seemed larger, vaster, the city more dramatic. Or maybe she just noticed the drama of the city more, looking out from the high, upper floors of the better hotels, the Mark or the St. Francis.

Before leaving the car, she reached under the seat for her good shoes, slipped them on, and flipped down the sun visor to redo her hair. The long tresses offered infinite possibilities. She pulled out the pins and combed it out, letting it fall over her shoulders.

Reaching into the backseat, she retrieved a large, floppy sun hat printed with pink flowers. Settling this low over her face, she applied a careful smear of hot pink lipstick. Peering up into the mirror at herself, she grinned, then slid out and headed up the street for the library, moving through alternate sun and shade beneath the oaks that spread across the narrow street. It wasn't such a bad village, picturesque in its way, though really too cute with all the steep roofs and balconies and gables. Maybe she'd hit two or three more Molena Point houses, then move on. Get out before the papers started about the cat burglar or before Captain Harper picked up a make on her car—though she'd been incredibly careful, painstaking in the switches she'd made.

Entering the library, she glanced around for the cat, hoping fervently to avoid it. How totally stupid, for a public office to keep a cat. There'd been a big fuss in the paper about how wonderful it was to have a "library cat," editorials, letters to the editor. And then that battle to get rid of the beast, headed up by the librarian who was allergic to cats. And people getting up petitions to keep the animal. What idiots. Half the village thought a library cat was just darling—and of course the tourists loved it. The cat was of no earthly use, just a common cat, shedding hairs and fleas, one of those ugly, dark-striped creatures—there were hundreds like it—that you could see in any alley.

Passing the checkout desk, she studied the adjoining rooms warily but didn't see the beast. It gave her the creeps to approach a table or the book stacks thinking she might suddenly see the cat wander out under her feet. Just thinking about it made her ankles itch, as if any minute it might find her and rub against her.

The woman behind the desk kept staring, so she smiled brightly back at her. What was she looking at? Watching her like she was some kind of character. Didn't she like floppy pink hats and pink lipstick?

Well I like them, and I'm the one wearing them. And she had to smile—if she was a character, that was just fine, she didn't give a fig what some librarian thought.

19

In Casa Capri, Dulcie woke beneath the parlor couch, curled up warmly on the thick Chinese rug. Joe was gone. Looking for him, out past the squat couch legs and through the glass to the patio, she stiffened to full alert.

The garden was alive with birds, with the swift flitting and chirping of sparrows among the low bushes and flower beds, with quickly winging finches darting under the leaves to harvest the morning's insects; that busy, winged feast beckoned and enticed, begging to be sampled.

She saw Joe at the glass doors, standing on his hind legs working at the latch, pawing at the lock, his teeth chattering as if he was already crushing succulent sparrow bones.

She settled back. She wasn't particularly hungry; really she felt too lazy to leave the soft, warm rug. She'd like to nap a little longer. Let Joe hunt, she'd catch breakfast later.

Rolling over, she pawed at the rug's intricate, labyrinthian patterns. Then, rolling onto her back, she reached a paw above her to stroke the bottom of the couch. Through the black gauze dust cover—it did smell dusty—she could see the rows of springs and the couch's thick wooden frame. Patting at the black gauze, smoothly she let her claws slide into the thin, flimsy fabric.

She raked hard, ripped down through the thin material a long, straight tear, felt her blood surge at the delicious sound of ripping cloth.

She clawed again. Again. In long straight gashes. She had no idea why the underside of a couch roused such an irresistible urge to tear and shred. She was about to kick with all four feet, really give the dry, frail gauze a workout, when she heard the front door open.

Flipping over, she peered out toward the front entry.

The door opened slowly, as if someone were not sure of a welcome. A nurse slipped in, a small woman, and thin. She wore the requisite immaculate white uniform, white oxfords, a white nurse's cap tipped over her dark, sleek pageboy. Her hair was beautifully done, not a strand out of place, as if she had just come from an expensive beauty parlor. Her face was made up with blusher and dark eyeliner, and with a touch of green eye shadow that made her brown eyes look larger, made her look far older and very sophisticated. Her lipstick was bright and carefully applied, her gold earrings small and tailored.

But even beneath the scent of cosmetics, the young nurse still smelled like Dillon. Dulcie hardly knew the child—a casual observer would guess this young woman to be at least eighteen.

She watched Dillon move away quickly toward the social room and on through, among the couches, to the dining room. Watched her push the door open with casual assurance and slip into the kitchen. The door swung back and forth behind her, slowed to a stop.

Dulcie watched the closed door, expecting any minute to hear angry scolding from within, and see Dillon come flying out again.

Nothing happened. There was a long silence. She waited nervously, her tail twitching, her paws growing hot with wary anticipation. Any minute she was going to hear enraged shouts, and Dillon would be hustled out by some irate kitchen employee, would be roughly scolded and sent packing for her effrontery.

But after a few minutes the door swung out again and a breakfast cart appeared. Dillon pushed it out swiftly and efficiently, letting the door swing closed, looking as if she did this job every morning. The top shelf was heavily laden and covered with a white cloth, the rubber tires made the same soft sticky hum that the snack cart had made over in the Nursing wing.

Dillon pushed the cart past her toward the admitting desk and around the corner toward Nursing, trailing the scent of eggs and toast. Dulcie was about to follow her when Joe returned from the patio, licking blood from his whiskers, slipping under the couch beside her.

He stared toward the passing cart, sniffed the child's scent, got a glimpse of her sleek hair and grown-up face. "What the . . . That can't be Dillon?"

Dulcie smiled. "Would you take her for twelve years old?"

Joe licked his whiskers. "More power to the kid. She might get away with it."

"But if they catch her again, what will they do? Those nurses . . . She's only a little girl. Would they . . . ?"

"They won't hurt her. Get a grip. Why would they hurt her? This isn't some den of murderers; it's an old people's home. If they catch her, they'll give her hell and pitch her out and maybe that would do the kid good. Got to admit she's pretty nervy."

"How did she learn to make herself up so beautifully? If I didn't know her . . ."

"She's a girl, Dulcie. Girls are born reaching for the eyeliner. To a girl, that stuff comes naturally, you ought to know that better than anyone. Look at how you fuss over silk nighties, dragging them home. And you should see Clyde's sleep-over girlfriends. Lipstick and junk all over the dresser. They drive Clyde crazy, hogging the bathroom mirror."

"But she's only twelve. She—"

"So she's twelve. So look at those child models you

read about. Eleven years old, and they look like they could buy a double martini."

He slipped out from under the couch and returned to the glass, fixing his gaze again on the birds. "I could eat another; guess I didn't get my fill. Come on, we can—" But when they heard footsteps and a sharp voice in the hall, he slid back under.

Around the corner, a woman was hurrying down the hall, scolding. The nurse rounded the corner, pulling Dillon along by one arm.

Dillon had abandoned her cart. Her nurse's cap was gone, and her pretty pageboy hair was all mussed, her uniform awry, and one white shoelace untied. But though the nurse was scolding, pushing her out into the entry toward the front door, Dillon didn't look repentant. She looked mad, red-faced and scowling.

The nurse reached around her, opening the door. "If I see you back there again, young lady, if there's a hint of trouble because of you—if I lose my job over this, you're going to be a sorry little girl." The woman pushed her out onto the porch. Dulcie crouched to leap after Dillon, but Joe grabbed her leg in his teeth. She stared at him and hung her head.

The nurse slammed the door, shutting Dillon out, and turned away.

"What were you going to do?" he whispered. "Run after her and tell her you're sorry?" He licked her ear. "She'll be okay. She'll cry and then go home." He groomed Dulcie's ears and her face until she calmed. He was washing his own whiskers when they heard a car door close softly, heard high heels on the walk, heard the knob turn.

Adelina came in quickly, seeming preoccupied. She did not seem unduly upset, had evidently not seen Dillon slinking—the kid must have gotten out of there fast. Adelina was dressed in another little black suit, this one with a low-cut jacket over a fluff of white lace. She wore patent spike heels, black sheer stockings. Behind her, as the door swung in, they glimpsed the pearl red Bentley standing in the drive.

Slamming the big double door, she moved toward her office, her black skirt swishing in soft friction against her silky legs. Her keys jangled, and they heard the click of the lock opening. She disappeared into her office, leaving the door ajar.

Dulcie crouched, tail twitching, eyeing the open door. The next instant, she was gone, had fled through, not waiting for Joe. Without asking for his opinion, without asking if he was coming, she was gone into Adelina Prior's lair. Within the room a blue light came on, and Joe could hear the click of computer keys. He waited to see if Dulcie got pitched out again.

When nothing happened he stifled his urge to beat it out of there and, slinking, followed Dulcie.

Just inside the door and to his right stood a little seating group, a purple leather love seat and matching chair, and a dark, polished corner table. He slid beneath the love seat, flattening himself down into the white carpet. The piece was so low he had to belly along like a snake. Oozing along in the dark space, he realized he was alone, that Dulcie wasn't there, the space was unoccupied except for a spider huddled inches from his ear, clinging to the squat mahogany leg. This schlepping around under furniture was getting old. He felt as if he'd spent his whole life underneath couches and beds and desks, like some weird mole-cat, living entirely in a four-inch-high world beneath heavy furniture. Why was he doing this? He was a cat, not an earthworm; he was a freewheeling tomcat born to the wind and high places.

From this vantage, all he could see of Adelina were her well-turned ankles and spike heels, the desk legs, and the five-castered pedestal of her wheeled desk chair.

Slipping out to the edge of the love seat for a wider view, he studied the sleek black desk and the computer behind which Adelina sat, her smooth profile bathed in green light, her black hair a shining wing pulled back into an elegant roll, her diamond earrings catching green sparks with the movement of her typing. He did not see Dulcie. She wasn't under the desk, nor under the upholstered chair. Searching for her, he crept farther out, careful to stay out of Adelina's line of sight. Surveying the room, he was not impressed by the decor of purple and black against the lavender walls. And who would want paintings of flat, purple, naked humans that looked like they were drawn with a ruler? The work had no passion, was like purple cutouts, or as if the artist had filled in the outlines for a street sign.

Adelina stopped typing, removed a tissue from her top desk drawer, and delicately blew her nose. She smoothed her hair, touching the intricate dark coil, then resumed her work. He could not see the computer screen, it angled toward the window at her back. The window was open a few inches above a long window seat covered with decorative pillows. There was no screen on the window. Dulcie could, if she'd lost her nerve, simply have slipped on out. Escape out the window, through the scrolled iron bars and away, leaving him in the lurch.

If she'd ditched him, if she'd cut out of here, she'd never hear the end of it. He judged his distance, ready to leap across and follow her. One jump into the cushions, and he'd be through before Adelina could grab him. The pillows were done in such a maze of wild patterns and colors they dizzied him, a tangle of intricate tapestry, a panoply of color and texture that must have cost a bundle. He suddenly saw, tucked between the lavish weavings, a pair of green eyes watching him.

Swallowing back a laugh, he crept out and winked at her. Among the pillows, she looked exactly like a puff of dark, striped embroidery.

She cut her eyes at him, then blinked them closed, was at once invisible: a little commando hidden in jungle camouflage.

She had positioned herself directly behind Adelina,

where she could see clearly the computer screen. When she opened her eyes again, she glanced at him, then watched the screen intently. She seemed impatient at what she was seeing. He could see, between the pillows, the end of her tail irritably twitching.

He wondered if Adelina was working on the files they had sought, on the information they'd searched for all night.

If she was, whatever it showed, Dulcie didn't look pleased.

Soon Adelina turned on the printer, and the state-of-the-art machine spit out five pages as fast as bullets. When the printing ended she punched a few keys, turned off the machine, then unlocked a desk drawer.

As she removed several files, Dulcie emerged from among the cushions and reared up behind Adelina, peering over her shoulder like some sudden, ghostly visitation. They watched Adelina remove an untidy sheaf of papers from the top folder, and a sheet of stationery. With a thin gold pen, she began to write. Behind her Dulcie stood taller, so fascinated, stretching up to see, that she rocked precariously on her hind paws, her front paws drooping over her pale belly, her tail switching for balance. Joe guessed they were both thinking the same thought: Why would Adelina turn off the computer and write a letter by hand?

Exchanging another glance, they watched her finish one letter, address the envelope, seal it, and drop it in her purse. When she opened a second file, she removed a large pad of lined paper, the kind a school child might use, and started a second letter, writing with a lead pencil. Adelina had written two pages when the soft scuff of shoes in the hall sent Dulcie diving into the pillows again and Joe slinking deep beneath the love seat.

The feet, in scarred, flat shoes, that scuffed across the carpet belonged to Renet. He caught her scent, and, as she went around the desk, he could see her, pale hair hanging ragged around her ears, no makeup—that plain face could use some help—her cotton skirt and cotton blouse wrinkled and baggy. She dropped a large brown envelope onto the desk. "Done. Good job if I do say so. Worked it out last weekend. Did the prints this morning, to make sure."

She sat down on the love seat, her light weight nearly squashing Joe. Maybe the love seat needed new springs. If she'd been heavy, he'd be flat as a twenty-cent hamburger. Belly down, he slid away to the other end, then out between the love seat and the wall.

From this vantage he watched Adelina remove a sheaf of photographs from the envelope and lay them out on the desk. She studied them solemnly.

"Yes. Very good. How long does this one take?"

"An hour to be safe. I hope that Mae Rose woman doesn't come snooping."

Adelina raised her dark, expressionless eyes. "Forget Mae Rose. You're fixated with the woman just because she knew Wenona." She gave Renet a long, chill look. "Wenona's dead, Renet. Please forget everything connected with her."

"But Mae Rose—"

"And as for Mae Rose going on about Jane Hubble, that's all talk. What possible connection could she make?"

"I don't like her. I think Mae Rose should—"

"Mae Rose has three daughters. Get your mind off her."

"They never visit her, they live clear across the country. I could easily—"

"She's not a suitable subject. For one thing, she's too small, you know that. Pay attention to the business at hand. If you do just one sloppy presentation, Renet, it's over. You'll have no need to worry about Mae Rose."

Adelina slipped the files back into the drawer, locked it, and put the photographs back in the envelope. "I don't know why these people have to visit the same day as that Pet-a-Pet business. And I don't know whether allowing those animal enthusiasts in here is worth the trouble, for the little PR it affords."

"Well it certainly wasn't my idea."

Adelina sighed. "Have you done all the errands?"

"Of course. What time?"

"Two-thirty. Don't leave half the box in the closet."

"I never do. What about that new nurse, that big slow woman? I don't—"

"I'll see that she's kept busy. Have you made any progress on her? I don't like keeping her when she—"

"So far, nothing. You should have looked deeper before you hired her."

"I didn't have any choice. It isn't easy to get help. Just get on with your job. Everyone has some skeleton in the closet, and you're to keep on until you find it. You've had two weeks, and you don't have a thing. If you'd pay more attention to business—"

"I've checked DMV. Five credit bureaus. Four previous addresses and talked with three of her landlords."

"What about NCI? That was foolish, to allow that Lieutenant Sacks to get married."

"What was I going to do, poison his dearly beloved? There'll be someone else. Max Harper—"

"You'll leave Harper alone; he's not to be approached. I don't trust him for a minute. What about that Lieutenant Brennan?"

Renet did not reply.

"If not Brennan, then you'll have to buy the information in San Francisco—that should be no problem."

"You needn't be sarcastic. And I might have other things to attend to."

"You had better plan your time around matters of first importance." Adelina rose. "Lock the door when you leave. And make sure you have your little party under control." And she disappeared into the hall, her black skirt swishing against her silken thighs.

Renet didn't move from the love seat for some time, but sat tapping her foot irritably. When she did rise, she stepped to the desk and tried the locked drawer. When she couldn't open it, she tucked the brown envelope under her arm and left the room, locking the door as she'd been instructed.

The instant they were alone, Dulcie slid out from between the pillows. Standing on the window seat she shook herself, licked her paw, swiped at her whiskers. "I'm all matted down—those pillows are hot as sin." She watched Joe slide out from under the love seat, pawing dust from his whiskers. He leaped up beside her, and they sat looking out to the drive and the gardens.

They could see no one. The red Bentley and Renet's blue van were parked before the door. When they were certain they were unobserved they slipped out beneath the open window, through the scrolled curves of the burglar grille, and dropped into a bed of marigolds.

Crouched among the sharp-scented flowers, they scanned the gardens. They saw no one.

"The smell of marigolds is supposed to keep away fleas," Dulcie said.

"Old wives' tale. Come on, we're out of here." Close together they raced across the drive away from the manicured grounds, flew down the hill into a tangled wood so wild and unkempt it could never be a part of Casa Capri. At once they felt safe again, and free.

Fallen branches and drifts of rotting leaves lay tangled against the trunks of the ancient, sprawling trees. Together they fled, leaping from log to log, plunging through piles of crackling leaves, shaking off the tight sense of closed rooms and locked doors and under-furniture niches that would hardly let a cat breathe. They were flying down through leafy tangles and branches when a shrill sound stopped them. A strange and muffled cry. They froze still, two statues, listening.

20

The woods angled downward, the old twisted oaks rising among fallen, rotted trees, among dead branches and dry, brittle foliage: a shadowed graveyard of dying trees. The cry came again, a muffled gurgle. Puzzled, the cats trotted down among the shadows, watching, leaping silently over logs, sinking down into drifts and damp hollows. Far below them, between a tangle of dead branches, they glimpsed something bright, a gleam of metal glinting from the dark tangles.

Slowly and warily padding down, they could soon make out the handlebars of a bike. The crying came from there. The rough, gulping sobs sounded more angry than hurt.

The bike leaned against the forked trunk of an ancient oak that had split down the middle, its two halves leaning jagged against their neighbors. At the tree's base, Dillon sat in a pile of dead bracken, her head down on her knees, her arms around her knees, bawling so hard she didn't hear them, heard no rustle of paws crunching leaves.

Dulcie dropped down beside her. Dillon startled, looked up. The child's face was smeared with tears and makeup, black eyeliner and lipstick and powder all run together. Dulcie climbed up into her lap, touched Dillon's cheek with a soft paw. Dillon smiled through her tears, grabbed Dulcie to her, hugging her, burying her face in Dulcie's shoulder—then began bawling again, crying against Dulcie until Dulcie's fur was wet. Joe sat watching, exasperated at the female display of weeping. All this because she'd been booted out of Casa Capri.

When at last Dillon stopped crying, she eased her grip on Dulcie and reached her fingers to Joe, touching his nose. "What are you two doing, way up here in the hills? You're miles from home. This isn't Pet-a-Pet day." She frowned, puzzled. But then she grinned through her streaked makeup. "You were hunting— Wilma said you hunt all over these hills."

She looked hard at them, and her eyes widened. "Did you hear me crying? Did you come down here because you heard me crying?"

Dulcie snuggled against her, but Joe turned nervously to lick his paw. Had they shown more than a normal cat's interest? The kid didn't need to get any ideas about them.

But she was only a kid. All children believed in the sympathy and understanding of animals; most kids thought their dogs understood every word they said. Kids grew up on fairy tales featuring helpful animals, and even on *Lassie* reruns—a helping animal was no big deal, to some kids as natural as a loving grandmother.

Dillon wiped her tears with the back of her hand, smearing black and red. "I only wanted to see Jane. They acted like I was some kind of criminal." She gave them a deep, confiding stare. "She isn't there. Why else would they be so nasty. And they know that I know she isn't there." She gave them a determined look, her brown eyes blazing with anger. "Well they can go to hell. I'm going to find out what's going on.

"Yesterday I called her trust officer, but the switchboard said to leave a message. Voice mail—big deal. I gave my name and phone number, but now I'm sorry. My folks'll have twenty fits."

Dulcie reached a soft paw again, patting the child's face. Dillon gathered them both into her arms, pulling

Joe into her lap with an insistent little hand. She held them against her as if they were rag dolls, pressing her wet face into their fur. The child was warm, and smelled of the perfumed cosmetics.

"I love you both. I wish you could tell me what to do." She kissed Dulcie's pink nose. "They were so gross, marching me out of there like a baby." She looked at them bleakly. "Jane isn't there. And no one will believe me."

Unblinking, Dulcie stared at the child, so intent that Dillon widened her eyes, looked into Dulcie's eyes deeply, suddenly alarmed. The two gazed at each other for a long moment, in a strange, silent aura of communication.

Dillon whispered, "What, Dulcie Cat? What is it? What are you trying to tell me?"

Joe wanted to shove Dulcie away, she wasn't behaving like an ordinary cat. He could feel her concern for Dillon. If the people of Casa Capri were this adamant about keeping out strangers, then maybe there was reason to fear for the child.

Dillon said softly, "Are you afraid of them, too?"

When Dulcie looked almost as if she would forget herself and speak to Dillon, Joe pushed her aside.

Scowling, she jumped down, turned her back on him, began to wash herself, contrite suddenly, and embarrassed.

They sat with Dillon for a long time, until at last she sniffled, blew her nose. Finally, she picked up her bike and began to drag it through the woods, heaving it over the tangles, heading for the road.

They didn't follow her.

At the top of the hill she blew her nose again, looked down at them once more, puzzled, then kicked off and sped away, coasting down the dropping street. They watched her small, lone figure until she disappeared around a curve.

They were licking Dillon's salty tears from their fur,

licking away her makeup, when suddenly Dulcie gave him a wild look and exploded away through the sunshine, racing up across the hills—too wild to be still another instant. Shedding the restraint of cautious hours last night and this morning, shedding the tension of dealing with Dillon, she leaped invisible barriers, careened around bushes and through dead grass and across driveways and gardens, across the open fields. Joe sped behind her, infected by her drunken lust for freedom, their ears and whiskers flattened in the wind, their paws hitting only the high spots.

Dulcie paused at last, half a mile north of Casa Capri in a favorite field where three boulders thrust up. The smooth granite glinted hot with morning sun. Leaping to the top, she stretched out across the warm stone, twitching her tail, rolling in the heat. She chased her tail, then lay on her back, letting her paws flop above her, idly slapping at a little breeze.

Joe lay in the warm grass below, nibbling the tender new blades which thrust up between last year's growth. "The kid's going to get herself in trouble, nosing around."

"Not if we find out what's going on first."

He looked up at her, exasperated. "So what was Adelina writing? I'm surprised she didn't feel you breathing down her neck."

Dulcie lifted her head, her eyes slitted against the sunlight. "Personal letters. She was writing to a friend of Lillie Merzinger. The file had Lillie's name on it, and there were letters to Lillie in a scrawly handwriting, and some snapshots of two ladies standing beside a lake, with pine trees behind. There were graduation announcements, too, and wedding invitations, little personal mementos, the kind of personal stuff people save."

She rolled over to look at him. "There were machine copies of letters from Lillie to Dorothy. Adelina spread them all out, as if to refer to them, before she began to write."

She rolled again, to warm her other side. "What did she do, open Lillie's mail? Open the letters Lillie wrote, before they were mailed, and make copies?"

"What did the letter say?"

"Boring stuff. About Lillie's poor digestion, and about Dorothy's old dog and about Cousin Ed. Dull, personal things. Why would Adelina write the letter in the first person, and sign Lillie's name?"

"So Lillie Merzinger's too sick to answer her mail," Joe said. "Someone has to answer her letters, or her family would worry."

"But why doesn't she tell Lillie's family she's too sick to write? Why wouldn't she type a regular letter on the computer? Print it out with the rest of her letters. Tell them how Lillie's feeling, that she's taking her medicine, maybe getting a little better. And if someone's really sick, wouldn't she phone the family?"

Dulcie's eyes narrowed to green slits. "And the other letter, the one she wrote on lined paper—she wrote it in a totally different handwriting. She signed it James. Addressed the envelope from James Luther."

She snatched at a flitting moth, caught it in curving claws, chomped and swallowed it, then fixed him with a hard green gaze. "And why was her handwriting different for each letter? Why was she forging those letters?"

They both thought it: *Because Lillie and James aren't there anymore.* Their thought was as sharp on the wind as if they'd spoken.

Joe slapped at a wasp, turned away and began to wash his back.

Normally he'd be as eager as Dulcie to find out what was going on, but this situation made him edgy. He felt as though very soon they were going to wish they'd kept their noses to themselves. Casa Capri, with its locked doors, gave him the fidgets.

"And what," Dulcie said, "is Renet's mysterious presentation tomorrow? Like a speech? Why would Renet give a speech? A speech about what?" She sat up tall on the warm boulder, her eyes narrowed, thinking. She shivered once, then lifted a paw and began to clean her pink pads, licking fast and nervously, tugging fiercely at each claw. Tearing off each old sheath, she angrily released the sharper rapiers beneath. She was wound tight, edgy and irritable.

Joe wanted to say, *You thought visiting the old folks would be all kippers and cream*, wanted to say, *Casa Capri didn't turn out like you expected*. But she glared at him so crossly he shut his mouth.

As he bent to tend to his own claws, suddenly she leaped from the boulder and streaked away across the hills again, all nerves and temper. He stared after her, watched her vanish into the tall grass, watched the heads of grass shake and thrash in a long undulating line as if a whirlwind fled through.

He took his time about following her, lingering to sniff at the sweet dusty smells, at masses of yellow poppies which seemed to have bloomed overnight, at old scents of mouse, at rabbit droppings. She was headed diagonally across the hills moving north, and occasionally he stood on his hind legs, so as not to lose her.

He couldn't see her cross the crest of the hill but he could see the grass shaking. Beyond them to the north, the hills were black from last fall's fire but were slowly turning green again, as new spring grass sprang up between the remains of that terrible burn. He could still smell burned wood on the wind, and wet ashes. And against the sky there still stood the skeletons of black, dead trees, and a lone chimney, an abandoned sentinel, though some of the houses had been rebuilt.

Janet Jeannot's studio had been replaced in a way Janet might not like if she were alive to see it. It was now a second-floor apartment, an inoffensive cedar structure without any of the excitement of an artist's studio. To the east of Janet's house, up beyond the highest homes, he could see where the drainage culvert emerged from the hills, the place where he and Dulcie had discovered the final key to Janet's killer.

Dulcie had disappeared. He leaped to the highest hillock to look for her. Gazing down the rolling hills, he thought how they must have been a century ago, before there were ever houses. A wild land, all open, alive with animals far larger than the creatures he and Dulcie hunted, a land of cougars, of wolves and bear, a land belonging to beasts that would send *Felis domesticus* scooting for cover.

And though the wolves and bears were gone, still sometimes the cougars and coyotes came down out of the mountains, driven by thirst or hunger, and by encroaching civilization—where tracts of new houses covered their hunting territories—wild animals moving closer each year to human dwellings. Now sometimes in the small hours, a lone coyote wandered the street of a coastal town, hunting domestic cats and small dogs. And already two humans had died at the claws of attacking cougars. He was gripped with amazement that a shy, totally wild creature would dare enter the world of houses and concrete and fast cars.

But the animals, if they were starving, had little choice. He was no philosopher; the only conclusion he could draw was that if humans kept pushing the animals off the land they needed to survive, then humans had better sharpen their own teeth and claws.

Rearing above the grass, still he did not see Dulcie, saw no thrashing where she sped through, only a faint susurration all across the grass tops where the breeze fingered. He heard no sound above the hush of wind and the churr of the buzzing insects.

But suddenly he knew where she was headed, and a chill of fear touched him.

High above the last houses, an ancient barn stood rotting and half-fallen in, its silvered boards leaning inward, its roof torn open to the sky. Dulcie would be there, he'd bet on it. Hunting the rats that ruled that dim, cavernous ruin.

Someday the remains of the old barn would collapse and rot to nothing, but now it belonged to wharf rats. Having long ago cleaned out the last kernel of grain in the feed bins, they subsisted on roots and on mice and lizards, and on whatever smaller creature ventured into their domain.

Some of the rats had migrated down to the boatyards again, but the biggest and boldest had remained to challenge whatever predator invaded their dark and rotting home. Raccoons did not bring their kits to hunt there. A fox had to be full-grown before it would face those beasts.

A stupid place for Dulcie to go, insane to go alone. Terrified for her, he raced across the hills, hoping he was wrong, but knowing she was there. That rat-infested mass of timbers was exactly the place she would go to work off frustration from their night of confinement. He wished she wasn't so damned volatile.

Ahead, the old barn towered drunkenly, its timbers balanced precariously against one another. He was on the crest of the hill some ten feet above when he saw Dulcie, crouched in shadow among the fallen walls. She seemed, at first, a part of the shadows. She moved slowly, slinking beneath the timbers, her belly hugging the ground. She was poised to leap, but he could not see her quarry. He watched her swing her head from side to side, sorting out some tiny sound that he could not yet hear.

He sped down soundlessly, but he did not approach close enough to spoil her attack. He waited, ready to leap, every muscle and nerve jacked into high voltage, watching her creep deeper into the blackness.

She froze, remained still, the tip of her tail flicking.

She was gone in a sudden blur, flashing through shadows into the blackness.

Silence. No sound, no movement. He could see nothing within that dark, rotting world. He crept swiftly closer.

A scream jarred him, the enraged scream of a rat. A board fell, thundering. Dulcie yowled. He dived for the blackness, charging in, storming in beneath fallen boards.

She screamed again, then another rat scream. He saw its eyes red in the blackness. The two were thrashing; it was a huge rat, a monster. Joe piled into the thudding squealing flailing bodies, grabbing at rat fur. He found the rat's face and bit deep. Pain burned him. Dulcie twisted and shook the rat so violently she shook him, too. His ears rang with rat screams and with the thuds of his own body. The three of them slammed into timbers, into the earth. His blood pounded, he felt teeth in his leg.

And then, silence.

His mouth was filled with the bitter taste of rat. The beast lay between them, unmoving, their fangs in it, Dulcie's in its throat, his seeking its heart, its ribs crushed against his tongue. It was a huge, grizzled beast, its body as long as Dulcie, its coat rough with age, its pointed muzzle knobby with old scars. Its eyes even in death were cold and mean.

They rose, spit out rat hair.

But they did not turn away from the kill in the usual ritual to wander aimlessly, cooling down and letting off steam. They remained watching, one on either side of the rat, staring at that giant kill.

It was the biggest rat Joe had ever seen. He wanted to yell at Dulcie for having attacked such a beast, for having been so damned stupid. And he wanted to cheer her and lick her face and laugh. His lady had killed the monster, had killed the king of rats.

She gave him a green-eyed grin of triumph and leaped up. She spun, clawing at the timbers. She leaped over the rat, racing and whirling among the fallen boards, careening in circles; she laughed a human laugh; she spun and danced, driving out the built-up tension, ridding herself of that last terrible violence and rage. She careened into him broadside, pummeled him.

"We killed the king—king of rats—we killed it." She was insane, rolling and spinning and chasing her lashing tail. "The king, we killed the rat king." She was crazy with victory and release.

She collapsed at last and lay still. He sat beside her, washing himself. They licked the blood and cobwebs from each other's faces and ears, licked the deep wounds that would, too soon, begin to hurt like hell.

Joe's paw and leg were torn, and his cheek ripped. There was a gash across Dulcie's pale throat, another up her shoulder. They cleaned each other's wounds carefully, though they would be tended again at home. Joe could hear Clyde now, ragging him about how septic rat bites were. And Wilma would pitch a fit.

But they had demolished the great-great-granddaddy of wharf rats.

The midmorning sun warmed them. Dulcie rubbed against him sweetly and smiled. A gleam of sunlight picked out the shingles and boards of the old barn, the rusted nails, and the rat's mangled body. Joe supposed that some possum coming on the rat in a week or two would be thrilled, would maybe drag the moldering rat away to its babies. Possums would eat anything, even the blood-spattered cobwebs.

He watched Dulcie stretch out limp across the grass, her green eyes closed to long slits, her purr rumbling with little dips and high notes. Life had turned out better than he'd ever imagined. If a cat really did have nine lives, he hoped he and Dulcie would be together in all the lives yet to come.

Last summer, his alarm when he found himself able to speak human words had nearly undone him. He knew himself to be a freak, an abnormal beast fit only for a side show. He hadn't dreamed there was, anywhere in the world, another like himself.

But then he'd found Dulcie, and he was no longer alone in his strangeness. She was the most fascinating creature he had ever met; their love had changed his very cat soul. Lovely Dulcie of the dark, marbled fur, her pale peach paws and peach-tinted nose so delicate, her green eyes watching him, laughing, scolding, emerald eyes set off by the dark stripes perfectly drawn, like the eyes of an Egyptian goddess.

Only a master artist of greatest talent could have composed his lady. And she was not only beautiful and intelligent, she'd beaten the hell out of that rat.

She rolled over, her green eyes wide. "I'm starved. Too bad rats are so bitter."

"How about a nice fat rabbit?"

She flipped to her feet and stood up on her hind legs, looking away across the grass to where the hills rose in a high, flat meadow bright with sun, a meadow so riddled with rabbit burrows that any human, walking there, would fall through to his arse pockets. And within minutes, high on the sun-baked field, they were working a rabbit, creeping low and silent, each from a different angle, toward a shiver of movement within the dense grass.

No normal house cat hunted as these two; ordinary *Felis domesticus* hunted only as a loner. But Joe and Dulcie had developed a teamwork as intricate and beautifully coordinated as any team of skilled African lions. Now they crept some six yards apart, moving blindly through the grass forest, rearing up at intervals to check the quarry's position. They froze, listening. Slipped ahead again swift as darting birds.

Joe stood up, twitched an ear at her.

She sped, a blur so fast she burst at the cottontail before it had any clue. It spun, was gone inches from her claws. Joe cut it off. It doubled back. Dulcie leaped. It swerved again, angling away. They worked together hazing, doubling, then closed for the kill.

The blow was fast, Joe's killing bite clean. The rabbit screamed and died.

They crouched side by side, ripping open its belly, stripping off fur and flinging it away. Joe ate as he plucked the warm carcass, snatching sweet rabbit flesh

in great gulps. But Dulcie devoured not one bite until
she had cleaned her share of the kill, stripped away all
fur. When the warm meat lay before her as neat as a
filet presented for her inspection by a favorite butcher,
she dined.

They cleaned the rabbit to the bone. They washed.
They cleaned one another's wounds again, then climbed
an oak tree and curled together where five big limbs,
joining, formed a comfortable nest. The breeze teased
at them, and, above the oak's dark leaves, the blue sky
swept away free and clean. Below them, down the
falling hills, where the village lay toy-sized, their own
homes waited snug and welcoming. Home was there,
for that moment when they chose, again, to seek human
company.

But at that moment the cats needed no one. They
tucked their chins under and slept. Joe dreamed he was
a hawk soaring, snatching songbirds from the wind and
needing never to touch the earth. Dulcie dreamed of
gold dresses and of music, and, sleeping, she smiled, and
her whiskers twitched with pleasure.

They woke at darkfall. Below them the lights of the
village were beginning to blink on, bright sudden pricks
like stars flashing out. The smell of cooking suppers
rose on the salty wind, a warm and comforting breath of
domesticity reaching up to enfold them.

Galloping swiftly down the hills, within minutes they
were trotting along the grassy center median of Ocean
Avenue beneath its canopy of eucalyptus trees, their
noses filled with the familiar and comforting aromas of
Binnie's Italian and an assortment of village restaurants,
and with the lingering scent of the greengrocer's and
the fish market; how comforting it was, when home
smells embraced them. Their wounds were beginning
to burn and ache.

They parted at Dolores Street, Dulcie trotting away
toward the main portion of the village, where, beyond
the shops and galleries, her stone cottage waited. Joe

turned left, crossed the northbound lane of Ocean, and soon could see his own cat door, his own shabby white cottage. He pictured Clyde getting supper, pictured the kitchen, the two dogs greeting him licking and wagging.

He stopped, sickened.

Only Rube was there. Barney would never again greet him. He approached the steps slowly, riven with sadness.

His plastic cat door was lit from within, where the living-room lights burned, and he heard the rumble of voices. Looking back over his shoulder toward the curb, he realized that he knew the two cars parked there—both belonged to Molena Point police officers.

Turning back across the little scraggly yard, he leaped up onto the hood of the brown Mercury. It was only faintly warm; Max Harper had been here a while. Sitting on Harper's dusty hood studying the house, he tried to decide—did he want to spend an evening with the law?

He didn't relish Harper's cigarette smoke. But he might pick up some useful information. And it amused him to hassle Harper, and to spy on the police captain, to lie on the table among the poker chips, listening. Learning things that Harper wouldn't dream would go beyond those walls. And even if his eavesdropping didn't prove useful, it was guaranteed to drive Clyde nuts.

Flicking an ear, he leaped down and trotted on inside.

21

The letter had been folded many times into a tiny rectangle no larger than a matchbook. It had been stuffed between layers of cotton filling in the belly of the doll, and the doll's stomach sewn shut again with the ragged green stitches. The letter had lain concealed for more than three months, and the doll hidden and forgotten.

Dear Mae,

I don't know if I'm being foolish in writing this. Maybe my distress and unease are only a result of my condition or of the medication they give me. Maybe that causes my shaky handwriting, too. I do feel odd, off-balance, and my hands don't work well. I was so hoping you would visit me here and that we could talk. The nurses say you haven't asked about me, but I don't believe them. I've longed to come over to your room or the social room. You're so near, just beyond this wall, but it's as if a hundred miles separate us.

The doctor told me to walk, so I have been all around the halls, but always accompanied by a nurse, and none of the nurses will let me come over to the social room. They are so needlessly strict, and I haven't the strength to defy them, not like I once had. Six months ago I wouldn't have stood for this high-handed treatment.

I haven't seen anything of your friends, Mae, though I have watched the doors where the charts are posted. I don't think any of them are here. Their names are not on the doors, and I've looked carefully.

If your fears continue, maybe you should talk to the police. But I wouldn't ask these nurses questions, they get terribly cross.

I heard the supervisor scolding one of the nurses when she thought I was asleep. Though I don't know much Spanish, just a few words, I'm sure she was saying something about a phone call and your friend Mary Nell Hook. I think she told the nurse not to answer questions from anyone, told her to tend to her own job unless she wanted—something "guardia," something about the police. Though I didn't understand much of it, the conversation frightened me. The supervisor mentioned Ms. Prior, too, in a threatening way. I think Adelina Prior can be very cold, I would not want to cross her.

I don't know if there's any connection, but twice late in the night I've awakened to see a man standing across the hall inside a darkened room, just a shadow in the blackness, looking out. And once when I woke around midnight I thought someone had been standing beside my bed watching me. Not one of the nurses but someone studying me intently, and I felt chilled and afraid—but maybe it was only my overactive imagination, or maybe the medication is affecting my nerves.

I'm putting this note inside Mollie, and I mean to ask Lupe to bring her back to you. I'll tell her that I don't want her anymore, that the doll makes me sad. I know you'll make Mollie a new dress. When you do, you'll find my stitching hidden under her skirt and slip—I just hope

Lupe doesn't find it. I'll use green thread so you won't miss it—but you wouldn't miss it, my hands are no better for sewing than for writing.

I know I seem very depressed. I suppose that's natural, given my illness. Though I do wonder if the medicine doesn't make me feel worse.

I long to see you, Mae, but I'm so very tired, too tired to argue. I miss you. And I long for my friend Dillon, too. Since I came here, she hasn't written, though I have written to her several times. How strange the world has become. I feel very disoriented and sad.

With all my love,

J.

22

Joe pushed in through his cat door and headed for the kitchen, toward the cacophony of good-natured male voices and the click of poker chips. He heard someone pop a beer, heard cards being shuffled. When he heard Clyde belch and politely excuse himself, he knew there were ladies present. And that meant a better-than-usual spread from Jolly's Deli. He could already smell the corned beef, and wished he hadn't eaten so much of that big cottontail rabbit.

As he quickly shouldered into the kitchen, the good smells wrapped him round, the thick miasma of smoked salmon and spiced meats and crab salad, this gourmetic bouquet overlaid with the malty smell of beer, and, of course, with a fog of cigarette smoke that he could do without. His first view of the group as he pushed in through the kitchen door was ankles and feet among the table legs: two pairs of men's loafers below neatly creased slacks; a pair of well-turned, silk-clad legs in red high heels; and Charlie Getz's bare feet in her favorite, hand-made sandals. Clyde, as usual, was attired in ancient baggy jogging pants and worn, frayed sneakers. On beyond the table, Rube lay sprawled listlessly across the linoleum, the big Labrador's eyes seeking Joe's in a plea of lonely grieving.

Slipping between the tangle of feet, Joe lay down beside Rube, against the dog's chest. He tried to purr, to comfort the old fellow, but there was really no way he could help. He could only be there, another four-legged soul to share Rube's loneliness for Barney. Rube licked his face and laid his head across Joe, sighing.

Clyde had buried Barney in the backyard, but he had let Rube and the cats see him first. Dr. Firreti said that was the kindest way, so they would know that Barney was dead and would not be waiting for him to return. He said they would grieve less that way. But, all the same, Rube was pining. He and Barney had been together since they were pups.

Joe endured the weight of Rube's big head across his ribs until the old dog dozed off, falling into the deep sleep of tired old age, then he carefully slipped out from under the Labrador. Rube didn't stop snoring. Joe was crouched to leap to the table when he glanced toward the back door and saw the latest architectural addition to the cottage: Clyde had installed a dog door. He regarded it with amazement. The big plastic panel took up nearly half the solid-core back door, was big enough to welcome any number of interested housebreakers. Clyde had evidently reasoned that Rube would need something to distract him from grieving. Surely this new freedom, this sudden unlimited access to the fenced backyard, couldn't hurt. Too bad Barney wasn't here to enjoy it.

The other three cats would certainly find the arrangement opening new worlds. They had, heretofore, been subject to strict supervision. They were kept shut away from the living room so they couldn't go out Joe's cat door, and Clyde let them into the yard only when he was with them. In the mornings and evenings he let them have a long ramble, but strictly inside the yard. With the aid of a water pistol, he discouraged them from climbing the back fence. Two of the cats were elderly, and disadvantaged in any neighborhood fight, and the little white cat was so shy and skittish she was better off confined. Joe wondered what they'd make of their new liberty. Clyde must have been really worried about Rube to instigate this drastic change in routine.

As for himself, he had never been confined, not from the very beginning of their relationship, when he was six months old and Clyde rescued him from the San Francisco alleys. For the first week he'd been too sick to go out, too sick to care, but when he was himself again and wanted access to the outer world, and Clyde refused, he'd pitched one hell of a fit. A real beauty, a first-class, state-of-the-art berserker of snarling and biting and raking claws.

Clyde had let him out. And from that moment, they'd had a strict understanding. They were buddies, but Clyde would not under any circumstances dictate his personal life.

Leaving Rube sleeping, Joe leaped to the poker table, gave Clyde a friendly nudge with his head, and watched Clyde deal a down card. This group seldom played anything but stud. If the ladies didn't like stud, they could stay home. Max Harper glanced at his hole card, his expression unchanging. Harper had the perfect poker face, lean, drawn into dry, sour lines as if he held the worst poker hand in history.

Harper had gone to high school with Clyde—that would make him thirty-eight—but his leathery face, dried out from the sun and from too many cigarettes, added another ten, fifteen years.

The other officer was Lieutenant Sacks, a young rookie cop whose dark curly hair and devilish smile drew the women. Sacks had recently married, the heavily made-up blonde with the nice ankles and red shoes had to be his new wife. Joe thought her name was Lila. Absently he nosed at Clyde's poker chips until the neat round stacks fell over, spilling chips across the table.

"Oh, Christ, Joe. Do you have to mess around?"

He gave Clyde an innocent gaze. Clyde's second card was a four of clubs, and Joe wondered what he had in the hole. With Clyde's luck, probably not much. He

tried to think what he'd done on poker nights before he
understood the game. Just lain there, playing with the
poker chips. The smell of the feast, which had been laid
out on the kitchen counter, was making his stomach
rumble. Clyde always served fancy, in the original paper
plates and torn paper wrappers. He tried to remember
his manners and not dive into Clyde's loaded plate,
which sat on the table just beside him, but the smell of
smoked salmon made his whiskers curl. Watching the
bets, he studied the two women.

Charlie Getz was Clyde's current squeeze, a tall, liber-
ally freckled redhead, friendly and easy, the kind of
woman who did most of her own automotive repairs and
didn't giggle. She wore her long red hair in a ponytail,
bound back, tonight, with a length of what looked like
coated electrical wire in a pleasant shade of green.
Charlie tossed in her chips to raise Harper, and absently
petted Joe, then handed him a cracker piled with smoked
salmon. Across the table the little blonde watched this
exchange with distaste.

He tried to eat delicately and not slop salmon onto
the table, but when he took a second cracker, this time
off Clyde's plate, the blonde shuddered, as if he'd con-
taminated something. *Who the hell are you, to be so picky?*

Though the fact did cross his mind that he'd recently
been gnawing on a dead rabbit and had, moments before
that, bitten and ripped at a flea-infested rat.

Sacks bet his king, and Lila folded on a six of hearts.
On the last card, Clyde dealt himself another four.
Across the table, Max Harper's lean, leathery expression
didn't change. There ensued a short round of bluffing,
then the hole cards came up and Harper took the pot on
a pair of jacks. Charlie made a rude remark, rose, and
filled her plate. She prepared a plate for Harper, too,
and set it before him, then fixed a small plate for Joe, a
nice dollop of crab salad and a slice of smoked salmon
cut up small so he needn't make a mess, so he wouldn't
have to hold it down with his paw and make a spectacle

of himself chewing off pieces. Charlie did understand cats. He feasted, standing on the table beside her, thoroughly enjoying not only the fine gourmetic delicacies, but the scowling blonde's disgust.

When he had finished, he gave Lila a cool stare and curled up next to Charlie's chips, ducked his head under one paw, and closed his eyes. He was dozing off when Charlie said, "Oh, hell," and tossed her three cards toward the center of the table.

Joe reared his head to look. Harper had a pair of aces showing. With Harper's luck, probably his hole card was an ace. Clyde started to bet, glared at Harper, and changed his mind. He folded. Sacks and Lila folded.

"Bunch of gutless wonders," Harper said, gathering in the few chips. "What kind of pot is this?" He did not turn over his hole card, but shuffled it into the deck.

"His luck won't last," Sacks said. "It's the full moon—screws up everything." Sacks rose and opened the refrigerator, fetched five cans of beer, and handed them around.

Lila gave her bridegroom an incredibly sour look. "Honey, that's such a childish idea. I wish you wouldn't talk like you really believe in that stuff."

Harper looked at her. "Believe in what stuff?"

"In these silly superstitions—that the full moon changes your luck. The moon can't affect people. The moon—"

"Oh, it can affect people," Harper told her. "You'd better read the arrest statistics. Full moon, crime rate soars. Moon's full, you get more nutcases, more wife beatings, bar fights."

Charlie, petting Joe, had discovered his wounds. She sat examining them, parting the fur on his paw and leg, holding his head so she could see his cheek. Anyone else tried that—except Clyde—he'd get his hand lacerated. But for Charlie, he tried to behave, waited patiently as she rose, opened the kitchen junk drawer, and fetched the tube of Panalog. Returning to her chair, she began to doctor him, drawing from Lila a look like Lila might throw up.

"The presumption is," Harper said, "that the increase of crime is caused by the pull of the moon, same as the moon's pull on the ocean causes the tides. That people emotionally or mentally unstable lose what little grip they have on themselves, go a little crazy, teeter on the edge."

Lila studied Harper as if he had suddenly started speaking Swahili.

"It's the same with animals," Charlie said. "Ask any vet. More crazy things happen, more cat fights, runaway animals, dog bites during the full moon."

Lila looked at them as if *they* came from the moon. Joe had never seen a more closed, disgusted expression. The woman had no more imagination than a chicken. He wanted badly to set her straight, tell her how he felt when the moon was full—like he was going to explode in nine different directions. The full moon made him wild enough to claw his way through a roomful of Doberman pinschers.

But he couldn't speak; he could tell Lila nothing. She wouldn't buy it, anyway. She stared at Charlie and Max Harper as if they were retarded. "You can't really believe that?"

"Come down to the station," Harper said. "Take a look at the stat sheets, check them with the calendar. Right now, today, full moon. Seven domestic violence, five dog poisonings, and one little old lady brought in a human finger."

Lila shuddered.

Joe raised his head, watching Harper.

Clyde said, "A finger?"

"Nettie Hales's mother-in-law called the station." Harper sampled the crab salad from the plate Charlie had fixed for him. "The Haleses live up the valley, a little five-acre horse farm up there. Her terrier brought the finger in—just a bare bone, dirt-crusted."

Harper tilted his beer can, took a long swallow. "The old lady didn't know where her dog had been digging. Said he'd brought the bone in the house and was chewing on it." Harper laughed. "Gumming it. Old dog doesn't have a tooth in his head. Still, though, even gumming it didn't please the lab. Bone was fractured, and covered with dog slobber. Don't know what kind of evidence it might have destroyed."

Lila's blue eyes had opened wide. "You mean it might be a murder? Al, you didn't tell me there'd been a murder. You didn't tell me anyone was missing."

Sacks gave his new bride a sour look. "The finger is old, Lila. Old and dark and brittle. And when do I ever talk about that stuff?" He glanced uneasily at Harper.

Lila grew quiet.

It was Joe's turn to study the blonde. *This woman isn't only a snob, she isn't too bright.* He didn't realize he was staring until Clyde began to stroke his back, pressing down with unnecessary insistence. He lay down again and shuttered his eyes, tried to look sleepy.

Clyde said, "What did the lab come up with?"

"Nothing yet. That finger'll be sitting under a stack of evidence until Christmas. They're so backed up, the place looks like a rummage sale. The court's putting all criminal investigations on hold, waiting for the lab. Victims' relatives can't even collect insurance until the lab is finished, can't do anything until they get a death certificate. Thirty investigators working the county lab, and still they can't stay on top."

Harper sipped his beer. "That Spanish cemetery up the hills, it may have come from there—that old graveyard on the Prior place. It's only a mile from the Haleses' house." For Charlie's benefit, because she hadn't lived in Molena Point long, he said, "It was part of the original Trocano Ranch from Spanish land-grant days. Family members were buried at home, tradition to be buried on family land. Even after the land passed down to the children and grand-children, the family still buried their dead there. The funerals—"

"Isn't there a law against that?" Lila interrupted.

Harper looked at her, a hard little pause as expressive as an explosion. He did not like interruptions. "No one would enforce that law, with the Trocanos," he said shortly. "Long after Maria Trocano married Daniel Prior, they buried family at home. Both Daniel's and Maria's graves are there.

"When Adelina came of age she sold off all but five acres. Kept the original old ranch house and the cemetery, turned the house into servants' quarters," Harper said. "Built that big new house for herself and Renet, and I guess Teddy's there part of the time. Turned that fine stable into garages. Not a horse left on the place.

"That was quite some stable in its day," Harper said. "Some of the finest thoroughbreds in California came off the Trocano Ranch."

He drained his beer. "When Mrs. Hales brought in the finger bone, we had a look at the old cemetery. Thought the dog might have dug into one of the old Spanish graves, but not a clod disturbed. The Priors keep the grounds nice, the grass mowed and trimmed around the old headstones.

"We've got three men out walking that area looking for where the dog was digging, and I've ridden every inch of that land. So far, nothing." Harper lived on an acre up in the hills several miles north of the Prior estate. He kept only one horse now, since his wife died.

"I told Mrs. Hales to keep her terrier in before he picks up something worse than a finger bone. The dog poisonings were in that area, too. Three dogs this week, dead of arsenic poisoning. We've put two articles in the *Gazette* telling people to keep their animals confined." He looked at Clyde. "That would go for cats, too. If I recall, that tomcat's a real roamer." He studied Joe intently. Joe gazed back at the police captain. Harper was talking more tonight than Joe had heard in a long time; Harper got like this only occasionally, got talky.

But it wasn't until Lila left to use the bathroom that

Harper told Clyde, "One good thing turned up this week, we got a line on that old truck that hit Bonnie Dorriss's mother."

"That's good news. Wilma will be glad to hear it, too, she's fond of both Susan and Bonnie. How'd you get the lead? Another anonymous phone tip?"

"No, not another anonymous phone tip," Harper snapped. Those phone calls were a sore subject for Harper. He hadn't a clue that his anonymous snitch was sitting on the table not a paw's length from him.

"That auto paint shop out on 101," Harper said. "They fired one of their painters, Sam Hart." He grinned. "Getting fired made Hart real mad. The guy plays baseball with Brennan, and he told Brennan about this pickup he'd painted. It was a job his boss wanted done in a hurry, and the truck's owner had acted nervous. Hart thought maybe the vehicle was hot.

"A week after he was fired, Hart spotted the truck up in Santa Cruz in a used lot. He was up there looking for a fender for a '69 Plymouth he was rebuilding. He saw this Chevy truck with fresh brown paint. Same model, same year. He could still smell the new paint, and when he checked the front bumper there was the same little dent. Looked like someone had scrubbed at it with maybe a Brillo pad.

"Brennan had filled him in on the green truck we were looking for, so Hart called Brennan, and Brennan hiked on up there."

Harper shook his head. "By the time Brennan got there, just a couple of hours, the dealer had sold it. Described the woman who bought it as a looker, tight leather skirt, long auburn hair.

"We ran the new registration but it came up zilch. False ID. And the previous plate was stolen, registered to an L.A. resident, guy with an '82 Pinto. Plate had been stolen three months before."

Lila had returned. Clyde rose, and set the sandwich makings on the table with a stack of fresh paper plates.

"We're trying to get a fix on the woman," Harper said. "Samson did a sketch from the dealer's description, but the guy didn't remember much about her face, he was looking at her legs."

Charlie grinned.

Lila looked annoyed. This woman, Joe decided, wasn't going to be a cop's wife very long.

There was a long silence while sandwiches were constructed. Rube went out his dog door, barked halfheartedly, and came back in again. Charlie fixed Rube a corned beef sandwich. It was near midnight when the poker game broke up and the officers and ladies left. Charlie's parting remarks had to do with an early repair to a rusted-out plumbing system; she seemed actually eager to tackle the challenge.

Clyde opened the back door and the window to air the kitchen, shoved the remains of the feast in the refrigerator, and emptied the ashtrays in deference to the animals who had to sleep there. Joe left him stuffing beer cans and used paper plates into a plastic garbage bag, and lit for the bedroom.

Pawing the bedspread away so not to be disturbed later, he stretched out on his back, occupying as much of the double bed as he dared without being brutally accosted. He was half-asleep when Clyde came in, pulling off his shirt. "So how was Pet-a-Pet day?"

"What can I say? Paralyzing."

"You are such a snob."

"My feline heritage. And why are you so interested?"

Clyde shrugged. "When you weren't home last night, I figured maybe you liked those folks so much you moved in with them, took up residence at Casa Capri."

"Slept in a tree," Joe said shortly. He did not like references to his nocturnal absences. He didn't ask Clyde about *his* late hours.

But then, he didn't have to. It was usually apparent where Clyde had been, the clues too elemental even to mention, a certain lady's scent on his collar, his phone book left open to a certain name, hints that did not even add up to kindergarten training for an observant feline.

He did not mention that he and Dulcie had searched the Nursing unit at Casa Capri, and had run surveillance on Adelina Prior in her private office. No need to worry him.

"Harper said, before you came slinking in tonight, they think the cat burglar is getting ready to move on up north."

"What made him say that?"

"This morning's police report had an identical operation in Watsonville, and another at Santa Cruz. Harper thinks she's testing the waters up there. That's what happened down the coast, a couple of isolated incidents weeks apart before she moved in for the action."

Clyde wandered around in his shorts, belatedly drawing the shades. No wonder the elderly matrons in the neighborhood turned pink-faced and flustered when they met him on the street. "The *Gazette* is going to do an article on the cat-lady angle. Max never did like keeping that confidential, but he didn't want to scare her away. Once that paper hits the street, she'll be gone." He picked up the remote from beside the TV and turned on the late news.

"Pity," Joe said, "that a police force the size of ours didn't have the skill to nail her. Do you think they'd like the make on her car?"

Clyde turned off the volume, turned to stare at him.

"Your mouth's open," Joe said, yawning. He burrowed deeper against the pillow.

"So what's the make? I won't ask the details of how you got it."

"Blue Honda hatchback. Late model, not sure what year. California plate 3GHK499 with mud smeared on it."

Clyde sighed and picked up the phone.

But he set it back in its cradle. "I can't call him now.

Where would I have gotten that information, just a few minutes after he left?"

Joe gave him a toothy cat grin. "Where else?"

Scowling, Clyde settled back against his own pillow and turned up the volume, immersing himself in a barrage of world calamities, avoiding the subject he found far more upsetting.

Joe rolled over away from him, curled up, and went to sleep. But he did not sleep well, and in the small hours before the first morning rays touched the windows he rose and padded into the kitchen to the extension phone.

The time was 3:49 A.M. as he punched in the number of the Molena Point PD and gave the duty officer the make on the blue Honda: the color, style, and license number. The officer assured him that Harper would get the information the minute he walked into headquarters.

And that, Joe figured, would be the end of the cat burglar's long and lucrative spree. Harper would have her cold. And if a twinge of sympathy for the old girl touched him, it wouldn't last. *Dulcie's the easy mark, not me. She's the sucker for thieving old women, not Joe Grey.*

23

 Eula rose hastily from the couch, spilling Joe to the cushions. Scowling, clutching the back of the couch to support herself, she stood looking out the glass doors across the patio toward the empty corner room. "There's someone over there; the curtains are open. There's a light on—there, in Jane's old room." This was Joe's second visit. Again, he'd been paired with Eula.

Mae Rose came alert, wheeled her chair around, almost upsetting it, staring out. On her lap, Dulcie rose up tall, looking, her tail twitching with excitement, her green gaze fixed across the patio on the corner room, where figures moved with sudden activity.

Joe leaped to the back of the couch, looking out, nipping at his shoulder, pretending to bite a flea, as he gave the distant view his full attention. Across the patio, through the loosely woven draperies, a bedside lamp shone brightly, picking out three busy nurses. The room seemed to brighten further as the sky above Casa Capri darkened with blowing clouds.

Along the length of the patio garden, each room was lit like a bright stage. In some, the occupant was reading or watching TV; other rooms were empty, though residents had left lights burning while they came to the social hall. Dillon came to stand beside Joe, leaning against the back of the couch, stroking him, but her attention was on the far room.

He hadn't expected to see Dillon again after finding

her bawling in the woods, after the nurse booted her
out. He'd figured she was done with Casa Capri, that
she'd give up looking for Jane Hubble, but here she was,
fascinated by that far bedroom, her brown eyes fixed
intently on the action behind the curtain.

Suddenly, everyone moved at once. Dillon fled past
him out the sliding door, leaving it open to the wind. Mae
Rose took off in her wheelchair toward the front entry
and the hall beyond, moving faster than he thought that
chair could move, Dulcie balanced in her lap, stretching
up to see. Eula followed behind Mae Rose's wheelchair,
hobbling along in her walker as fast as she could manage.

Joe delayed only a moment, then nipped out the glass
doors behind Dillon.

The kid stood across the patio beneath an orange
tree, pressed against the glass, shielded by the partially
open draperies, looking in, her hands cupped around
her eyes. Joe, slipping along beneath the bushes, rubbed
against her leg. She looked down and absently scratched
his ear with the toe of her jogging shoe. She must think,
with the patio darkening and the room so brightly lit,
and the flimsy drapery to shield her, that she wouldn't
be noticed. He sat beside her in the shadows, watching
the three white-uniformed nurses within. One was setting out some books on the dresser, another was filling
the dresser drawers with folded garments: neat stacks of
lacy pink nighties, quilted satin bed jackets, and what
appeared to be long woolly bed socks. The closet door
stood open, but the space within did not contain hanging clothes.

The closet was fitted with shelves, and the shelves
were stacked with cardboard boxes, wooden boxes, plastic bags, small suitcases, several small flowered overnight
bags, and two old-fashioned hatboxes. Dillon seemed
fascinated with the jumble; she peered in as if memoriz-
ing every item. She looked away only when a fourth
nurse entered the room, wheeling a patient on a gurney,
a thin old lady tucked up beneath a white blanket, her

face pale against the white pillow, her body hardly a puff beneath the cover. The nurse positioned the gurney beside the hospital bed and set its wheel brakes.

Two nurses lifted the patient. Working together they settled her onto the taut, clean sheets of the hospital bed and tucked the top sheet and blanket around her. She squinted and murmured at the light from the bed-side lamp, and closed her eyes. A nurse turned the three-way bulb all the way up, forcing a moment of bright glare, switching on through to the lowest, gentle setting. For an instant, in that brief flash of harsh light, something startled Joe, some wrong detail. Something he could not bring clear.

He had no notion what had bothered him, whether some detail of the room, or something about the patient, but soon the feeling was gone. If something was off here, he didn't have a clue. Probably imagination. Annoyed at himself, he lay down across Dillon's feet, watching the room as the nurse pushed the gurney out into the hall.

Another nurse attached an IV tube to the patient's wrist where a needle had already been inserted, and hung a bottle on the IV stand. The old lady was dressed in a lacy white nightie with a high, ruffled collar, and on her hands she wore little white cotton gloves.

"The gloves," Dillon whispered, looking down at him, "are so she won't scratch herself. Wilma says their skin is like tissue paper when they get old. Mae Rose's skin is thin, but I don't remember Jane's being like that."

He wondered if a cat's skin got thin and fragile in old age. Old cats got bony. Old cats looked all loose-hinged, their eyes got bleary, and their chins stuck out. Old cats had a lot of little pains, too. Maybe arthritis, maybe worse.

He didn't think he wanted to hang around after he got frail and useless; he'd rather go out fast. End it quick in a blaze of teeth and claws, raking the stuffings out of some worthy opponent.

Slowly Dillon backed away from the glass. "It's not Jane," she said sadly. She picked him up, buried her face against him. But soon she moved closer to the glass again, peering in as if the sight of that poor old soul fascinated her. He still couldn't figure out what was off about the scene—the old woman looked comfortable and well cared for; the room seemed adequately appointed.

The old lady was very pale, but so were a lot of old people. Her white hair fanned out in a halo onto the white pillow, hair so thin he could see her pale pink scalp beneath. Her wrinkled cheeks and mouth were drawn in, her pale blue eyes were rimed with milky circles. Her lids were reddened, too, and at the corners of her eyes liquid had collected. Dampness shone at one side of her mouth in a small line of drool.

A nurse bent to wipe her face, taking such gentle strokes she seemed hardly to touch the old woman. Behind the nurses in the hall, two visitors appeared, figures robed in black, stepping heavily into the room, two square and hefty old women dressed all in black like two Salvation Army bell ringers.

Their gray hair, frizzed close to their heads, formed little caps as kinky as steel wool. Their shoes were black and sturdy, their black skirts reached nearly to the floor. They seemed as ancient as the bed's occupant, but of a different breed. These two ladies looked indestructible, as if they had been tempered perhaps by some demanding religious sect. Or maybe the vicissitudes of life, alone, had toughened them, just as old leather becomes tough.

The shorter of the two carried a brightly flowered handbag of quilted chintz, its yellow and pink blooms screaming with color against her sepulchral attire. The taller lady bore in her outstretched hands a small bowl covered with a white napkin. Adelina Prior moved behind them, shepherding them inside. She wore beige today, a tailored suede dress that showed less leg, and she wore less makeup, her eyes almost naked, her lips a flesh-colored tone.

The women paused uncertainly by the foot of the bed, watching the patient. She lay with her eyes closed, whether in sleep or out of shyness or bad temper was impossible to tell. The two black-robed ladies leaned forward, peering.

"Mary Nell? Are you awake? It's Roberta and Gustel."

"Mary Nell? Can you hear us? It's Cousin Roberta and Cousin Gustel."

When the patient didn't open her eyes, Ms. Prior took the ladies' arms and guided them to a pair of upholstered chairs that had been drawn up at the side of the bed, the backs to the wall and facing, across the bed, the glass doors. The black-clad women sat woodenly. The shorter lady leaned forward. "Mary Nell, it's Roberta. Are you awake?" As she leaned, she deposited her flowered handbag on the floor. The tall lady remained silent, clutching her bowl in her lap.

Joe, dropping down from Dillon's arms, slipped behind the orange tree, then leaped up into its branches. The sky had grown darker, and the clouds were moving fast. A damp wind scudded through the branches, shivering the leaves. He settled in a fork where he could see out between the moving leaves, directly down upon the bed, upon Mary Nell Hook and her two sturdy cousins. He could see, as well, beneath the bed, Dulcie's two hind paws and the tip of her twitching tail.

Dulcie's view was restricted to the floor, the bed legs, a corner of the blanket hanging down, and the high-topped black shoes of the visitors. Each woman, when seated, kept her feet flat on the floor as if to assure adequate balance. Above their ankle-high shoes, two inches of leg were encased in thick, black corrective stockings— a sharp contrast to Adelina's silk-clad ankles and creamy pumps, her sleek narrow foot tapping softly beside the bed. The two ladies smelled of mothballs, a strange mix when combined with Adelina's perfume and the sweet aroma of vanilla from the bowl that Gustel held. These, with the strong air freshener that had been sprayed earlier, left her nose nearly numb. But she did catch a whiff from the bed above, of nail polish remover. This seemed a puzzling aroma to be associated with a frail, bedridden lady. But maybe she liked nice nails—though one couldn't see them beneath the white cotton gloves.

She could see Dillon standing beyond the glass door and draperies, a shadow among shadows in the darkening patio, a subtlety probably not detectable by human eyes. She had seen Joe streak for the tree—he was hidden, now, high among the leaves—but she caught a glimpse of his yellow eyes, watching.

A chair creaked as if the short lady had leaned forward. "Mary Nell? Mary Nell, it's Roberta. Open your eyes, Mary Nell. It's Roberta and Gustel."

There was a rustle of the covers as if Mary Nell had turned to look at her visitors.

"Mary Nell, Cousin Grace sends her love," Gustel said. "I've brought you a vanilla pudding."

Mary Nell murmured, faint and weak.

"Her husband Allen's son is graduating from Stanford, and we came out to the coast for the ceremony, and, of course, we wanted to see you; it's been years, Mary Nell."

Mary Nell grunted delicately.

"Do they treat you well? We talked with your trust officer, and she said they are very kind here."

Another soft murmur, a bit more cheerful.

The conversation progressed in this vein until Dulcie had to shake her head to stay awake. From Mary Nell's responses, the patient, too, was about to drift off. The cousins took turns talking, as if they had been programmed by some strict familial custom which allowed exactly equal time to all participants. Mary Nell's answers remained of the one-syllable variety. Not until Gustel began to talk about the old school where Mary Nell had taught did the patient stir with some semblance of vigor.

Gustel, holding her pudding gently on her lap, told about the grandchild of one of Mary Nell's students, who was now vice principal of that very same school. When she described for Mary Nell the new modern gymnasium with a skylight in the dome, this elicited from Mary Nell her first decipherable comment. "A light in the roof. Oh my. And little Nancy Demming, just imagine, she was no bigger than me."

"We have all your old history books and cookbooks, Mary Nell; we're keeping them for the great grandchildren."

"A regular window," Mary Nell said. "A regular window in the roof." The springs grumbled as if she had shifted or perhaps leaned up for a better look at her cousins. It was at this moment that Dulcie saw Mae Rose.

Mae Rose had abandoned her wheelchair and was creeping along the hall. Walking unsteadily, clutching at the wall, she was headed for the open door.

Dulcie had left Mae Rose near the front door, in the parlor. When Mae Rose stopped to wait for Eula, Dulcie had lost patience, leaped down, and streaked in through this door behind the nurses' feet. She thought that not even Dillon peering in through the glass had seen her as she slid beneath Mary Nell's bed.

She didn't know why Mae Rose had left her wheelchair; it frightened her to see the little woman walking so precariously. She did not see Eula, though she could see a good slice of hall from where she crouched; it was only close up that her view was limited to chair legs and feet. Mae Rose crept along to the door, clutching her little doll Lucinda and hanging on to the wall. Moving inside, she approached the bed, drew so close that Dulcie could see only her pale, bare legs and her bright pink slippers. The smell of air freshener was so strong she couldn't even catch Mae Rose's sweet, powdery scent. Just the chemical smell of fake pine.

Wanting to see more, she reared up behind the bed, shielded by Mary Nell's plumped pillows, and peered out through a tiny space beside Mary Nell's left ear. She watched Mae Rose lean over the bed, smiling eagerly at Mary Nell, holding out the doll. Mary Nell grunted, perhaps startled at the proximity of the doll. When she leaned up a few inches from the bed, Mae Rose pressed the doll toward her, as if by way of a loving gift.

The cousins, sitting beside the bed like two black crows, watched this exchange with blank stares. And Dulcie drew back imperceptibly, deeper into the shadows behind the bed.

She felt that if either cousin spotted her, escape would be imperative. And now suddenly Eula appeared in the hall, stumping along in her walker. Behind Eula came a scowling nurse, pushing Mae Rose's empty wheelchair.

Soon the nurse had forced Mae Rose away from the bed, back into her rolling chair, and started away with her, pushing determinedly. But then the nurse seemed to take pity. She turned back again, rolled the chair back into Mary Nell's room, and up to the bed.

Again Mae Rose held out the doll. "Mary Nell, do you remember Lucinda?"

"I remember her," Mary Nell said weakly.

"She's for you, to keep you company. She's your doll now." Mae Rose thrust the doll at Mary Nell. The bed creaked as Mary Nell reached. Dulcie watched intently through the tiny space between the two pillows. Mae Rose and Mary Nell looked silently at each other. Mae Rose said, "I've missed you, Mary Nell. And I miss Jane. Do you see Jane over in Nursing?"

"She's not well," Mary Nell told her. "She misses you. She said—she said, if I saw Mae Rose, to give her love." Her voice was weak and shaky. The effect on

Mae Rose was to bring tears; Mae Rose's face crumpled. And at the same moment, Adelina appeared.

Adelina paid no attention to Mae Rose's weeping; she dispatched the tearful old lady back to her own wing, and Eula with her; sent them both away, escorted by two nurses.

The two cousins had sat scowling and silent through the little episode. Seated firmly, their feet planted, they gave each other a meaningful look, then rose as one. Moving slowly, with a measured precision, Roberta clutched her flowered handbag. Gustel turned away from her sister only long enough to deposit her vanilla pudding on the dresser beside the books.

As the two cousins made their good-byes to Mary Nell, Dulcie studied the hall and the glass door, weighing her chances. She could likely unlatch the glass door, but she didn't want Dillon to see her do that. She was assessing the traffic in the hall when she saw the foot.

The nurses had wheeled the empty gurney back into the room. Even as the cousins departed, clumping away, they prepared to lift Mary Nell onto the rolling cart. Wrapping Mary Nell's blanket around her, and one nurse lifting her shoulders while the other supported her hips, they set Mary Nell on the cart for her return to Nursing. But as they slid her acquiescent body off the bed and onto the gurney, her blanket caught and was pulled awry, pulling her off-balance. She kicked out against the bed, to right herself.

Dulcie, looking up from beneath the bed, saw Mary Nell's bare foot kick out beyond the edge of the cart. A slim, smooth foot, without the blue veins and knobby joints of an old woman. A lightly tanned foot that might easily run and dance.

She paused, frozen with amazement, then reared up beneath the blanket for a closer look. Staring at that healthy, slim foot, she was so fascinated that she forgot herself and let her whiskers brush Mary Nell's skin, catching a whiff of disinfectant from the blanket. At the

tickle of her whiskers, Mary Nell grunted, startled, and
reached to scratch her instep. Dulcie dropped down,
crouching deep beneath the bed, in the far corner. Mary
Nell scratched her foot vigorously with a white-gloved
hand, drew her foot back beneath the covers, and pulled
the blanket closer around herself. And she was wheeled
away.

Dulcie remained hidden until they had gone, her
mind fixed on that slim, smooth foot with its neat, professional pedicure of bright red toenails, and on the sudden, vigorous movements of that frail old lady.

24

It was getting dark in the grove. Susan knew she should head back, should turn her wheelchair around. She had only to speak to Lamb, and he would circle back toward Casa Capri. Bonnie would be wanting to leave; she had scheduled this afternoon an hour later than usual, having had to work later, and now it looked like rain, the clouds so dark and low overhead they seemed to cling in among the oak trees. Beyond the grove, the lights of the dining room and the long line of bedrooms shone brightly, the big squares of the glass doors marching along behind the wrought-iron fence. She could see, down at the end, a portion of Teddy's wheelchair behind his open drapery, saw movement as if perhaps he sat reading. He didn't stay long at the Pet-A-Pet sessions. Mae Rose thought the proximity of so many animals annoyed Teddy, irritated him.

The wind was picking up. Speaking to Lamb and stroking him, she gave him the command to turn back. Willingly he led her around, pulling her chair in a circle off the path and back again. It was at that moment, as they turned, that she saw Teddy rise from his wheelchair, stand tall, move away from it.

She spoke to Lamb, and he stopped in his tracks, stood still.

She watched Teddy walk across the room to the other side of the glass doors. No mistaking him, his hanging stomach forming a pear-shaped torso.

She watched him reach to pull the draperies, saw him pause a moment, looking out—then step back suddenly against the wall, out of sight.

Saw the draperies slide closed as if by an invisible hand, from where he had concealed himself.

He had seen her, despite the gathering dark. Had seen some glint, maybe her white blouse, seen her here in the grove. Seen her watching him.

She shivered deeply, unaccountably frightened.

Now the draperies obscured the room. Those drapes on the outside windows were not like the thinner casement curtains that faced into the patio. These window coverings, facing away from Casa Capri, were opaque, totally concealing.

She sat still, watching the obscured glass door, still shaken, chilled.

Teddy couldn't walk. Not at all. His spine had been crushed. He was completely incapacitated from his waist down, could use only his arms. Drove his car with special hand equipment.

That is what they had been told. That is what Adelina Prior told them.

Ice filled her.

And in her fear she made some movement, some little body language that made Lamb whine and nose at her. Stroking him, hugging the big poodle to her, she felt very alone suddenly, the two of them, too vulnerable alone here in the gathering night.

But Bonnie would be waiting. She spoke to the poodle, urging him on, and headed fast for the social room. Wanting Bonnie, wanting company, wanting to be around other people.

25

The cats read the newspaper article while
standing on the front page, on the Damen
kitchen table. They were not amused at the
evening *Gazette*'s treatment of Max Harper.
Behind them at the stove, Clyde and
Wilma were cooking lasagna, boiling pasta and making
sauce, Wilma's silver hair tied back under a cloth, Clyde
wearing an ancient, stained barbecue apron. The steamy
kitchen smelled deliciously of herbs and tomato
sauce and sautéed meat; and the room reverberated
with banging from the roof above, where Charlie was
at work replacing shingles. Working for her supper.
There was, Joe thought, nothing *very* cheap about
Clyde.

Dulcie sat down on the paper and read the article
again, her tail lashing with annoyance. "This is really a
cheap shot," she said softly.

Joe agreed. He might make fun of Harper, but when
the *Gazette* put Harper down, that made him mad.

"Not only bad for law enforcement," Clyde said,
chopping cilantro, "but bad politics."

"And poor taste," Wilma said, glancing up toward
the roof. Further banging told them Charlie was still
out of hearing. "Max Harper is a fine man. He keeps
this town clean, and that's more than I can say for some
city officials."

There was a big difference, Joe thought, rolling over
on the newspaper, between his own good-natured and

secret harassment of Max Harper, and the *Gazette*'s caustic misinformation.

POLICE FAIL TO NOTICE OPEN GRAVE

Molena Point Police, searching earlier this week for the body from which a finger bone was stolen supposedly by a neighborhood dog, failed to find during their investigation of the Prior estate, the wide-open grave of Dolores Fernandez. The excavation, in plain sight in the historic Spanish cemetery, had been dug into so deeply that the dirt was scattered across the grass and the body uncovered. Police gave reporters no explanation for their failure to find the body until their second visit to the estate, just this morning.

On Tuesday of this week, the human finger was brought to Captain Harper's attention by Mrs. Marion Hales, who had taken the bone away from her dog. Harper claims his men searched the cemetery at that time but says they failed to find any ground disturbed. Yet this morning, inexplicably, the Prior caretaker reported the grave open, the body revealed, and the finger missing.

The grave of Dolores Fernandez is an historic landmark. Fernandez, who died in 1882, was first cousin of Estafier Trocano, one of the original settlers of Molena Point and founder of the Trocano Ranch. The Prior estate is part of the original Spanish land grant given to the Trocano family by Mexico. Police have sent the finger, and samples from the body, to the State Forensics Lab in Sacramento for analysis.

Sacramento forensic expert Dr. Lynnell Jergins told reporters that several weeks may be required to make positive identification.

Dr. Jergins said the county forensic laboratory is facing a large backlog of work because of a shortage of scientific personnel. The grave is not open to public observation, and is under police surveillance until their investigation is completed. The Prior Ranch is private property and is patrolled.

Joe rolled over and began to wash. Above their heads, Charlie's pounding came steady and loud as she fitted in new shingles. Last night's rain had flooded Clyde's hall closet, drenching half a dozen jackets, Clyde's suitcase, and an old forgotten cat bed. It was about time Clyde got around to some repairs. Typical, of course, to get the work for free, if he could manage it.

But better free than not at all. In this household, it was a big deal if he remembered to buy lightbulbs before the old ones burned out.

Joe felt eternally thankful that cats didn't have to replace lightbulbs, repair shingles, and paint walls. And, of course, no cat would write such a misleading newspaper article. This display of bad taste was beneath even the scroungiest feline. The *Gazette* had no reason for their caustic slant; it was obvious to any idiot that the grave had been dug up after Harper's men searched the Prior estate. Probably someone at the paper had a grudge against Harper, not uncommon in the politics of a small town.

He could see that regardless of the slant, the story of the open grave fascinated Dulcie. You could bet your whiskers they'd be up there digging before you could shake a paw. And he had to admit, whatever scoffing he'd done about missing patients, the fact that a skeleton had turned up, and that maybe the finger bone belonged to that body and maybe it didn't, shed a new light. His interest had suddenly shifted into high gear. His feline curiosity sat up and took note.

Glancing at Dulcie, he knew they were of one mind: investigate the grave. Maybe, as well, they could get into the Prior house. Who knew what they'd find, maybe more photographs like the ones of Mary Nell Hook that Renet had put on Adelina's desk yesterday morning.

There was no doubt the pictures were of Mary Nell—Dulcie had seen them clearly, and she had seen Mary Nell clearly. They had no idea what use Adelina had for such pictures. She hadn't given them to the two black-robed cousins; they had left empty-handed except for Roberta's flowered handbag. He supposed Adelina could have given them the pictures as they stepped out the front door, but when Adelina appeared in the hall earlier, she hadn't been carrying them.

Dulcie hadn't dared follow the cousins; there had been nurses all over. Besides, she'd been too busy watching young Dillon. The minute the room was empty, Dillon had slipped in through the glass doors, making directly for the closet. And as Joe and Dulcie watched, Joe from the orange tree and Dulcie from under the bed, Dillon had removed from the crowded shelves one item. She had known exactly what she wanted.

Dillon had only an instant alone, before two nurses returned and began straightening the room, opening drawers, and putting Mary Nell's clothes into cardboard boxes. In that instant she had removed a wide, flat oak box with metal corners. Carefully lifting it out, watching the door to the hall, she had opened the lid—and caught her breath.

From the tree, Joe could see into the box clearly. It was like a little portable desk, with a slanted top for writing, and with small compartments inside. He could see that some of the spaces still held stamps, a pen, some white envelopes. But in the largest compartment, which was probably meant for writing paper, lay a doll.

Her porcelain face looked dusty, her pale hair matted,

her blue-and-white crinoline dress wrinkled and limp with neglect. Dillon lifted it out quickly and tucked it inside her shirt, where it made a large lump.

She closed the box, looked undecided for a moment, then shoved it back into the cupboard. As she slipped out through the glass door, Dulcie had nipped out behind her, crowding against Dillon's heels. They were hardly out when two nurses entered. Just as Joe slipped down from the tree, the rain hit. By the time the three of them reached the social room, racing across the garden, they were soaked. The cats had sat behind the couch, dripping onto the carpet, washing themselves, as Dillon squinched across the carpet to Mae Rose and laid the doll in the old lady's lap. She had kept her back to the room, and her voice low.

"Is this the doll you gave Jane Hubble? The one you told me about?"

"Oh yes." Mae Rose's smile shone bright with surprise. "This is my little Becky. Where did you find her?" She cuddled the doll, staring up at Dillon, then immediately slipped the doll out of sight beneath the pink afghan, tucking the cover around her. "Where did you find her? Did you see Jane? I gave her to Jane before she was moved to Nursing. Where. . . ?"

"She had a little writing desk, a lap desk."

"Of course. It's one of the few things Jane asked her trust officer to bring from home." She looked up at Dillon, her blue eyes alarmed. "Jane wouldn't give up her little desk and give up Becky. She wouldn't give her up if she . . . No matter how sick she was. How did you know about the desk?"

"We were neighbors; she kept it on a table by the living-room window. She'd carry it to her easy chair before the fire to write letters. Fix herself a cup of coffee and sit by the fire to pay her bills, or write a letter to the editor of the *Gazette*—she loved doing that. She didn't have any close friends to write to."

Dillon looked down at Mae Rose, touching the arm

of Mae's wheelchair. "I found the doll in the desk, and the desk was in the cupboard of that room—the room where you went, where Mary Nell was. But why would they take Jane's desk away from her?"

Mae Rose stroked the afghan where the doll was hidden. She didn't reply.

Dulcie and Joe glanced at each other. Dulcie shivered. She told Joe later that it was Dillon's finding the doll and the desk that made Wilma decide to go to Max Harper.

26

She had a sudden change of mind about stealing from one of the oceanfront houses. After what happened Thursday afternoon, she decided to give it a shot; how could she resist. The conversation she overheard in the drugstore, the exchange between this Mrs. Bonniface and the pharmacist seemed destined specifically for her enlightenment. And Friday morning, when she woke and saw the fog thick outside her windows, fog heavy enough to give her total cover approaching and leaving the Bonniface house, there was no decision to make. She was on her way. Not only would the fog conceal her, but the beach would be virtually empty, the tourists all in bed, warm in their motel rooms, or bundled up drinking hot coffee in the little restaurants. And the cops, with minimal beach attendance, wouldn't put out a full patrol.

In the drugstore, Mrs. Bonniface, whom she had seen around town, of course, had been standing at the pharmacy counter waiting for a prescription. Bonniface was a big name in Molena Point—he was the founding partner of Bonniface, Storker, and Kline. Dorothy Bonniface was thirtysomething, one of those beautifully groomed blondes, perfect haircut and professional makeup, one of those women who could walk into the Ritz Carleton wearing out-of-style jeans and a worn-out sweatshirt and still have the entire staff falling over themselves to serve her.

Mrs. Bonniface, standing at the pharmacy counter, had told the druggist conversationally that Donald was in Japan wrapping up a sales contract with some Sony subsidiary, that he would be home a week from Friday. They talked about little Jamie's cough, which was not bad enough to keep her out of school. The prescription was for Jamie. She said the other two children were just fine, she was on her way to pick them up from school and drop them at a birthday party. Her shopping list, lying on the counter beside her, included a flat of pansies and a flat of petunias and six flats of ajuga ground cover, presumably from the local nursery. This meant, with any luck, that Dorothy Bonniface might be spending the next morning in her garden, putting in the tender plants, leaving her house unattended.

She had left the pharmacy, walking out behind Mrs. Bonniface, feeling high, a delicious surge of excitement. She had stopped in at the Coffee Mill two doors away to look up the Bonniface address in the Molena Point phone book.

There were three Bonnifaces; she knew they were related. The Donald Bonnifaces lived at 892 Shore Drive. Leaving the Coffee Mill, she got her car and took a swing by the Bonniface house, cruising slowly.

The nicely kept two-story blue frame featured a huge patio in front, with expensive wrought-iron furniture. The handsome outdoor sitting area, walled in by glass to cut the sharp sea wind, reached to within ten feet of the sidewalk, and was given privacy by a row of pyracanthas. The entry walk, the lawn, and the flower beds were to the right of this, with a wide expanse of bare earth where some kind of bedding plants had recently been removed.

She had glimpsed behind the house another bricked terrace, sheltered by a series of freestanding walls, these supporting espaliered bushes, and offering privacy from the neighbors' windows. As there were openings between them, it was a perfect setup. She could park on the back street a block away and slip through the neighbors' yards and into the Bonniface yard calling for her lost kitty.

Friday morning she did just that: parked on the back street and wandered on through, calling softly for Kitty. She was certain no one noticed her moving through the fog; she could hardly see the neighbors' flower beds and fences. Approaching the Bonniface house, she wandered innocently to the back steps.

Wiping the damp from her feet, she surveyed what she could see of the neighbors' windows, which wasn't much. But no one was watching. She tapped lightly at the back door, though she didn't expect an answer. As she drove by the front, she had seen Dorothy Bonniface already on her knees in the dirt, hard at work setting out her petunias. The woman was an early riser. The pansies were already in place, perky and bright in the pale fog; and the flat of ajuga stood waiting. There was no car in the drive, as if a maid might be working within, and no car nearby on the street. Most Molena Point families, except for those with estates in the hills, hired help only for housecleaning and to assist at dinner parties.

No one answered her knock. She tapped again, hoping she wouldn't be heard from the front yard, and after a safe interval she turned the knob. The door was unlocked. Smiling, she slipped inside.

Dorothy Bonniface had left the coffeepot on, and the cooking brew smelled as strong as boiled shoe polish. The morning paper lay folded on the table as if Mrs. Bonniface had saved it, perhaps to read during a mid-morning coffee break. The kitchen was handsome, all creamy tile, deep blue walls, and whitewashed oak cabinets. Under one of the upper cabinets was installed a nice little miniature TV set. She wiggled it in its bracket. Yes, it would slip right out. And, in the fog, it wouldn't be too noticeable beneath her tan raincoat.

She'd get it as she left. Moving on into the dining room, she spent a few minutes assessing the Spode and crystal in the china cabinet. These items weren't much good unless she took a whole set, and she had no way to carry so much. The china was lovely. Maybe she'd come back later, load up her car, do things a bit differently for a change.

Down the hall, the master bedroom faced the front, opening with sliding doors onto the glassed terrace. Standing at the dresser, she broke the lock on Dorothy Bonniface's jewel chest and surveyed an impressive collection of gold and diamond earrings, amethyst and emerald chokers, a topaz pendant, a few gold bracelets. Dorothy Bonniface liked color, though all the pieces were delicate and in good taste. She was lifting them out, tucking them away in the various pockets beneath her coat, when the phone rang.

There was only one ring. When the phone stilled without ringing again, a stab of alarm touched her. Had Mrs. Bonniface come into the house? Had she been passing the phone when it rang?

But when she stepped to the bedroom window, she saw Mrs. Bonniface still kneeling on the walk, talking on a remote, holding the phone gingerly so not to dirty it with her soiled gardening glove. Her trowel lay in the half-empty box of petunia plants. She was not speaking, now, but listening. She glanced once toward the house, glanced up the street, and made a short reply. When she hung up, she rose and headed for the front door, studying the living-room windows.

At the porch she removed her shoes, stepping through the front door in her stocking feet. Someone had snitched, some nosy neighbor.

Moving fast down the hall and through the kitchen as Dorothy Bonniface crossed the living room, she slipped quickly out the back door, moved quickly away through the fog-shrouded backyards. Softly calling the cat, she glanced around toward the neighbors' indistinct windows, wondering which busybody little housewife had made that phone call.

Ambling around through a neighbor's garden to the street, she moved slowly down the sidewalk, still calling for Kitty, but wanting to get out of there fast. She was half-wired with nerves, and half-strung with amusement. Heading through the fog for her car, she glanced back several times.

The houses behind her had nearly vanished.

She had not brought the blue Honda, and she had put a Nevada plate on this car, along with half a dozen bumper stickers pointing up worthwhile wonders to be seen around Nevada. She had applied the stickers with rubber cement so she could tear them off in a hurry.

She drove eight blocks up the beach to where the houses ended, where the dunes rambled away to the south. Getting out, she left the engine running as she removed the stickers and stuffed them in her purse. Then she headed for the village and across it to The Bakery, craving a cup of coffee and a chocolate donut.

She left her coat and slouch hat in the car and changed her shoes. In the restaurant she chose a veranda table, where she could enjoy the fog-muffled sea. She ordered, then headed for the rest room.

In the little cubicle she tore the bumper stickers into tiny pieces and flushed them away, then worked her loose hair into a knot.

Returning to her table, to her steaming coffee and an incredibly sticky, nut-covered donut, she got her first look at the morning edition of the Molena Point *Gazette*.

The paper lay on the next table; she nearly had palpitations before the occupant left, and she could snag the front page.

The Molena Point *Gazette* paid little attention to world events. People could buy the San Francisco

Chronicle or *Examiner* for that. Village news, the small local stories, that was what sold the *Gazette*. Yesterday evening's paper, putting Max Harper down about missing the open grave, had been sufficiently amusing. But this article in the morning edition, though it, too, put down Harper—and that pleased her—this article did not cheer her. She felt, in fact, a chill depression, an emotion which perhaps had taken some time to build, and which she did not care to examine closely.

She might enjoy this newspaper column later, about the cat burglar, and she would certainly save it, but at the moment it presented only a personal warning. And though maybe it wasn't that warning alone that frightened her, whatever emotions caused this hollowness in her belly, she knew it was time to go, time to leave Molena Point.

CAT BURGLAR ON THE PROWL

The recent rash of Molena Point burglaries, police report, are very likely attributable to a shabbily dressed old lady that local police have dubbed "The Cat Burglar" but whom they have not been able to apprehend. Captain Max Harper was not able to explain to reporters the failure of his officers to arrest the lone woman who has entered and burglarized more than a dozen Molena Point homes.

As the woman prowls Molena Point neighborhoods, she pretends to be looking for her lost cat. If questioned, she gives a plausible story about the escape of the cat from her car. The woman's operation is not unique to Molena Point. Within the past year, she has burglarized countless homes in cities up and down the coast, including San Diego, La Jolla, Ventura, Santa Barbara, Paso Robles, San Luis Obispo, and smaller towns between. She is in and out of a house so quickly she seems to move like a cat herself, as silently and with as furtive intentions.

To date, in Molena Point, she has burglarized fifteen homes. None of the stolen items has been recovered. And while Captain Harper has been unable to apprehend her, he warns homeowners to keep their doors locked even when they are at home, either inside or working in their yards.

"This is the time of year when everyone likes their doors open to enjoy the spring breeze," Harper said. "Leaving a door unlocked is an invitation. The old lady will wander the neighborhood where people are working in their gardens or enjoying their swimming pool. She slips into the house quickly, looking for jewelry, cash, and small collector's items. If she is discovered inside by a surprised homeowner, she claims to be looking for her lost cat."

Besides cash and jewelry, she favors expensive cameras, the more expensive brands of small electronic equipment, and she has been known to take small pieces of artwork. Missing from the home of John Eastland on Mission Drive is a complete set of rare ivory chess pieces, and from an unnamed residence in the hills, five valuable, limited edition collector's dolls of unusual beauty. From the Elaine Garver residence the woman has stolen a small etching by Goya valued at a hundred thousand dollars, and for which there is a generous reward. The rash of burglaries is an unfortunate stain on the reputation of Molena Point. Anyone having information about the identity of the woman, or about the stolen items, should contact Captain Harper of the Molena Point Police.

She set down her coffee cup, staring at the newspaper. Mrs. Garver's claim of a missing Goya so amazed her she had almost choked. There had never been a Goya. She'd seen no etching by Goya in that house, nor had she seen any valuable artwork there. The woman was flat lying. Planning to rip off her insurance company for a cool hundred thousand, and using her as the patsy.

The fact that someone would piggyback a scam of that magnitude on her own modest operation was both annoying and, in a way, flattering. But then she started to get mad—mad that this Garver woman would set up a poor little old bag lady to take the rap for a hundred-thousand-dollar painting.

The idea so angered her that by the time she finished her coffee and paid her bill, she was seething. The woman wasn't going to get away with this.

Returning to the ladies' room, she dropped a quarter in the pay phone and called the Molena Point PD.

She was able to reach Max Harper himself, and told him there was never any Goya etching. "I expect the Garvers' insurance agent will be pleased to have that information." And because she was feeling so mad, and because she had to prove to Harper that she spoke the truth, she gave him a complete list of the items she had taken from the Garver house, gave him a far more detailed accounting than was in the paper.

Hanging up the phone, she stood a moment, letting her pounding heart slow. Then she got out of there fast.

In the car she pulled on her coat again, against the chill of the fog, and headed on through the village. That insurance company would nip Mrs. Garver's scam, jerk her up short. And as far as Harper tracing her phone call, he hadn't had time. She knew how long such a thing took; she'd researched phone tracing carefully. Anyway, she'd be out of here in a day or two, and on up the coast. With *cat burglar* smeared all over the front page, the whole village was alerted, she didn't dare hang around. Just a few loose ends to take care of, and she'd be gone. In Molena Point she'd be history.

27

Max Harper left the police station at mid-morning, heading up the hills to have another look around the Prior estate. He didn't intend to pull into the Prior drive in his police unit. He thought he'd stop by his place, saddle Buck, and take a ride. He'd been using Buck all week to quarter the hills above the residential areas, looking for human bones or a shallow grave. And he could do with a break this morning, get out of the station for a few hours. The morning had not started out well, everything he'd touched seeming as murky and vague as the fog itself. Driving slowly uphill through the thick mist, he went over this morning's and last night's phone calls, looking for some detail he might have missed.

He had come in just before eight, parking in his reserved slot in the lot behind the station. He was pouring his first cup of coffee when his phone buzzed. The caller was a woman; she wouldn't give her name. She told him that Elaine Garver had lied about the Goya etching, said there was no etching. He couldn't dismiss the call; the woman gave him a detailed list of stolen items, information that only the Garvers or the burglar herself could know—or one of his own people, and that wasn't likely. If he prided himself on anything, it was on the quality and honesty of his officers, in a world where that wasn't always the case. Nothing made him as deeply angry as hearing some report about a bad cop, about someone's inner departmental decay.

When the anonymous caller hung up, too quickly to trace, Wilma Getz was on another line. She wanted to come in with the little Thurwell girl, see him for a few minutes. She said just enough to make him uneasy, make him think the problem might be tied in with Susan Dorriss's phone call late last night.

He would never peg Susan Dorriss as one to pass on wild stories, any more than he would think of Wilma that way. Yet the story Susan gave him was the same wild tale he'd heard weeks ago from that Casa Capri patient, little Mrs. Mae Rose.

Last night, Susan had called from her daughter's car phone, sitting in the parking lot of Casa Capri. Said she didn't want to use a phone inside Casa Capri. She had called her daughter at about ten, and Bonnie came on down and wheeled her out to the car.

Susan had called Bonnie just after Mae Rose came to her with the note she had supposedly found inside an old doll, a note from the woman Mae thought was missing, from Jane Hubble. Susan said the note and the doll smelled musty from being closed up in a locked closet. His immediate reaction was, what was he supposed to do about a note some old lady found inside a doll? And maybe he'd been short with Susan. When she read the note to him, his temper flared. He'd wanted to say, maybe it was something in the water up at Casa Capri that made everyone nuts, that he'd rather deal with any kind of straightforward crime than some groundless mystery that had just enough truth to turn him edgy. And when Susan told him about seeing Teddy Prior get out of his wheelchair and walk, that set him back. Everyone knew Teddy was incurably crippled—everyone thought they knew that.

And then this morning when Wilma brought the kid in, little Dillon Thurwell, to tell him about the doll, neither Wilma nor the kid knew that Susan had called him with the same story. Neither Wilma nor the kid knew about the note; Mae Rose had found that hours

after the two of them left Casa Capri yesterday afternoon, and Mae Rose had taken the note to Susan.

He'd never known Wilma Getz to go off on a tan-
gent. She'd worked her whole life in corrections and
wasn't the kind to buy into some nut story. Unless
Wilma herself was getting senile. On the phone, she'd
said, "I guess it's all nonsense, Max. I know it sounds
crazy—but you know that little niggling feeling? That
ring of truth that's so hard to shake?"

"Go on."

"I saw Dillon take the doll from the closet, I could
see clearly across the patio, from where I stood in the
glass doors of the social room. I watched her slip inside,
remove the lap desk, open it, and take out the doll. She
shoved the desk back, hid the doll in her shirt, and made
a dash out the door just as it started to rain. The
cats . . ." She'd paused, stopped talking.

"The cats? You started to say, what?"

"Oh, that the cats were out in the rain, too. You
know, the Pet-a-Pet cats."

"So?"

"I don't know—so they got wet. What time can I
come in?"

"Come on in," he had said, sighing. "I can give you a
few minutes." He had hung up, poured another cup of
coffee, and gotten some paperwork done. Not twenty
minutes later, there was Wilma coming into the station
with the kid. Threading their way back through the
crowded squad room, Wilma herded the kid along, her
hand on the little girl's shoulder, the child looking fascinated by all the uniforms, and looking scared.

He'd poured coffee for Wilma and got the kid a
Coke. Dillon was real silent for a while, but when she
saw the picture of Buck on his desk she brightened right
up. He told her about Buck, and they'd talked about
horses. She started talking about Jane Hubble's horse,
and the next thing she launched right in, telling him
that Jane was missing, that she'd tried three times to see

Jane and every time had been run off from Casa Capri. Told him how yesterday afternoon she'd found Jane's lap desk with the doll inside.

He didn't point out to Dillon that she had no business in that closet and that she was taking things that weren't hers. The kid knew that. She described the closet shelves as stuffed full of small boxes of folded clothes and purses and shoes, items which, she thought, must belong to several people. Maybe, she said, to the six people Mae Rose said were missing.

The irritating thing was, Dillon seemed like a sensible kid. He knew her folks; they were a decent family, no problems that he knew of. Helen Thurwell was one of the most reliable Realtors in the area. And Bob, for a literature professor, was all right—he seemed a no-nonsense sort. Dillon Thurwell did not seem the type to go off on wild fancies, any more than Wilma did.

And what disturbed him was, the kid's story dovetailed exactly with Susan Dorriss's phone call.

That made him smile in spite of himself, and made him know he'd better pay attention—better to be wrong than plain bullheaded, and miss a bet. He'd hate like hell to be outflanked by a team of juvenile and geriatric amateur sleuths.

Driving slowly up the hills through the thick fog, he topped out suddenly above the white vapor blanket into sunshine. The hills, above that dense layer, shone bright, the sky above him clear and blue. Maybe he was getting old and soft-headed, and he'd sure take a ribbing from the department if he followed up on this doll business, but it wasn't something he wanted to ignore.

Turning south, he soon swung into his own narrow drive and headed back between the pastures. Across the pasture he saw Buck lift his head, looking toward the car. The gelding stood a minute, ears sharp forward, then headed at a trot for the barn, knowing damn well if Harper was home in the middle of the day that they'd take a ride. Buck loved company, and he was rotten spoiled.

Harper parked by the little two-stall barn behind the house, wondering idly how Dillon Thurwell would get along with Buck, or maybe with one of the neighbor's horses.

No one knew better than he that kids could be skilled liars, that Dillon could be jiving him. The kid could have gone along with Mae Rose's fantasy just for the excitement, could have made up more details and embroidered on the story just for fun, could have put that note in the doll herself, sewn it up, hidden it in the cupboard—ragged stitches like a child's stitches.

He'd hate like hell to get scammed by a twelve-year-old con artist.

But he didn't think Dillon had done that.

His gut feeling, like Wilma's, was that the kid, though her imagination might have colored what she saw and was told, did not mean deliberately to mislead them.

In the house he changed into Levi's and boots and a soft shirt, and clipped his radio to his belt. Stepping out to the little barn again, he brushed Buck down, saddled him, and swung on. Buck ducked his chin playfully as they headed over the hills toward the Prior place.

Within half an hour he was crossing the hill above the old hacienda, looking down into the old, oak-shaded cemetery. The estate lay just above the fog, and as he studied the wooded cemetery and the ancient headstones, a mower started up near the stables. Buck snorted at the noise and wanted to shy. He watched the groundskeeper swing aboard the machine, and as he started to mow around the stable Buck bowed his neck and blew softly; but he was no longer looking at the mower, he was staring toward the old graves.

Scanning the grove, Harper saw a quick movement low to the ground as something small fled away into the shadows. Maybe a big bird had come down after some creature, maybe a crow. Or maybe it had been a rabbit or a squirrel, frightened by something. The breeze shifted, rustling the oak leaves; and as the light changed within the woods, he saw it again. Two cats streaking away.

He guessed if there were cats around, still alive, there wasn't any poison nearby. Or maybe cats were smarter than dogs about that stuff. He rode on down, pulling Buck up at the edge of the woods. And he saw the cats again, watched them disappear into the bushes near the main house. That gray cat looked like Clyde Damen's tomcat, but it wouldn't be way up here.

He was getting a fixation about that cat. Ever since that hot-car bust up at Beckwhite's last summer, when Damen's cat got mixed up in the action and almost got itself shot, ever since then he thought he saw the cat everywhere.

But he did see it more than he liked. Every poker night there it was on the table, watching him play his hand. Who, but Damen, would let a cat sit on the table. It gave him the creeps the way the cat watched him bet, those big yellow eyes looking almost like it understood what he was doing. He could swear that last night, every time he raked in a pot, the cat almost grinned at him.

Harper sighed. He was losing his perspective here.

Getting as dotty as the old folks at Casa Capri.

Yet no amount of chiding himself changed the fact that there was something strange about Damen's cat, something that stirred in him a jab of fear, or wonder, or some damned thing. He sensed about the cat something beyond the facts by which he lived, something beyond his reach, some element he should pay attention to, and would prefer not to consider.

28

Earlier, on a hill above the Prior estate, the two cats crouched, looking down at the old hacienda, enjoying the warm sunshine after climbing up through fog so thick they thought they were under the sea. Licking hard at their damp fur, energetically they fluffed their coats, licked beads of fog from their whiskers and paws. Directly below, the old hacienda and stable stood faded and dusty-looking, their tile roofs bleached to the color of pale earth, their adobe walls lumpy with the shaping of patient hands long since gone to dust.

Beyond the old buildings, the main house rose sharply defined, its tile roof gleaming bright red, its precision-built walls smooth and white, and its gardens and lawns neatly manicured. The hilltop estate at this moment was an island, the sea of fog lapping at its gardens and curved drive. Far away across the top of the fog, the crowns of other hills emerged: other islands, an archipelago. And the real sea, the Pacific, and the village beside it were gone, drowned in the heavy mists.

Above the estate, on the sun-drenched hill, the warm grass buzzed with busy insects, ticking away beneath the cats' paws. And as Joe and Dulcie rested, washing their ears and faces, from below came the soft cadence of Spanish music, electronically broadcast songs from somewhere within the hacienda, music plucked out of the air in a manner never dreamed possible when this hacienda was built, when the only music available came from live musicians blowing and jigging and strumming.

Three cars were parked before the old homeplace, all late-model American makes. Evidently the house staff, like the employees of Casa Capri, were well treated.

"If Adelina hires so many Spanish-speaking people," Dulcie said, "she must speak Spanish herself. How could she control someone if she didn't know what they were saying?"

Joe smiled. "Or if no one knew she spoke Spanish, she'd be ahead of them all. Could really keep them in line." He batted at a grasshopper, knocked it off its grass stem, but released it. "Whatever's going on at Casa Capri, those nurses with no English might not have a clue."

He studied the cemetery below them, off to their right, the dark, misshapen headstones set among thick old oaks. They could see the police barrier of yellow ribbon at the far side, strung around a rectangle of raw earth. Dolores Fernandez's open grave. "What makes Harper think no one will bother the grave just because he tied a ribbon around it?"

"Maybe there's a guard."

"Do you see a guard?"

She shrugged, a brief twitch of her dark tabby shoulder. "Maybe the gardener or handyman?" They could see no one on the grounds, though they could hear someone tinkering, an occasional metallic click above the radio music, coming from the direction of the old stable. Dulcie yawned, stretched, and they trotted on down into the shadowed woods of the cemetery.

The grass beneath their paws was clipped short and smooth, was as well kept as any park. It had been cleared of leaves, and was trimmed neatly around the thick oak trunks and around the old headstones. Some of the graves had sunk, forming shallow depressions. The old granite markers were deeply worn by water and wind, their crumbling edges blackened with dirt, their ornately written Spanish epitaphs dark with soil, some nearly illegible. Several headstones featured the angel of death, with hands beckoning and wings outspread. Other grave markers were carved with hollow-eyed, bony skulls. They found one happy-looking angel, a cherub-faced child with a broken nose. Farther on, two blackened angels joined hands, dirty-faced and naughty. They did not know the meaning of the epitaphs, but *muere* appeared twice, and Dulcie thought it meant death.

Se muere como se vivi.

No se puedo creer eso ella es muerto.

Walking softly, they approached the cordoned-off grave and trotted under the barrier of yellow police tape.

The body had been removed; only a hole remained, neatly excavated. The investigating team had not taken only bone samples, as the newspaper said.

Circling the raw earth mound, they sniffed at the shovel marks and at an occasional shoe print where the police and the forensics examiner had been working. Outside the ribbon barrier, clods of raw earth lay scattered across the grass.

They did not know precisely what they were looking for—but they were looking for anything strange, any small detail the police might have missed, but that a cat would see or smell. The grave did not smell of death; it smelled of moldering earth.

There were marks in the earth where pieces of the casket had lain, and they could see the bristle marks of a small brush, as if the excavation had been as carefully attended as an archaeological dig.

"We could dig deeper," Dulcie ventured.

"And find what? They have the bones. And don't you think they dug deeper beneath the body?" He prowled beyond the grave, nosing among tree roots, sniffing at the grass.

Once, they thought they caught Teddy's scent, but

they couldn't be sure. They could find no wheel marks from Teddy's rolling chair. Quartering the cemetery, trotting over the smooth turf and protruding roots that bisected the lawn like huge arteries, they moved in a careful grid, working back and forth. Twice more they caught Teddy's scent. But it was old, faded, and mixed with the sharp perfume of grass and leaves and earth.

But then, suddenly, a powerful smell stopped them. The stink made Joe bare his teeth in a grimace of disgust, made Dulcie back away.

The smell of death, of rotting flesh.

Approaching a heap of dry oak leaves, where the smell came strongest, Dulcie froze.

"Cyanide. I smell cyanide, too." The smell made her gag and grimace. The leaves were piled against a tree, as if they had been missed by the lawn-care equipment, by the vacuum or blower or mulching mower. It was the only pile of leaves in the neatly manicured cemetery. Dulcie lifted a reluctant paw, lightly pulled away leaves, hating the cyanide smell. She had, earlier this year, been shocked to find the same deadly chemical lacing her freshly served salmon.

Now she raked angrily at the tangle, pawing it away.

Revealing, half-hidden beneath the pile of leaves, a lump of dark, raw meat.

She thought at first it was a lump of human flesh, then she saw that it was hamburger, half-rotted, a disgusting mound several days old. The combined stink of rotting meat and the almondlike smell of the cyanide forced bile into her mouth. She turned away quickly, gagged, and threw up on the grass.

Joe regarded the bait with disgust. "We can't leave that mess for a dog to find." A cat, of course, would have better sense than to go near it; no cat likes rotten meat, no cat would roll in rotten meat the way a dog does.

Holding their breath, they dug a hole deep into the sandy loam, and, by pushing a heap of leaves against the meat, they managed to paw it in. They had covered the hole with earth and leaves and had moved away where the air was fresher, were scuffing their paws in the grass to clean them, when Dulcie stared at the turf between her paws.

"There's a little crack here. Look at this. A little thin crack in the earth, under the grass."

The line was as straight as a ruler. She pressed her nose against it. "And the grass blades go in a different direction."

When they followed the line, they found another, crossing it. Pacing, they made out an even grid of crossing lines. Someone had laid sod here, piecing it so cleverly that one would never see the cracks unless one's nose was practically against them. From a human's view, they thought, the turf would seem undisturbed. Fascinated, Dulcie skinned up a tree for a look from a person's height.

Yes, from six feet up the grass stretched away smooth as velvet, a clean, unbroken turf. "No one would know. They could . . ." She paused, watching the hills above. "There's a rider coming. Do the Priors keep horses?"

"Harper said they don't. Remember, he sounded disgusted that Adelina would waste such a nice barn." Joe grinned. "He was really annoyed that she didn't have the place full of horses."

Horse and rider were too far away to be seen clearly, and on the crest of the hill they stopped; the rider sat his horse, looking down toward the cemetery.

"Can he see us?"

"I doubt it. And what difference?"

She studied the rider's tall, slim form, his easy seat, the tilt of his head. "I think that's Harper. Let's get out of here." She leaped out of the tree, and they moved away, going deeper among the shadowed headstones. They had just settled down where they knew they wouldn't be seen, when the roar of a motor started up, coming from the stable and heading in their direction.

Rearing up, they could see a big riding mower, the dark-haired driver wheeling it directly toward the grave-yard. Irritated, they moved out of his path, into shadows between the trunks of six big oaks.

But the mower turned, making straight for them again, toward the exact spot where they crouched. Unnerved, they ran, quitting the grove, racing flat out toward the main house.

Azalea bushes bordered the back patio. They crouched beneath that shelter, at the edge of the wide brick terrace. "Nice," Dulcie said, looking out. The sunny expanse was furnished with heavy wrought-iron chairs cast in the patterns of flowers and twining leaves and fitted with soft-looking, flowered pillows. Pots of red geraniums set off this outdoor sitting area, and at its edge, wide glass doors opened into the living room and the dining room, where they could see polished floors, and rich, dark furniture.

From within the house they could hear the roar of a vacuum cleaner, accompanied by the same Spanish radio station that played behind them in the old hacienda, the brassy cadences of a metallic horn and guitar.

The French doors to the sunken living room stood open. They glanced at each other and grinned. There was no need to break and enter—they could waltz right on in. If cats could do a high five—and did not find such antics beneath their dignity—they would have been slapping paws.

In fact, they could enter the house almost anywhere; nearly every window stood open, welcoming the sunny morning. Along the second floor, six sets of French doors stood ajar, giving onto a row of private balconies. And far to their left, facing the patio, the kitchen door was wide-open. Beyond the corner of the house, they could see two cars parked, the door of one open, as if someone were unloading groceries or perhaps ready to leave.

Behind them, the mowing machine grew louder; it had not entered the grove after all, it had gone along the edge, then turned back. Roaring past the terrace, its spinning blade cut swiftly across the short lawn just above them.

They were about to make a dash into the living room when the maid with the vacuum cleaner entered—stepping on stage right on cue, Dulcie thought, annoyed. Her machine roared across the wood floor, then was muffled by the thick oriental carpet.

They headed for the kitchen. Moving swiftly beneath the azalea border, around the edge of the patio, they pressed against the wall of the house beside the kitchen door, then slipped along to peer in.

The kitchen shone bright with sunlight, light poured across the rosy tile floor and across the tiled cooking island. The aroma of something meaty, with cilantro and garlic, forced a moment of involuntarily whisker licking.

A maid stood at the sink washing tomatoes, surrounded by hanging pots of herbs and flowers; her view through the window was of the wide blue sky and of the cars parked beside the kitchen. Dulcie sat very still, admiring the bright room. Joe never ceased to wonder at her love of anything beautiful; as if her little cat spirit had, in some life past, been a reveler among the arts. There was, within his lady, far more knowledge and spirit than any ordinary cat could ever contain.

"Move it," she said, nudging him.

The maid had turned her back to them. They sped past her and through the kitchen into the dining room. They paused within the shadows beneath a huge, ornately carved, black-lacquered banquet table, a monster of Spanish elegance.

Looking back toward the sunny kitchen to see if they were observed, they watched the maid dancing and jiggling to the brassy trumpet. And they saw, as well, trailing across the kitchen's clay tiles, two lines of fresh, damp pawprints.

"They'll dry," Dulcie breathed hopefully. But the prints would leave little dirty paw marks; they both knew that too well. The fact had been pointed out to them more than once, by their respective housemates.

Crouching among the forest of carved table legs, Dulcie nosed appreciatively at the Persian carpet, its colors as vibrant as an oil painting. She rolled over, luxuriating in its dense, soft weave. Joe was watching her, amused, when the vacuum cleaner headed their way. Between the mower outside and the vacuum cleaner within, the world seemed inclined toward a science-fiction horror scene of sucking and slicing adversaries. As the machine approached they fled again, racing for the foyer, where they could see the front stairs.

A gold-framed mirror hung beside the carved front door, reflecting the curving stairway; the stairs' soft carpet was woven in patterns as bright and intricate as a bird's feathers. Quickly they raced up, listening for any sound from above. Who knew how many people Adelina Prior employed to keep her house?

Upstairs they followed the central hall, followed a hint of Adelina's perfume. Where the first door stood open, Adelina's scent was strong. They slipped inside, tensed to leap away. The room was huge, done all in white. They crossed the thick white carpet and slid beneath a chair, half-expecting to be yelled at, to have to run again, this time for their lives.

29

Crouching beneath the chair in Adelina's private chambers, they could hear no sound. Beyond the dazzling white parlor, they could see into her bedroom and mirrored dressing room; the walls of mirrors reflected all three rooms, and reflected the huge, luxurious bath—as if the layout had been planned, not only for ample reflection of Adelina's perfectly groomed image, but to afford complete and instant surveillance of her private quarters.

They could see that the suite was empty, that they were alone. They could hear faintly, from downstairs, the hum of the vacuum cleaner.

The deeply padded white leather couch and chairs looked as soft as feather beds. The rooms smelled of the expensive leather and of Adelina's subtle, smoky perfume, the scents combining into the aroma of wealth, tastefully and egocentrically displayed. But it was the vast expanse of thick, snowy carpet that fascinated Dulcie. She pawed at it and rolled on it, her purrs rising to little singing crescendos. "This is better than rolling on cashmere. Why didn't Wilma put in carpet like this when she redecorated?"

"Because this stuff would cost her life savings; I'd bet several hundred bucks a yard." He gave her an arch look. "Adelina lives pretty high, considering those old folks at Casa Capri make do with Salvation Army castoffs for their sitting room."

The white carpet stretched away to pure white walls unsullied by any ornament or artwork, and to a white marble fireplace so clean that surely no smallest stick of wood had ever burned there. That pristine edifice was flanked by tall French doors standing open to the balcony, where three large pots of bird-of-paradise stood guard. Adelina's view would be down over the front drive to the dropping hills and the village and the sea beyond.

The large, carved desk was the only piece of dark furniture. Dull and nearly black with age, it stood alone on one long white wall, its four drawers fitted with black, cast-iron handles. As they approached this impressive vault they heard, from the garden below, the mower rounding the corner, making its way toward the front lawn. Its vibrating rumble, louder than the vacuum cleaner, would mask any sound of a maid approaching, or of Adelina herself entering her chambers.

Together they fought open the bottom drawer and pawed through desk supplies: unused checkbooks, notepads, labels, pens, all neatly arranged, nothing that seemed of great interest. The next drawer up contained packets of canceled checks tied with red string, a stack of used check registers, bundles of paid bills. Dulcie wanted to take the checks, but the packets were too bulky. At the bottom of the drawer, beneath these neatly tied records, lay a small black notebook. Joe took it in his teeth, lifted it out, and on the carpet they pawed it open.

Each page was marked with a Spanish name accompanied by a short personal history that included arrest records; convictions, mostly for such offenses as failure to file income tax, failure to report as a noncitizen, failure to file social security papers, or, in some cases, passing NSF checks. All the names appeared to be female, but who could be sure, unless one knew Spanish.

Joe's yellow eyes gleamed, he pawed at the pages, smiling. "Personal dossiers."

"Blackmail material."

"I'd be on it."

The next drawer held stationery and printed envelopes, but tucked beneath the thick creamy paper they found a list of numbers, each with a date entered beside it, and some with two dates. These extended over a fifteen-year period. The list made no sense—yet. They slipped it into the notebook and slid this beneath the desk, far to the back.

Before they left the sitting room, Dulcie licked away cat hairs from the white rug, where they clung prominent as a road sign.

Moving into Adelina's bedroom, they avoided the white velvet bedspread, which cascaded onto the carpet; probably it would pluck hairs from them like sticky paper. The bed and dresser were of black wood, light-scaled, and slender, maybe of Danish design. They rifled the dresser drawers but found no papers or photographs among the expensive silk lingerie; the silk and handmade lace were more than Dulcie could resist. She rubbed her face against the neatly folded garments, rolled on them, slid her nose beneath a satin teddy.

"Come on, Dulcie, leave the undies in the drawer. You go trotting out of here dragging that black lace, and we're dog meat."

She smiled sweetly.

"And don't curl up in there; you're leaving cat hairs."

Reluctantly she leaped out. "How often do I get to look at lingerie from Saks or Lord & Taylor? Don't be so grouchy." She cut him a green-eyed smile and licked up a few cat hairs that she had left on the lace.

In Adelina's mirrored dressing room they were surrounded by roaming cat reflections; the sudden feline entourage, the crowd of mimicking cats unnerved them both. Soon their paws felt bruised from fighting open drawers, and their efforts netted nothing more than a half hour survey of fashion that numbed Joe's brain and caused Dulcie to speak in little hushed mewls. Adelina's designer outfits offered a degree of luxury that left the little cat giddy and light-headed.

Outside the bedroom, below the open glass doors, the mower chugged back and forth, guttural and loud, the air perfumed with the clean scent of cut grass. Leaving the suite, they listened at the hall door, then slipped out, tensed to run.

The hall was empty; and the next door opened on a room so plain it must belong to Adelina's maid.

The tan bedspread was of the variety seen in the boy's rooms section of an old Sears catalog, and the desk and two chests could have come from the same page. The room was strewn with skirts and sweaters dropped and tossed across the floor and across every available surface. Maybe the occupant had made many costume changes, this morning, before settling on an outfit for the day. Or maybe she liked to have everything handy, within quick reach, not stuck away in the closet. The skirts were long and gathered, some in flowered patterns, some plain. The sweaters were baggy, and snagged.

Dulcie said "Renet. This is Renet's room."

"That figures. It looks like Renet. What it is about that woman, she's such a nothing."

Dulcie moved toward an inner door. The room smelled faintly of Renet, and of some sharp chemical, a scent pungent and sneeze-making. "It smells like those photographs. The ones Renet gave Adelina."

"Photographer's chemicals?" Joe said. "Maybe she has a darkroom."

"Why would she go to the trouble of a darkroom, when she can take her film to the drugstore?" Pressing her nose to the crack, she sneezed. "Yes, it comes from here." She switched her tail, and leaped, twisting the doorknob and kicking at the door.

"Maybe she's a professional photographer," Joe said. "They don't use the drugstore. To a professional, that's like taking your Rolls Royce to a Ford mechanic."

"How do you know so much?"

"Clyde used to date a photographer."

Dulcie crossed her eyes. "Is there any kind of woman he hasn't dated?" She leaped again, kicking harder, but the door didn't budge. And there was no little knob to turn the dead bolt. Only a key would open it. She dropped down, ears flat, tail switching.

The dresser drawers were no more enlightening, yielding nothing more exciting than Renet's white cotton underwear and flannel nighties and more baggy sweaters. Besides the closet, which was nearly empty, Renet's clothes being kept handily on the floor, there was a built-in wall cupboard with drawers beneath.

The drawers were locked, but the cupboard itself, when they pawed the doors open, revealed shelves filled with assorted small cardboard boxes, a few children's toys, some cheap china knickknacks, and several cameras. Crammed among the clutter was a doll; they could see just a wisp of blond hair and a flick of white lace. Dulcie reared up, looking. "Is that the doll Mae Rose gave to Mary Nell Hook?"

"Why would Renet take the doll away from Mary Nell? The old woman seemed really happy to have it. Why would Renet want . . . Well hell, she is a mean-hearted broad."

Dulcie crouched to leap up onto the shelf, tail lashing for balance, but she dropped back again as, from the hall, the sound of the vacuum cleaner approached, sucking and roaring, its bellow suddenly louder as it slid from the hall runner onto the bare hardwood, heading for Renet's door. They froze, staring, then streaked away through the open French doors to Renet's balcony.

Crouching behind a clay pot planted with ferns, they watched the machine, guzzling and seeking, come roaring into the room; and they shivered.

They were not inexperienced kittens to cower at a vacuum cleaner, but that kind of machine stirred a deep, primal fear, a gut terror about which neither Joe nor Dulcie could be reasonable.

Besides, any machine that could suck up crew sox and sweater sleeves was to be respected.

The maid guided the blue upright around the discarded clothes, moving nothing, circling each cast-off item, scowling as if this business of a messy room might be some private vendetta between herself and Renet. She'd be damned if she'd move one item. She was a middle-sized, middle-aged, dumpy, and unremarkable woman, her black uniform and ruffled little cap reminiscent of an English comedy on TV. A few strands of gray hair protruded from beneath the edge of the frilly cap. Moving toward the cupboard, she paused as if to close its two doors, but instead she lifted out the doll, seemed very familiar with it, as if perhaps she had done this before.

Her back was to them, but they glimpsed the movement of the doll's pale hair and could see a flash of white and a long slim leg. The maid's arm moved as if she were stroking it or smoothing its hair. Clutching the doll, she seemed about to carry it away with her, but then she sighed and returned it to the cupboard, tucking it back among the boxes.

Shutting the cupboard doors, she moved on into the adjoining bath—they could hear the water running as she scrubbed the sink and tub—and began to sing. Her words were in Spanish, the melody sad and slow and enhanced by the heavy echoes of the tiled walls.

Even a cat's singing resounds better in the bathroom; the reverberations from the surrounding hard surfaces tending to make one's voice seem full-bodied and professional. They remained on the balcony listening, a captive audience, until she returned at last, drying her hands on a paper towel. Before she left Renet's room, she tried the inner, locked door.

She twisted the knob and pushed, and when the door wouldn't open, she pressed her ear against the panel. But at last she turned away, with a closed, dissatisfied expression.

Pausing again at the cupboard, she reached as if to open it, then seemed to change her mind, headed for the hall.

"Why was she so interested in the door, interested in the next room?" Dulcie said softly.

Joe didn't answer; he stood rigid, looking intently in, at the locked door.

"Maybe," Dulcie began . . .

But he was gone; the balcony beside her was empty. She whirled around, caught a flash of gray as he vanished over the rail into empty space.

30

Dulcie crouched on the balcony, staring across empty space where Joe had disappeared. He was not on the next railing eight feet away, and when she pushed out between the wrought-iron bars to look down far below to the concrete, the curved drive stretched away unbroken. Stories shivered through her, of cats who had fallen, sometimes to their deaths—it was another human myth that cats invariably landed on their feet.

But no pitiful accident victim lay below her, no gray tomcat flattened and unmoving or trying to right himself.

Looking again to the far terrace, she hopped up onto the balcony rail and gathered herself, crouching, and steeled herself, wondering if she could make that eight-foot span.

If she'd had a good purchase, a solid platform, or if her target was somewhat below her, no problem. But the tiny, slick metal rod beneath her paws felt like a tightrope, and the other rail was no wider.

She could see that the glass doors stood open, and she caught a scent of the harsh chemicals. Surely Joe had gone in there, but why couldn't he have waited for her. Talk about impulsive—he was always on *her* case for being impetuous.

She knew she was procrastinating, afraid of a simple eight-foot hop.

No good thinking, just do it. Why would she fall? She crouched tighter, a coiled spring, and took off with a hard thrust—was in midair when Joe appeared from out the glass doors, springing to the rail. She nearly plowed into him, nearly fell; landed beside him hissing. The chemical smell hit her so hard she doubled over, choking and sneezing. She glared at him angrily.

"Why didn't you wait for me? I thought . . ."

He gave her a sideways smile and licked her ear. "You okay?"

"I guess."

He trotted on inside, couldn't care less that she was mad enough to claw him. "Come on, Dulcie, this is too good to miss."

She followed, swallowing back her anger.

Beyond the glass doors, shutters had been partially closed, dimming the room within. The chemical stench came so strong she could taste it, like swallowing some disgusting prescription medicine.

The room seemed to be half dressing room, and half some kind of workroom. A stainless-steel worktable occupied the center of the large space, and around it the walls were crowded with cabinets and built-in drawers. On their left was the locked inner door to Renet's bedroom. Across the room to their right were two doors. One stood open. But the chemical smell that came from beneath the closed door was so strong one did not want to press one's nose against that crack; Joe sniffed as close to the space as he could manage.

"It's a darkroom. I'd bet on it."

Occupying most of one wall was a large dressing table, an elaborate affair with a hinged, three-way mirror, its glass top cluttered with bottles and jars and, at one end, a stack of round, old-fashioned hatboxes. Dulcie paused, torn between the dressing table and the two doors. The room seemed a wealth of possibilities, a treasure trove perhaps bristling with clues hidden inside the cupboards or on the dressing table.

Leaping up, she wandered among the bottles and crowded jars, stepping carefully, sniffing at the lids, trying to identify the contents. Makeup, certainly, but some smells were very strange. Stepping over an array of lipsticks and little boxes of eye makeup, over eyebrow pencils, cotton swabs, and a pair of tweezers, she paused to look into the three-way mirror, enchanted by her multiple reflections. To see herself from all angles at once, see herself from the back as if looking at another cat, was like an out-of-body experience.

Forgetting Joe, preening shamefully, she heard, from the drive below, from somewhere beyond the kitchen, a car start up and pull away, heard it move around the front of the house and head off up the long drive.

A miniature chest of drawers stood beside the hat-boxes, a little, perfect piece of furniture no taller than her shoulder. She nosed at it, and with a careful claw she pulled out one of the drawers—and she raised her paw to strike, her eyes blazing.

But these were not mice. In the small drawer, the furry bodies looked, in fact, more like dead caterpillars lying fuzzy and still.

Some were gray, some brown, some nearly white. They did not smell like anything that had ever lived. Puzzled by the lifeless fuzzy creatures, she shoved the drawer closed and opened the next.

She froze, staring.

Eyeballs. The drawer contained human eyes.

Pairs of eyes lay jumbled together, blue eyes, green, light brown, hazel. Each pair had been placed inside a tiny transparent box. Some were faded, their color drained away at the outer rim to a ring of foggy white. Her heart raced.

These were not disembodied human eyeballs.

She sat down and coolly regarded the little pairs of contact lenses.

"What's with you?" Joe said from the floor below. Rearing up below the dressing table, he had pawed open its larger drawers. She looked down into a drawer full of neatly folded nighties, soft and beautifully made, with high, ruffled necklines. Tucked into the corner of the drawer were several pairs of neatly folded gloves, white cotton gloves.

They could no longer hear the vacuum cleaner; for some time the upstairs rooms had been silent. Joe pushed the drawer closed and leaped up beside her, to the dresser. Tramping heavy-pawed among the delicate bottles, he posed before the mirror, twitching a whisker, giving her a toothy grin. Panning and turning, he glanced over his shoulder, studying his stub tail and his tomcat equipment. She hadn't known he was such a ham.

She had known cats who were afraid of mirrors. And, of course, a kitten's first experience with its own reflection puzzled and frightened it. She knew a cat once who, when he was laughed at for growling at his mirror image, leaped to the lap of his tormentor and slapped her face.

Leaving Joe leering and clowning, she left the dressing table and approached the adjoining room, which she could see through the open door. It was a huge space, and bare, nearly empty. Bare floor, bare walls, hardly any furniture. A room so hollow that her startled mewl bounced back at her in a sharp echo.

At first glance, the vast space looked like the set for a low-budget science-fiction film. Five tall metal tripods stood about like spindly space aliens. The only other furniture was a hospital bed, with its nightstand, alone in the far corner.

The bed was neatly made up with a white blanket, the corners tucked under with rigid precision. Over the metal headboard hung a gray electrical cord fixed with a squeeze button so a nurse could be summoned. There was a clip-on light, too, like the ones used at Casa Capri, and a stand for an IV bottle.

Joe, having abandoned his multiple reflections, trotted in and pressed against her, his warmth and solidity suddenly very comforting. She did not like this room.

He scowled at the bed, his ears back. "Does Renet keep some patient here? One of the missing women?"

She shivered; they stood looking at the bed as if a patient might suddenly materialize beneath the smooth covers, a pale, thin figure softly moaning. Standing on their hind legs, they sniffed the bed warily. They could smell nothing but laundry soap.

Each of Renet's three rooms—bedroom, the peculiar dressing room, and this hollow chamber—had its own detached balcony. Perhaps at one time these had all been separate bedrooms, had been joined together for Renet's convenience. Another solid door led from this room, the smells beneath it were of fresh air and newly cut grass. They sniffed deeply.

"Must be an outside stairway," Joe said. "I think we're above the kitchen." He leaped for the knob and swung. It turned, but the door was locked with a dead bolt. They sniffed beneath it again, a good lungful of fresh air, then returned to the dressing room.

Approaching the door that closed away the sharp chemicals, again Joe leaped, clamping his paws on the knob. Swinging and pushing, he managed to force the door open.

The room was small and windowless, very dark. As their eyes adjusted, they could see another metal table; it occupied most of the space. Along the back wall stretched a counter with drawers below and shelves above. Four red lightbulbs hung over it, and Dulcie could just make out the switch, beside the door.

Three leaps, and the red lights shone like canned fire. The blaze turned her paws pink, stained Joe's white face and white markings to the color of thin blood. The shelves held gallon jugs reeking of developer, their labels clearly visible. Leaping up to the stainless-steel sink, the cats balanced on the edge.

"That's the printer, there on the table," Joe said. "And, I think, an enlarger."

Clawing open cupboards, they found four big cameras,

and when they pawed into a long, thin drawer, it contained slick photographic paper. A deeper drawer held hanging files filled with negatives in plastic envelopes, items nearly too slick for paws and claws. They managed to pull out several with their teeth. All were portraits of people, but the reversed images showed faces strange and unnatural. The strong smells in the warm enclosed space were beginning to dizzy the cats.

"So this," Joe said, "is where Renet printed the pictures of Mary Nell Hook. If the pictures were taken here, in that hospital bed, if they're keeping that old woman here, we'd better look for her." He leaped to the cold metal table, stood licking his shoulder. "A darkroom, a hospital bed, that elaborate dressing table . . ."

"The sod in the graveyard," Dulcie said. "The missing finger . . . Like parts of a puzzle that all seem to fit, but when you try to put them together, the key piece is missing."

She felt, not enlightened by the varied bits of information, but as if they'd lost their way.

"It takes time," Joe said. "Like playing with a mouse. Let it run free, then catch it again. Maybe you have to play with the facts. Let them run free, catch them from another angle."

"There's a car pulling up the drive."

He heard it and stiffened. They both came to attention as the car stopped beside the house, near the kitchen.

The car door slammed. Footsteps came up the back stair, keys jingling. They leaped together at the light switch as they heard the dead bolt slide back, felt a suck of wind as the door opened.

31

The fog was breaking apart, blowing in tatters. Pulling Buck up, beside a stand of eucalyptus trees, Max Harper watched a black Toyota come up the Prior drive and around the house toward the kitchen. A gray-haired woman got out, probably one of the maids returning from an errand. He could hear no sound now from within the house—the radio and the vacuum cleaner were silent.

He had ridden in a circle around the Prior land along its outer perimeter, crossing the long drive down the hill, then making a second pass closer to the house, looking for any sign where the ground might be disturbed, any sign of digging, just as he had searched every foot of these hills. Though very likely forensics would identify the finger as belonging to Dolores Fernandez.

He wondered how a venerable member of the Spanish aristocracy would view the vandalism and dismemberment of her ancient, frail remains.

Maybe Senora Fernandez wouldn't care, maybe what happened to her earthly self would mean nothing to her now—or maybe would even amuse her.

He pressed Buck in the direction of the cemetery though Buck wanted to shy, began to fuss, didn't want to approach the shadowed grove. When Harper forced him on, the gelding tried to whirl away, snorting rollers. Buck was seldom spooky, and never without cause. He kept ducking and staring into the grove.

Buck's nervous attention was fixed on a spot where three old thick trees stood close together, casting heavy shadows. Harper could see nothing moving there, but Buck was watching something. Max heard, behind him, the car door slam, then footsteps going up the outside stairway at the far end of the house, and in a minute he heard a door open and close. He forced Buck to the edge of the grove, where the gelding tried again to whirl away, snorting and staring like some green colt. Max squinted into the shadows between the heavy oaks, pressed Buck on, amused by their stubborn-willed contest. He seldom had a problem with Buck. But suddenly the breeze changed. Came sharper. And he knew what was wrong with the horse.

He caught the smell himself, the smell of rotting flesh.

Frowning, he let Buck spin around and move away, and at the far end of the grove, upwind from the stink, he swung out of the saddle. Undoing his rope, he made a halter of it and tied the gelding to an oak tree.

He stayed with Buck, talking to him until the gelding calmed, then left him. Walking slowly, he quartered the cemetery around the old graves, looking. Could not pinpoint the source of the putrid scent as it shifted on the wind, could see no sign of digging, but as he neared the three close-growing trees, the smell came so strong it gagged him.

The only thing that looked out of place on that smooth turf was the heap of dry leaves piled against a tree.

Poking around with a branch, he found a small portion of earth disturbed beneath the leaves and, scraping the leaves aside, digging into the dirt, his stick hit something unnaturally soft, something that wasn't earth.

He knelt, gently brushed soil and leaves away with the tip the branch, uncovered a small lump of what looked like rotting flesh, a dark and stinking mess buried in a shallow hole. Covering his nose and mouth with his glove, he knelt to look closer.

It appeared to be hamburger, chopped meat of some kind. And he could smell, besides the rotting meat, the distinctive scent of cyanide.

He had found not a body as he'd expected, but a lump of poison bait.

And as he knelt studying the meat and the disturbed earth, he saw not only scrape marks from digging, but faint pawprints—as if perhaps some animal had been after the meat, and had been frightened away.

Except, the pawprints were *under* the leaves, not indentations on top. These animal tracks had been made before the leaves were scraped over.

Had some animal buried the stinking mess and scraped leaves over it?

Exploring further, he found where the bait had originally lain, some two feet from where it was buried.

What kind of animal would move rotten meat and bury it? Would dig a hole, push the meat in, and scrape dirt and leaves over it?

Cats buried offal, buried their own offensive mess.

He stood looking into the gloom of the cemetery, then fished his handkerchief from his back pocket and, with the stick, scraped the cyanide-laced meat into it.

Leaving Buck tied, carrying the rotten meat, he headed for the old adobe stable, where he could hear a hose swishing and could glimpse, through the open gates to the stable's inner courtyard, the caretaker at work, hosing off the wheels of the big riding mower. Moving quickly, Harper stepped inside the big double gates.

32

As the door opened, the cats streaked from the darkroom, through Renet's dressing room, and out onto the balcony, and crouched against the wall beneath a spindly iron chair. There were no potted ferns here to conceal them. They heard the outer door close, and as footsteps crossed the room, Dulcie peered around through the glass—and went rigid.

"That's not Renet. That's—oh my God. She hasn't come here. What colossal nerve."

"*Who* hasn't?" He pressed against her, to look.

"Your cat burglar. That's your *cat burglar*."

The frowsy old woman was dressed, today, not in her tentlike black raincoat, but in a tan model, equally voluminous. A floppy, matching rain hat was pulled down over her straggling gray hair—perhaps she found the fog just as distasteful as a pouring rain. She crossed the room as brazenly as if she owned the place. Joe watched her with blazing eyes, enraged by her nerve—yet, highly amused. He felt a sudden, wild admiration for the old woman. Talk about chutzpah.

She had walked right into the Prior household, and in the middle of the day. Walked in, with who knew how many maids and other household help on the premises, walked in here bold as brass balls on a monkey.

"And where did she get a key?" Dulcie whispered. "From one of the maids? Did she bribe one of the maids? And didn't the yardman or anyone see her, didn't anyone wonder?"

Entering Renet's dressing room, the woman pulled off her raincoat and laid it carefully on the metal worktable. It was lumpy, its inner pockets loaded. Her baggy black skirt and black sweater made her look even more ancient. She stood looking around the room, then approached the dressing table.

Staring into the three-way mirror at her wrinkled old face and shaggy gray hair, she winked. Winked at herself and grinned. Seemed as pleased with her reflection as if she were young and beautiful.

Sitting down at the dressing table, making herself right at home, she removed the floppy hat, shook out her long gray hair, and eased off her shoes. She seemed unafraid that someone would burst in and find her. She undid the waistband of her skirt, rose, and pulled it off.

"What's she doing?" Dulcie breathed.

"Maybe she's planning to wear some of Renet's clothes when she leaves." As he reared up for a better look, he glanced down over the balcony and saw the horse and rider crossing the drive, headed up toward the cemetery. "There's Harper." And he grinned, his yellow eyes gleaming. His voice in her ear was barely audible. "Perfect timing. We'll get Harper up here. She's a sitting duck; Harper will nail her."

The woman tossed her skirt onto the table, atop her coat. She removed her black sweater, and her blouse and slip, then turned back to the dressing table. Stood in her pants and bra, looking in the mirror. The cats were so amazed they couldn't have spoken, if their lives depended on speech.

But the cat burglar did not seem distressed. The shocking contrast between her young, firm, smooth body and her ancient wrinkled face seemed not to phase her.

She looked like a young woman wearing the mask—the living mask—of a Halloween witch.

She sat down at the dressing table, lifted up her gray hair, and removed it with one smooth motion as casually as she had removed the floppy hat. Beneath the vanished wig, her own pale hair was wispy and matted. She brushed it and tried to fluff it, and sighed.

Putting the wig in one of the hatboxes, she arranged it as if the box might contain a little stand, perhaps one of those white Styrofoam heads with no face. The cats crept closer to see, moved in through the balcony door, into the room, staying behind the metal table.

Lifting a large bottle, she uncapped it, releasing a smell like nail polish remover. Pouring the clear liquid into a little dish, she soaked a cotton ball and began to scrub at her eyebrows, then rubbed the sharp-smelling liquid into her wrinkled face.

She did this several times, and then, working quickly, she peeled away her thick gray eyebrows and began to peel off her wrinkles, wadding them in handfuls, dropping the refuse in the wastebasket. Revealing young, smooth skin beneath.

Slowly Renet's face emerged, smooth and plain. A face totally unremarkable, as quickly forgotten as bland generic cat food.

Halfway through this task she stopped her work and turned, looking nervously around the room. Behind the table, the cats froze. Did she sense someone watching?

But she did not look in their direction, her glances across the room were higher up—looking for a human spy. And as she rose and turned, the cats slipped away to the balcony again, sliding beneath the questionable shelter of the lacy iron chair, into its thin, openwork shadow.

She tried the door leading to her bedroom and seemed relieved that it was securely locked. She stepped to the darkroom and stood in the doorway, looking in, then returned to the dressing table. The cats hunched close together, watching her cup her hands over her face and lean down, removing her contact lenses.

She cleaned the contacts carefully, put them in their little plastic box, and slipped that into the small drawer of the tiny chest. Her face was red and blotched from the harsh chemical.

Now, still in her cotton pants and bra, standing at the worktable, she removed from the coat's inner pockets a handful of glitter, flicked on the gooseneck lamp, and held to the light several gold bracelets, three gleaming chokers, four pairs of glittering earrings. She studied each, then turned away, leaving the jewelry scattered across the table.

Unlocking the door to her bedroom, she moved inside. They heard her open the cupboard, but from this vantage they couldn't tell what she was doing. Not until they slipped in again, to the bedroom door, did they see that she was holding the doll, cuddling it.

For the first time, Dulcie could see the doll clearly. She crept close, halfway into the room, took a good look. As they slipped away again to the balcony, she whispered so close to Joe's ear that her breath tickled.

"That's not the doll Mae Rose gave to Renet; that was a regular child's doll. This is something else. It's so real, like a real person. That's one of the stolen dolls, those valuable collector's dolls."

They watched Renet return to the dressing room, carrying the doll, touching its cheek with one finger. Sitting down again before the mirror, she propped the doll at the end of the dresser against the hatboxes, then began to work cream into her own chapped, red skin, using little round strokes as one might learn from a beauty magazine article on correct skin care. They were watching her with interest when, in the mirror, Renet's eyes caught theirs.

From the glass, she stared straight at them. Her eyes locked on their eyes.

They backed away, crouching to leap to the next balcony. She ran, dived for them. Before they could jump she was between them, cutting them off from each other and from the rail. Joe streaked between her legs into the bedroom. Dulcie fled toward the darkroom, swerved, slid behind the dressing table. Renet slammed the balcony door shut and turned, began to stalk them.

33

 Carrying the rotten meat in his handkerchief, Harper approached the old adobe stables that Adelina had converted to a maintenance building and garages. The structure was designed for maximum cooling, its rows of stalls set well back beneath deep overhangs, and its four sides facing an inner courtyard fashioned to trap the cool night air and hold it during the heat of the day. Entry to the stable yard was through an archway wide enough for a horse and wagon, so would easily accommodate any car. One row of stalls now served as garages—their inner walls extended out to the edge of the overhang, and individual garage doors had been added—providing a roomy eight-car area to house the Prior vehicles. All of the garage doors stood open, and a push broom leaned against the wall halfway down.

The spaces nearest him were empty; one of these probably belonging to Adelina's new Rolls, one to Renet's blue van, and a space likely reserved for Teddy's specially equipped van, for the times when he chose to stay here. The other vehicles showed him only a bumper, a bit of rear fender.

The courtyard was wet and slick where Carlito Vasquez was hosing down the wheels of the big riding mower. Vasquez was a middle-aged, lean little man, likable and generally responsible, who did not talk, as far as Harper knew, about his employer, about details of

her estate management, or about any personal business
he might be privy to.

Moving across the courtyard to where the hose
hissed and splattered, carrying the package of rotten
meat, Harper paused only briefly to take a better look
into the open garages.

A surge of surprise hit him. And a deep excitement.

In the last stall stood a blue '93 Honda. The plate,
where dried mud had flaked away, was partially legible:
California plate 3GHK . . .

It was days like this, when something unexpected and
significant was handed to him almost like a gift, that
made all the dirt he had to deal with seem worthwhile.

As he moved on toward Carlito, the groundskeeper
turned off the hose at the handheld nozzle. Harper
handed him the handkerchief-wrapped, stinking meat.
"You put this in the garbage, Carlito. You know what
this is. Show me where you keep the cyanide."

Carlito cringed, as if he'd been hit, and pointed
toward an open stall. Harper could see bags of fertilizer
piled inside and, along one wall, a shelf of cans and bottles, probably garden sprays, vermin poison.

"Leave the cyanide where it is, Carlito. My men will
take a look. Don't even go in that stall until I tell you."

Carlito nodded.

He gave the caretaker a long look, then waved him
away. "Go put that meat in the garbage. Put the lid on
real tight so nothing can get at it. *No mas animales
muerte. Comprende?*"

Carlito nodded again, dropping his glance before
Harper's angry stare. And, Harper thought, the man
had only done what he was paid to do.

"No matter what kind of orders Ms. Prior gives you,
if I find any more poison anywhere on this property,
you're going to find yourself sleeping in *la carcel.
Comprende?* Now vamoose, get rid of this stuff. I'll speak
to Ms. Prior."

Carlito left, carrying Harper's redolent handkerchief,

took off across the stable yard fast for the narrow arch at the back that led behind the stalls. The estate kept its garbage cans there, secured to the wall to keep local dogs and raccoons from overturning them.

When Carlito had gone, Harper moved on over to the garages. The ceilings were low, the shadowed spaces exuding cool air. He could hardly tell where the walls of the old stable ended and the new adobe had been added on, the work matched so well. Adelina didn't stint when it came to builders and construction work.

Scraping the remaining mud off the last three numbers, he stood grinning.

This was the one.

Feeling like a kid at Christmas, he circled the Honda, looking in through its closed windows, touching neither the glass nor the vehicle itself.

A flowered hat lay on the backseat beside a woman's blue sweater and a pair of flat shoes. He used the tail of his shirt to open the passenger door and the glove compartment and lift out the registration.

The car was registered to a Darlene Morton of Mill Valley. This was neither the name nor the address registered in Sacramento to this particular California plate.

Turning up his radio, he spoke to the dispatcher, asking for a team to dust the Honda and collect other evidence. When he signed off, he moved out through the arch again, stood idly watching the house, considering the possibilities of who the car might belong to.

He knew of no old, gray-haired woman in the Prior household, except that maid he'd seen.

That would be a gas, one of the maids into burglaries on her day off.

He found it impossible to imagine Adelina rigging herself up as the cat burglar; Adelina wouldn't waste her time on such foolishness. These burglaries were more like a lark, someone's idea of a little profitable recreation, B and E for a few laughs. And he didn't think

Adelina would stand for that misbehavior from her sister, not when it might cast a shadow on her own image.

Or would she?

Unless maybe they had some kind of trade-off.

The animal poisonings were another matter, and were easy enough to explain if Adelina didn't want dogs digging up the old, historical cemetery. She was big on historical landmarks, on civic pride; that stuff impressed other people.

As he stood watching the house he heard shouting and someone running inside on the hard floor. Renet's voice, shouting again. And a shadow that looked like Renet ran across the living room. At the same moment a streak of darkness fled, low, inches from the floor: out the door and across the terrace, disappearing into the bushes. One of those cats had sneaked in, he thought amused, and Renet had chased it out.

The next moment, Renet stepped out through the patio door, stood studying the terrace and bushes and the lawn beyond, then looking away toward the oak wood and graveyard.

When she turned at last, she seemed to see him for the first time. She gave him a friendly wave, and moved back inside.

Across the grove, he could see Buck standing easy now, only fussing idly at his rope, trying to get a mouthful of grass. He watched with interest the azalea bushes where the cat had disappeared. But when, after some minutes, nothing moved there, he turned away and headed back through the courtyard toward the back of old stables, where the garbage cans were kept, to make sure that Carlito had done as he'd been told—had put that poisoned meat where nothing could get at it. But, crossing the stable yard, he kept seeing the cat running from Renet, seeing that swift, low shadow.

34

Dulcie crouched high among the branches of an oak tree, looking down on the old graves and watching out through the dusky leaves to the Prior house. Watching for Joe. Nervously, she listened to Renet shouting, heard Renet running through the house across the hard floors—surely she was still chasing the tomcat.

Below her, at the base of the tree, the doll sat on the grass. Dulcie had gotten the lady out, had dragged her down the stairs and across the lawn despite the wild chase Renet gave them.

Renet shouted again, and Joe burst out the patio door, streaking across the terrace. As he dived into the bushes, Renet came flying out behind him, her robe flapping half-open over her pants and bra. As she hit the terrace, Dulcie saw Max Harper standing beyond, at the stables, watching her with interest.

Renet didn't see Harper, stood looking for Joe. Not until she headed for the bushes did she spot Harper. She stopped, waved to him, maddeningly casual, then turned away and went back into the house, her search foiled. Dulcie smiled, and watched Harper to see what he would do.

Earlier, when Renet attacked them on the balcony, driving them apart, she had fled straight for the dressing table. Leaping up, she had snatched the doll in her teeth. She was desperate to take away some evidence,

somehow to alert Harper—short of shouting the whole
story at him.

For a split second, as she grabbed the doll, her eyes
locked with Joe's, then they fled in opposite directions,
Joe leading Renet away, racing into the empty photo
studio. The minute they were gone, Dulcie dragged the
doll out, down the hall, and down the stairs, jerking it
along in a panic of haste, clumping down the steps, terrified she'd break the delicate lady. But she had no
choice. She needed the doll—this was the only plan she
could think of. As she gained the bottom stair she could
hear Renet running, just above her, chasing Joe through
Adelina's room. She prayed he could keep safe.

But if Renet caught that tomcat, she'd be sorry.
She'd be hamburger. Unless . . . unless he made a mis-
step, unless she threw something heavy and had good
aim. She heard Renet double back, shouting, could picture Joe dodging beneath the bed, beneath the white
leather chairs, pictured him leaping from one balcony to
the next and back again as Renet raced from room to
room in hot pursuit. If she hadn't been so terrified for
him, despite his claws and teeth—and so busy dragging
the heavy doll down the stairs—she'd have found the
humor in this, would have watched the charade, laughing.

Pulling the doll along through the living room, she
had reached the terrace and managed to jerk the doll
across into the azaleas. It seemed to grow heavier, every
step. She hardly paused to catch her breath; she raced
away again across the lawn, jerking the doll along and
praying no one was watching. When at last she dragged
it in among the tombstones, her insides felt as if they
were ruptured.

She felt better when she reached the hidden squares
of new turf. Working carefully, she had placed the
miniature lady between two squares of sod, arranged
her so she sat just on the crack, leaning over to touch
the grass. The lady's pale skin and white petticoats and

blue silk dress shone brightly against the dark woods. Dulcie had smoothed the doll's skirts with her paw and carefully pressed the doll's little hands down into the earth, into the thin seam between the sod squares.

Then she had scorched up into the oak tree.

As she watched the terrace, Joe burst suddenly from the bushes, a gray streak flying across the lawn and into the woods, crouching behind a headstone, staring out toward the house, wild-eyed. Renet must have given him a real chase.

"Here," she whispered, moving so he could see her.

He raced to the wood and stormed up the tree and onto her branch, his ears flat, his yellow eyes huge. He crouched beside her, panting, his sides heaving.

She licked his ear, but he shook his head irritably and backed away.

"Hot. About done for. That woman's as full of fight as a bulldog."

She was quiet until he had rested and caught his breath. At last he moved closer, settling against her. "You'd never think it to look at her. Three times she nearly creamed me, throwing things. She even threw a camera—damn thing could have killed me." He scowled down at the doll sitting on the turf below them.

"Very pretty bait, Dulcie. But even if Harper finds it . . ."

"I can hardly wait."

"He'll dig up the turf, all right. He'll find whatever's hidden underneath. But he won't connect the doll to Renet."

"He'll *know* it's one of the stolen dolls. You said the Martinezes gave him a good description."

"They did. Of course he'll know the doll is evidence, and Harper told Clyde those dolls are worth plenty. But that doesn't connect to Renet. And even if he did suspect her, he can't search the house without a warrant."

"He can *get* a warrant, call the judge. He's done that before. Judge Sanderson—"

"Harper finds a doll in the cemetery. Sanderson is going to issue a warrant on that?"

"If he dusts the doll for prints, finds Renet's prints—"

"That takes lab time. Computer time. And even then, there might not be a record. If she's never been arrested, then those prints from the burglarized houses will match those on the doll, but neither set will link to Renet."

Dulcie sniffed with impatience. Tomcat logic was so pedestrian. "First he has to find the doll. Then we'll take it from there. If he comes this way, he can't miss it. If he doesn't come into the grove, I'll lead him here."

"Fine. That's a clever move."

"*I* think—" She paused, looking past him. "He's coming." They watched Harper swinging toward them across the lawn. But at the same moment, two squad cars pulled down the front drive. The first black-and-white parked in front of the house. The other car moved on down the drive to the back, stopping beside Harper. The police captain stood leaning on the door. They couldn't hear much of the conversation over the static of the radio. When the car pulled away, Harper turned back toward the house.

Dulcie wasn't having that; she hadn't planted the doll for nothing. Like a flash, she dropped out of the tree, fled for the tethered gelding. Puzzled, Joe watched her from the branch, then realized what she was up to. He tensed to charge down and defend her as she leaped at the gelding's head, then raced around his hooves. Darting in, she slapped at his legs and spun away, harried him until he snorted and began to rear, jerking on his tie rope. When she jumped up at his neck, clawing him, the buckskin squealed and bucked.

Harper came running.

The horse jerked and squealed. When Dulcie saw Harper, she vanished. She was gone, behind headstones, behind trees.

Harper was totally intent on getting to the buckskin,

he'd never see the doll. Joe let out a bloodcurdling yowl,
a caterwaul that should stop a battalion of fast-moving
cops.

Harper paused; he was not six feet from the doll. He
stood looking.

Glancing away to the buckskin, seeing that the horse
had begun to quiet, Harper knelt, studying the little
seated lady, looking at her tiny hands tucked down into
the seam between the squares of sod. His thin, lined
face showed no emotion, not surprise, not incredulity. It
was a cop's face, stony and watchful.

But his fingers twitched as he carefully parted the
grass, studying the line in the dark, rich soil.

He didn't touch the doll. He moved to several posi-
tions, looking at the thin creases where sod met sod.
The gelding was quiet now, was, Joe decided, a sensible
horse not given to unnecessary histrionics. When the
danger passed, he forgot it.

As Harper walked the excavation, following the
nearly invisible lines, finding the cross seams, behind
him, among the headstones, Dulcie slipped past, returning quietly, swarming up the tree without sound, not
even a whisper of her claws gripping into the thick oak
bark.

They crouched close together watching Harper step
off the breadth and width of the excavation. When he
lifted his radio from his belt, Dulcie crept out along the
branch, flicking her tail with anticipation.

Harper called for two more squad cars. When he told
the dispatcher to patch him through to Judge Sanderson,
Dulcie grew so excited, waiting for the judge, shifting
from paw to paw, that she nearly lost her grip on the
branch. Joe nosed at her, pressing her back against the
trunk to a more secure perch, glaring at her until she settled down.

By the time the two police units arrived, Harper had
bagged the doll for evidence, had posted a guard beside
the two-by-six sod-covered excavation, and had stationed

another guard at the stables. The cats burned to know
what was there. Harper had not mentioned, to the judge,
anything about the stables, had told Judge Sanderson
only that he needed to excavate further in the cemetery,
and that he had new evidence about the string of burglaries. When Harper left the grove, so did Joe and
Dulcie. Slipping along behind him, keeping to the cover
of the headstones, they followed him toward the house.

Slinking from gravestone to gravestone in swift
dashes, streaking across the lawn behind Harper, they
gained the azalea bushes. Then under a chaise lounge,
working their way across the terrace toward the kitchen,
and past.

A tan Ford was parked by the back stairs. They
slipped up the narrow steps, listening. Beside Renet's
door they scrambled up a support post to the roof.

Within moments they were prowling the warm tiles,
the red clay expanse seeming as long as a city block.
Below them, on the front drive, the two black-and-
whites were parked, and four officers stood talking with
Harper. The other squad cars, behind the house, had
stopped beside the stable.

They watched the long front drive, as an unmarked
car turned in. Approaching the house it pulled up in
front. The driver handed Harper a white envelope.

"Search warrant," Joe said softly.

"I hope Renet hasn't already cleared out all the evidence, every necklace and bracelet. We could go down
there, distract her. Give Harper a chance to search. We
can just drop down onto her balcony and—"

"Yeah, right. We could do that."

"But . . ."

"I've had enough of her. The woman's a fiend."
Whatever bland, innocuous presence Renet managed to
exude in the course of everyday living, she was a Jekyll
and Hyde when it came to cats.

Dulcie nudged him, and he turned to look. Away
behind them, across the upper hills, two more police

cars were coming, making their way along a narrow, rutted back road. Behind them followed a dark, unmarked station wagon. The three vehicles turned downhill just above the grove, onto the dirt lane that bordered the cemetery on the far side, parking at the edge of the graves near the yellow police tape.

Four uniformed officers got out of the police units. The two men in dark suits who emerged from the station wagon each carried a backpack. Farther on, Harper's buckskin gelding, still tied to his tree, looked toward the men with interest. He didn't shy now; he was beautifully calm.

The six men stood talking beside the raw earth of Dolores Fernandez's grave, then moved on across the grove toward the patch of nearly invisible sod squares where Harper had found the doll, where he had left a yellow tape tied.

The two men in suits set down their packs and walked around the sod rectangle, then knelt to carefully probe at its edges. They worked at this for some time before one of the men fished a camera from his pack, adjusted some lens attachment, and began to take pictures.

Dulcie smiled with satisfaction, and settled more comfortably on the warm roof tiles. Joe yawned and curled down against the chimney in a patch of sun. When the photographer finished shooting pictures, both men walked the area, bending to pick up minute bits of evidence, dropping each into a little transparent bag. After some time, they produced long slim knives, working carefully at the sod, slipping the blades down into the hairline cracks. The cats were distracted only when two more cars came down the long drive: a black Lincoln and Adelina's pearl red Bentley, both vehicles squealing to a halt before the front door.

Car doors were flung open, two men in dark suits got out of the Lincoln, moving close to Adelina as she approached the house. At the same moment, as if she had been watching the drive, Renet slammed out the front door to join her sister. The cats could imagine phone calls from within, down to Casa Capri, could just picture Renet's panicked phone summons to Adelina. The two men had to be Adelina's attorneys.

From within the house, Max Harper appeared behind Renet. And as Renet and Adelina began to argue, the two men lit into Harper. They wanted to know what business he had bringing his police up here. They informed him that if he didn't leave at once, they'd have him in court.

"Lawyers," Joe said with disgust. "They'd better think again, if they plan to take *Harper* into court." He might rag Max Harper, but no one else had better give him a hard time. Harper did not seem pleased with the attorneys' abrasive attitudes. The cats had never before seen him really mad. They watched, highly entertained, kneading their claws against the clay tiles, as Harper worked the two attorneys over. They watched him back the lawyers toward their car, watched the two retreat inside the Lincoln and drive away, watched Harper herd Adelina and Renet into the house. That was the last the cats saw of the Prior sisters until they were escorted out the front door an hour later to a patrol car, where they were locked in the back behind the wire barrier. "Like common drunks," Dulcie said.

When the Prior sisters had been driven away, and the cats looked back toward the grove, the forensics team had removed two squares of sod and were lifting out a third, placing it on a plastic sheet, using tools as small as teaspoons. The two men stopped only long enough to pull on protective blue jumpsuits, to tie on white masks over their noses and mouths, and pull on rubber gloves.

Another half hour and the smell of decomposed flesh hit the air like a giant huff of fetid breath. Another hour more of tedious work, and the men had something new to photograph.

Within the carefully excavated grave, an arm and shoulder had been uncovered, protruding from the freshly dug earth, the body misshapen by decomposition. The smell was so strong that even Joe gagged. Dulcie turned away, retching. How could the police stand this?

It took several hours more for the officers to remove the remaining sod, to photograph and measure the body, to bag bits of evidence, and to dust for prints. The coroner had arrived, and later a forensic anthropologist who had been called down from San Francisco; the cats picked up this much from officers talking in the yard, and from the police radio. The sky began to darken, the roof tiles to cool. A little wind scudded up the hills, chill with approaching night. The two uniformed officers who walked the grove searching for additional unmarked graves soon were using highpowered flashlights, and the forensics men fetched portable spots from their cars.

Below the cats, the drive and gardens lit up suddenly, as the house lights came on, aprons of yellow brilliance casting their wash across the lawns and flowers.

Despite the untoward events which gripped the Prior estate, the household routine seemed unbroken. The cats could smell supper cooking, the scent of something meaty and spicy rising from the kitchen, as if perhaps the cook found it soothing to go on with her schedule in the face of confusion and perhaps disaster.

Joe licked his whiskers. "When did we eat last?"

"I don't remember. Seems like weeks ago. Supper smells so good, I'm tempted to go down and beg."

"Hey, we have to have some principles. I don't take handouts from anyone but George Jolly."

The mention of Jolly left them weak, feeling empty to the point of panic.

It was well after dark when the forensics team finished, and when, in the house, Harper's men were done bagging evidence, labeling and packing it and carrying it out to a squad car. Not until the police and the assorted experts had all gone, locking up the main house, leaving four officers on duty, sending the help back to their own quarters, did the cats come down from the roof and head home.

Just this one time, they wished they could have snagged a ride in a police car. They were beat. Drained. Trotting down the hills they were too tired even to hunt. They did find, before they left the Prior estate, enough water on the paving bricks of the stable yard to slake their thirst. When they slipped into the brick courtyard, the Mexican caretaker spoke to them in Spanish. But they stayed away from him, they could smell cyanide clinging around him, pervasive as a woman's perfume.

And even if he hadn't smelled of poison, they didn't need a friendly stranger just now. All they wanted was home and their own housemates, their own cozy houses and something warm and comforting in their supper bowls. The arrest of Adelina and Renet, the beginning of official police work on the tangle of events, had left them worn-out. Their comfortable homes, at that moment, had never seemed so sweet.

35

"No," Harper said, "there was not enough flesh on the body to take fingerprints. But we have positive identification—there's no doubt the body hidden beneath the turf was Jane Hubble's."

Mae Rose was very still, but she was calm; her primary emotion seemed to be her deep rage at Jane's death. Harper had wondered if he was being too graphic for these elderly ladies, but evidently not for Mae Rose. Her clear blue eyes were fixed on him not only with anger at Jane's murder but with a bright, intelligent attention. "It was not only the finger," she said, "but Jane's dental work that identified her?"

"Yes, and also an X-ray of an old multiple fracture of her left ankle."

"I remember that. She told me she broke her ankle when she was in college, on a ski trip. That old break pained her a lot in bad weather. And so the X-rays matched?"

"They did," Harper said. He supposed he was an incongruous figure, uniformed and armed, sitting at the delicate garden table in the beflowered patio of Casa Capri. At their small tea table, besides himself and Mae Rose, sat young Dillon Thurwell and Susan Dorriss. Susan had graduated from her wheelchair to a metal walker—it stood beside her chair—and the brown poodle lay beside it, napping. The entire Pet-a-Pet group was in attendance, the occasion a celebration hosted by the new management. At the next table were seated Clyde, Wilma, Bonnie Dorriss, and old Eula Weems.

"If the finger came from Jane's grave," Mae Rose said, "then the other grave, the open grave of Dolores Fernandez, that was just a red herring?"

"It was," Harper said. "After the dog dug into Jane's grave and took the little finger bone, Adelina had Dolores Fernandez's grave dug up to make it look like the finger came from there; and they put new sod on Jane's grave. Adelina must have had some wild idea— some silly hope, that we'd take the incident at face value, wouldn't bother to run the finger through the lab."

"But it didn't work," Mae Rose said with satisfaction. The little, doll-like woman amused Harper. Despite her fragile appearance, she'd been bull-stubborn in her insistence that Jane and the others had met foul play.

"When the dog dug up Jane's grave, that was when Adelina started putting out poison." Mae Rose shook her head. "Adelina had a regular shell game going, switching patients around."

"That's exactly what she had. It started when a Dorothy Martin died, fifteen years ago. We've identified Dorothy, too, from X-rays of her dental work. Adelina buried her secretly in the old cemetery, and told the other residents that Mrs. Martin had been moved over to Nursing, and she continued to collect the two thousand dollars a month for Dorothy's care. Though I guess the fee, now, is more like three thousand."

"Three thousand and up," Susan Dorriss said.

"Adelina did the same with the next two patients," Harper said. "It's possible both of those were natural deaths, forensics is still examining the remains. Neither death was reported, and the trust officers went right on paying.

"All three patients had bank-appointed trust officers looking after their incomes, paying their bills, people who had never even seen their clients. Bank trust officers aren't expected to visit their charges; they haven't the time, and they aren't paid to do that.

"And none of those three woman had any close relatives who might pop in for a visit. If a trust officer phoned to schedule a visit for some business reason, Renet did a stand-in, made herself up like the deceased."

"So Adelina buried her charges," Mae Rose said, "and went on collecting their monthly fees. No wonder she drives a new Bentley."

Harper nodded. "Adelina was able to keep most of her scam from her Spanish-speaking nurses, and she nearly doubled the salaries of the three supervisors. She's always hired nurses who wouldn't be apt to talk, who don't have much English and who've had a problem with the law. Women she can control through threats and blackmail." He sipped his tea, wishing he had a cup of coffee, and studied Mae Rose's overburdened wheelchair—all her worldly possessions. "That doll in your blue bag, Mrs. Rose, is that the doll that Jane had, where you found the note?"

Mae lifted the faded doll and fluffed its dry, yellow hair. "Yes, this is the doll I gave Jane. The doll that was Jane's cry for help." She gave Harper a long look. "A cry that didn't arrive until after she was dead." She stroked the doll sadly, and laid it in her lap beside the brindle cat curled asleep on the pink afghan. "Was there evidence of who—which one of those three—actually killed Jane? And of who buried her?"

"None," Harper said. "We know only that she was given a lethal dose of Valium mixed with other drugs. Drug traces in the body are a cause of death which is still detectable long after bruises and flesh wounds can no longer be found. We're assuming that either Adelina or Teddy buried her; forensics found hairs from both suspects around the grave. The lab had to separate them out from some animal hairs that forensics collected at the site, all of it was mixed together in with leaves and dirt and grass."

"What kind of animal hairs?" Dillon said.

"Cat hair," Harper said. "Some stray cat."

He did not look at Clyde, though Clyde was watching him. He was still ridiculously edgy about Damen's gray tomcat. The cat was, at the moment, perched above them in the orange tree, presumably asleep, though twice he had caught a thin gleam of yellow through its narrowly slitted eyes. Aware of the cat, he felt as he did too often lately, edgy, nervous, wondering if he was losing his grip.

The cat had got mixed into the case in a way that left him uncertain and short-tempered, left him so edgy he wouldn't care if he never saw another cat. Cats in the cemetery, some cat racing through the house with Renet in hot pursuit, cat hairs around the doll which had been set up for him to find. And the tiny indentations in the doll's arm, those marks, the lab swore, were the marks of a cat's teeth.

None of this helped his digestion. None of it was comfortable to think about.

If this had been the first time these two cats had got mixed up in a case, he'd shrug and chalk it up to coincidence, forget about it.

But it was not the first time. This was the third murder case within a year that, one way or another, these two cats had seemed to blunder into, leaving their marks, leaving their own perplexing trail.

And the worst part was, he had an uncomfortable feeling this would not be the last time.

Dulcie, lying on Mae Rose's lap, yawned and curled deeper into the pink afghan, pushing aside the doll. She had not looked up when Harper mentioned cat hairs on the grave, nor had she glanced up into the tree. Joe, crouched up there among the leaves, would be highly amused that Harper had sent cat hairs to the lab. If she dared look up at him, she'd see that stupid grin on his face. Grinning out through the leaves as smug as Alice's Cheshire cat.

Harper hadn't looked up at Joe, either. She hoped he wasn't putting some things together that were best left apart.

Still, if he was, she couldn't help it. He couldn't prove anything. She and Joe had, she considered, done an admirable job to assist Harper. But he'd never know for sure. If he insisted on feeling nervous, that was his problem.

"It's so strange," Susan said, "how the stolen doll got into the graveyard—and why Adelina's black book was hidden under her desk. Surely she'd have some better place to hide it." She glanced at Dillon. "It's almost like a child's prank, moving evidence around."

Dillon looked blank. Harper helped himself to another slice of lemon cake from the plate in the center of the table. Some details of the case did not bear close scrutiny.

They had a solid case, but there were unanswered questions that could prejudice the prosecution. He just hoped defense didn't claim the notebook was tainted evidence. They'd have to wait and see. Certainly the department had done a fine job sorting out the information in Adelina's black book, checking its entries against the backgrounds of her nurses.

The black book had contained, as well as the dossiers of two dozen employees, a separate sheet of paper with a code list of the dead patients. No name, just a number, with a birth date, and apparently the date he or she was secretly buried. Some had a second date when that person was given a public funeral and some other body buried. He had, when he removed the coded paper, found caught in the spine of the book one short dark hair, a hair varied in color like the hair of a dark tabby cat.

He had not sent this to the lab.

In the old cemetery, his men had found fifteen unmarked graves. They had found, as well, double burials in four of the Spanish graves where more-recent bodies had been tucked in to sleep, perhaps restlessly, beside ancient Spanish bones.

When he did the numbers on that, it looked like Adelina was raking in well over half a million a year on dead patients.

"It was with the fourth death," he said, "whatever the cause, that Adelina decided to have a funeral. By this time, the long-deceased Dorothy Martin would have been ninety-nine years old. Adelina probably decided that she'd better fake a death before Dorothy started receiving unwanted publicity for her longevity. She gave Dorothy a nice, though modest, send-off, using the body of a newly deceased Mary Dunwood. With Renet's background in the makeup department, it was no trick for her to make up the dead Mary Dunwood to look like an aged Dorothy Martin.

"Over the years," he said, "no one seemed to notice that Casa Capri always used the same funeral parlor, nor to think it unusual that the funeral director drives top-of-the-line Cadillacs which he trades in every year. Not likely anyone would have commented. No one takes a friendly view of funeral directors—people like to think of them as rip-off artists.

"For each prospect who fit Adelina's requirements—no close attachments, no close family—she kept a detailed record of any distant relative or friend, and she made copies of all their correspondence. It wasn't hard to learn to fake different people's handwriting. And she got personal information, as well, from what Teddy learned during his friendly little chats with the patients. Adelina knew more about those people than they ever imagined.

"And it wasn't hard for Renet, using her makeup and acting skills, to impersonate the dead patients. People change sufficiently as they age; five or six years can make a significant difference.

"Renet took photographs of the victims often, before they died. And she photographed herself made up like them, to compare. She made quite a study of how the patients would look as they aged; we found books outlining the changes that can occur. I'm guessing Adelina demanded that amount of commitment from Renet. Adelina is a perfectionist. She made sure, as well, that wherever Renet was living, up and down the coast, they were in touch. All Renet had to do, if she was needed, was hop on a plane. The nursing home made it known—an inviolate rule—that visitors must give twenty-four-hour notice. That patients did not like surprises, and did not liked to be disturbed during any small illness, such as a cold or an attack of asthma."

Susan and Wilma exchanged a look; Susan's dislike for the Priors was very clear. She had told Harper her suspicions about Teddy and how, the afternoon Adelina and Renet were arrested, there had been a major panic at the home. Susan said Teddy had spent maybe fifteen minutes in Adelina's office, then Adelina had left in a hurry; Teddy had wheeled to the front door, watching her drive away, then whirled his chair around, racing into the social room.

There he had confronted Susan, had wanted to know what she'd told the police, what she'd seen out in the grove, what she'd said about him.

Susan had played dumb, said she didn't know what he was talking about. She'd been terrified of him, said his eyes looked almost glazed, said she expected him to leap out of his chair and start hitting her.

Now, Harper watched Susan speculatively. He had been really distressed about Teddy's threat, thinking of Susan so vulnerable in the wheelchair. Strange, Susan was the only woman, since Millie died, who gave him that warm, totally honest, comfortable feeling, as if with Susan you could be totally yourself.

But he didn't need a woman in his life, not any more than he needed cats under his feet during an investigation.

Across from him, Wilma said, "How did the three Priors respond when you took them in for questioning?"

Max smiled. "Renet was upset, angry. And she was scared.

"Young Teddy went ballistic, threw a real tantrum—though he wasn't sufficiently out of control to abandon his wheelchair. Adelina was cool as ice, totally in charge of herself. And, of course, she already has her attorneys at work on her defense.

Mae Rose said, "*Were* there other murders besides Jane and Mary Nell? Or did the others die naturally?"

"Forensics is still examining the remains; there's indication that James Luther may have been a victim. With bodies that old, a murder can easily go undetected." He had to marvel at these old people. Some old folks would turn queasy at this much detail. These folks did not seem morbid in their interest, except maybe Eula Weems. They simply wanted information.

But Eula's hands fidgeted and plucked at each other. "How—how did they kill Mary Nell?"

"The way her skull was broken," Harper said, "she probably died relatively quickly. The murder weapon was a smooth, thin object, swung with force.

"One theory is that someone may have tried to smother her, and when she fought back she was hit a hard blow, possibly with the edge of a dinner plate. Such a blow would break the skull in just that way."

He would not ordinarily have discussed a case so openly, particularly when it was not yet in court, but the newspaper had got hold of most of the details; and these old folks did have a vested interest. Two of their close friends had been murdered, maybe more than two. These folks had a right to some answers when the very people who were entrusted with their well-being had betrayed them.

Dillon said, "Jane was desperate, to sew that letter in the doll praying someone would find it. And no one did, not in time."

"But we have her killers," Harper said. "And no one might ever have known, their little scheme might never have been discovered, if not for you and Mae Rose."

He thought he saw the tabby cat's expression change, a twitching of whiskers almost like a smile. But of course he was imagining that.

"The court won't let the Priors go free?" Eula said.

"No matter what happens in court, and I don't see them going free, Adelina Prior will not be back at Casa Capri, nor will Renet or Teddy. Judge Sanderson has promised that."

The home, left without management, had been placed under jurisdiction of the court and was being managed temporarily by a court-appointed chain of retirement homes. In the interest of public relations, the new manager had organized not only this little gathering today, but had announced several new policies, trying hard to counter the bad publicity and bad feelings.

He had opened the Nursing wing to patients' families and to all residents each afternoon, so they could visit those patients who felt well enough to have company. The Pet-a-Pet program would continue as a permanent part of the home's therapy, along with several other new programs, including a weekly reading of best-selling fiction by one of the local library staff and several evening classes to be presented as part of the continuing education offerings of the local college.

"Them college classes," Eula said. "Teddy talked about getting some kind of fancy schooling here, but it never happened." Eula sighed. "Teddy was all hot air." The old woman snorted. "He never did need that wheelchair. All the time, he could walk."

She half rose at the table, addressing her audience. "I bet it was Teddy dug those graves. Maybe took those poor old folks out of here, himself, in his van."

Minute particles of flesh and hair had been found in the van, identified as belonging to the dead patients. Clothing fibers were found matching threads from the graves. And similar particles had turned up behind the stable where, for years, an old truck had been parked. Harper's theory was that the bodies were transferred from the van to the truck late at night, and driven out into the cemetery.

And, even more interesting, the fragments of tire marks found behind the stable had matched the casts of tire marks taken from the scene of Susan Dorriss's accident. Same tread, same small L-shaped nick at one edge. The truck had been recovered three days ago in the small town of Mendocino, north of San Francisco.

At one time the truck had been legally registered to Adelina Prior—its original plates had been found in the old stable along with a dozen other plates hidden in a niche beneath the wooden bottom of an old feed bin in one of the stalls used for storage.

His theory was that either Renet or Teddy was driving the truck when it hit Susan, and that Renet had taken the truck to be painted. He hoped with time the department could establish that it was Renet who appeared at the paint shop dressed as a little frumpy Latino housewife, black hair, Spanish accent. He was hoping they could find hard evidence that it was Renet who later bought the truck from the used-car dealer, dressed in a short leather skirt, her hair a blaze of red curls, her legs shapely in black hose. The redhead who bought the truck had put a FOR SALE sign in the window, and two hours later had sold it cheap to a Mexican family moving to Seattle. When the truck blew a head gasket in Mendocino, they sold it for bus fare.

Mae Rose looked at Harper. "Strange that Renet would hit on the idea of calling herself The Cat Burglar. I had a friend once who used to joke that if she ever became a professional burglar, that was what she would do. Pretend to be looking for her lost cat."

She stroked Dulcie, watching Harper. "You said Renet worked in wardrobe, in Hollywood? So did Wenona. I wonder..." The little lady frowned. "It would seem strange, wouldn't it, if they knew each other? But Wenona lived in Molena Point when she was younger. She was forty when she moved to L.A.

Renet would have been about twenty then, doing those early films."

The little woman cocked her head, thinking. "Wenona used to go down to the wharf to feed the stray cats. She liked to feed them, but she was afraid of them, too."

Harper tried to keep a bland face, but Mae Rose's words hit home. When they locked Renet up, she kept shouting, *It was the cats. It was those damn cats that put me here.* No one had asked what she meant, she was in a violent temper. He hadn't asked, and he hadn't wanted to know.

Harper shivered. He didn't look up, but he felt, from the tree above, the yellow stare of the tomcat. And on the pink afghan, Wilma's cat didn't wiggle an ear, didn't open an eye, yet he could sense her interest as sharply as if she watched him.

And later, as Harper drove Clyde back to the village, he couldn't help glancing down at the the gray tomcat. The animal lay stretched insolently between them, across the front seat of his squad car. Clyde said taking a cat in the car was no different than taking a dog, and Clyde was so argumentative on the subject, you couldn't reason with him.

Everyone knew that dogs were fine in cars, dogs stuck their heads out in the wind, hung their tongues out and enjoyed. But cats—a cat was under the gas pedal one minute, then trying to jump out any open window. Cats weren't meant to ride in cars; cats were more attuned to creeping around in the shadows.

Besides, he wasn't keen about cat hairs in his squad car.

Though certainly Clyde's cat was obedient enough, it didn't make a fuss, didn't leap around clawing the upholstery, didn't go crazy trying to get out the window. It napped on the seat, purring contentedly. It looked up at him only once, a blank, sleep-drugged gaze, dull, ordinary, unremarkable, making him wonder what he thought was so strange about the animal.

If he thought this dull-looking cat had anything to do

with events at Casa Capri or at the Prior estate, maybe he needed a few days off, a vacation.

Pulling up before Clyde's white Cape Cod, he watched Clyde swing out of the car carrying the cat and set it down on the lawn. The cat yawned, glanced up blearily, and wandered away toward the house. Just a dull-looking, ordinary tomcat.

The tomcat, the minute Harper let him and Clyde out of the squad car in front of their cottage, headed for his cat door. Walking slowly, trying to appear stupid, he was nearly choking with amusement.

Pushing in through his cat door, leaving Clyde leaning on the door of the squad car talking, he moved quickly to the kitchen, where he might not be heard, leaped up onto the breakfast table, and rolled over, laughing, pawing the air, bellowing with laughter, working himself into such a fit that Clyde, coming in, had to whack him on the shoulder to make him stop. It took three hard whacks before he collapsed, gasping, and lay limp and spent.

"It's a wonder he didn't hear you; you were bellowing like a bull moose. You really have a nerve, to laugh at Harper."

Joe looked at him slyly. "Harper gets so edgy. Every time we wrap up a case, hand him the evidence, he gets nervous, starts to fidget."

"Just where would the case be, Joe, without Harper? You think Adelina and Renet would be in jail? You think you and Dulcie would have made a citizen's arrest? Hauled Adelina and Renet and Teddy into jail yourselves?"

"I wasn't laughing *at* Harper. I was laughing *because* of Harper."

Clyde looked hard at him. "You're not making sense."

"Harper's a great guy, but he's letting us get to him.

How can I help but laugh? He's developing a giant-sized psychosis about cats."

Silence. Clyde snatched the dish towel from its rod, folded it more evenly, and hung it up again.

"*You* can laugh at Harper," Joe said. "So why can't I? There he is, a seasoned cop with twenty years on the force, and he's letting a couple of kitty cats give him the fidgets."

Clyde sat down at the table, looking at him.

"In the squad car—he could hardly keep from staring at me. He knows we were up to something, and he can't figure it out. So we helped nail Adelina, so does he have to get spooked about it? We scare him silly. Can I help if he breaks me up?"

Clyde put his face in his hands and didn't speak.

But it was not until later, when Joe had trotted up through the village to meet Dulcie in the alley behind Jolly's Deli, that he realized the full import of what he and Dulcie had done and how their maneuvers would affect Harper. Why wouldn't Harper be upset? The man was only human.

"Three murderers are behind bars," Dulcie said. "A rash of burglaries has been stopped. And, best of all, now that those old people are free of Adelina, they're not afraid anymore. They're safe now, and looking forward to enjoying life a little, in their remaining years."

She looked at him deeply, her green eyes glowing. "And we did it. You and me and Dillon and Mae Rose."

"And Max Harper," he said charitably.

"Well of course, Max Harper." And she began to grin.

"What?" he said. "What are you thinking?"

"Renet in her underpants and bra, with that wrinkled old witch face." She rolled over, mewling with laughter, and soon they were both laughing, crazy as if they'd been on catnip. Only a sound from the deli silenced them, as George Jolly came out his back door bearing a paper plate.

They could smell freshly boiled shrimp, and the aroma

drove out all other thoughts. They looked at each other, licked their whiskers, and trotted on over, smiling. As they began to eat, old Mr. Jolly stood looking up and down the alley, wondering how those laughing tourists had disappeared so quickly. Only the two cats knew that there had been no tourists, and even for old George Jolly, they weren't telling.

And don't miss

CAT TO THE DOGS

the latest
Shirley Rousseau Murphy
mystery
featuring Joe Grey

A series of earthquakes have shaken Molena Point's quiet seaside village and stirred up a dangerous mystery. Dulcie and Joe Grey are on the case—and on the prowl.

SHIRLEY ROUSSEAU MURPHY
———— Mysteries ————

Featuring Joe Grey, a cat who not only solves crimes, but also talks!

CAT ON THE EDGE
105600-6 • $5.99 US/$7.99 Can

Joe Grey could handle having the ability to talk and understand humans. What worried him was finding himself in the alley behind Jolly's Deli the night Beckwhite was murdered.

CAT UNDER FIRE
105601-4 • $5.99 US/$7.99 Can

Joe Grey knows he's in trouble when his "girlfriend" Dulcie is determined to clear a man in jail for killing a famous artist by finding the real murderer—even if she has to get him killed doing it!

CAT RAISE THE DEAD
105602-2 • $5.99 US/$7.99 Can

Dulcie and Joe Grey must prove that an old folks' home is hiding more than just lonely seniors: a mysterious doll kidnapper, a severed finger, and a very, very busy open grave!

CAT IN THE DARK
105947-1 • $5.99 US/$7.99 Can

There's a new cat in town, Azrael, and he's masterminding a crime spree extrodinaire. Dulcie and Joe Grey must find a way to expose Azrael without revealing their secret.

Available wherever books are sold or please call 1-800-331-3761 to order.   SRM 0300

DEN OF ANTIQUITY MYSTERIES

by
TAMAR MYERS

LARCENY AND OLD LACE
78239-1/$5.99 US/$7.99 Can

As owner of the Den of Antiquity, Abigail Timberlake
is accustomed to navigating the cutthroat world of rival
dealers at flea markets and auctions. But she never thought
she'd be putting her expertise in mayhem and detection to
other use—until her aunt was found murdered . . .

GILT BY ASSOCIATION
78237-5/$6.50 US/$8.50 Can

THE MING AND I
79255-9/$5.99 US/$7.99 Can

SO FAUX, SO GOOD
79254-0/$6.50 US/$8.50 Can

BAROQUE AND DESPERATE
80225-2/$5.99 US/$7.99 Can

ESTATE OF MIND
80227-9/$6.50 US/$8.50 Can

And coming soon
A PENNY URNED
81189-8/$6.50 US/$8.50 Can